# Love is Murder

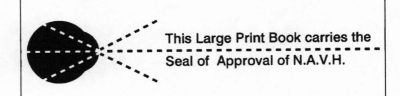

This Large Print Book carries the
Seal of Approval of N.A.V.H.

# Love is Murder

## Linda Palmer

**WHEELER**
**PUBLISHING**

Published in 2004 by arrangement with The Berkley Publishing Group, a division of Penguin Group (USA) Inc.

Wheeler Large Print Cozy Mystery.

The text of this Large Print edition is unabridged.
Other aspects of the book may vary from the original edition.

Set in 16 pt. Plantin by Christina S. Huff.

Printed in the United States on permanent paper.

**Library of Congress Cataloging-in-Publication Data**

Palmer, Linda.
    Love is murder / Linda Palmer.
      p.  cm.
    ISBN 1-58724-769-0 (lg. print : sc : alk. paper)
    1. Inheritance and succession — Fiction.  2. Television authorship — Fiction.  3. Women dramatists — Fiction.  4. Soap operas — Fiction.  5. Large type books.  I. Title.
PS3566.A528L68 2004
    813′.54—dc22                          2004054950

To D. Constantine Conte

As the Founder/CEO of NAVH, the only national health agency solely devoted to those who, although not totally blind, have an eye disease which could lead to serious visual impairment, I am pleased to recognize Thorndike Press★ as one of the leading publishers in the large print field.

Founded in 1954 in San Francisco to prepare large print textbooks for partially seeing children, NAVH became the pioneer and standard setting agency in the preparation of large type.

Today, those publishers who meet our standards carry the prestigious "Seal of Approval" indicating high quality large print. We are delighted that Thorndike Press is one of the publishers whose titles meet these standards. We are also pleased to recognize the significant contribution Thorndike Press is making in this important and growing field.

Lorraine H. Marchi, L.H.D.
Founder/CEO
NAVH

★ Thorndike Press encompasses the following imprints: Thorndike, Wheeler, Walker and Large Print Press.

# I am Grateful . . .

to Claire Carmichael (aka mystery novelist Claire McNab), a gifted writer and very generous instructor. You turned a screenwriter into a novelist — not an easy task.

to Normal Knight — a genuine "knight." Many people know that beneath your business attire is a suit of shining armor.

to Morton Janklow and Amy Jameson, who list themselves as agents, but are really a writer's gladiators. Thank you, too, for your suggestions that improved the manuscript.

to Allison McCabe, the amazing editor who saw clutter, repetition and missing information in a manuscript I could have sworn was "perfect." Thank you, Allison, for your enthusiasm and your tremendous editorial skill.

to the late (and irreplaceable) Rod Amateau. You hired me to write a screenplay before I knew how, and taught me to write what I most wanted to see, or to read. There's a huge hole in my life where you used to be.

to a wonderful group of diversely talented "test readers." Your reactions and questions were a great help: Arthur Abelson, Carole Christie Moore Adams, Henny Backus, Jane Wylie Boyd, Gail Temple Collyer, Ira Fistell, Judy Tathwell Hahn, Kevin Hing, Nancy Koppang, Susan Magnuson, Mari Marks, Jaclyn Carmichael Palmer, Kathy J. Segal, Dorothy Sinclair, Commander Gary Shrout, Nancy and Terry Smith, Corrine Tatoul, and Kim LaDelpha Tocco. Thank you all for your sharp eyes and for your encouragement.

to novelist, journalist, anchorwoman, and great dresser Kelly Lange, who said: "Oh no! Morgan can't wear *leggings* — that's so seventies! Put her in black jeans."

to Wayne Thompson of Colonial Heights, Virginia, for lending his professional background and part of his name to the character of "Chet."

and to Berry Gordy, for too many reasons to list here.

# 1

"Accidental incest. That's what ruined me."

"It's a mistake anyone could have made," I said.

I was trying to be sympathetic, but Helen Marshall was a hard woman to like. She was well known as a back-stabbing idea-thief. Small (about four inches shorter than my five feet six) with slightly protuberant eyes, she had fingernails like red claws, black hair cut in severe slashes, and made quick, darting movements as she spoke. Altogether, she reminded me of one of the lethal creatures in that old Hitchcock movie, *The Birds*.

We had met five months before, at the Daytime Emmy Awards.

The meeting had not been pleasant.

Overdressed in a gem-encrusted red Dior ball gown that must have cost as much as a midsize car, she had been seated at the *Trauma Center* table. I'd been nearby with my *Love of My Life* contingent. Wrinkling a nose that had undergone plastic surgery one too many times, Helen Marshall had pointed at me — specifically at my beige silk wrap dress — and in a voice loud enough for the three nearest tables of daytime television stars and executives to hear, said, "I saw that dress for sale on QVC. Don't you think she should wear something more . . . *soignée* to the Emmys?"

A zinger of a reply had been on the tip of my tongue. But I lost the chance to use it because my left-side dinner partner, Tommy Zenos, executive producer of *Love of My Life*, squeezed my hand to silence me. "Ignore her," he had said. "She's drunk, and I heard she's about to be fired." Tommy, at thirty-five, was at least fifty pounds too heavy for good health and much too young to have lost most of his hair.

My dinner partner on the right side was Jeremy Radford, the fifteen-year-old son of Tommy's and my boss, Damon Radford, the network's Vice President in Charge of Daytime Programming. In contrast to Tommy's balding head, Jeremy had enough bright red hair for two people. He was tall for his age, but competitive gymnastics had given him lean muscles and the physical grace to spare him from going through a gawky stage. Jeremy leaned over to me and whispered, "I think you look beautiful."

"Thank you, Jeremy," I said.

Then he gallantly buttered a dinner roll for me.

Two hours later, the show had finally progressed to the last four awards. I was dying to go home. My back ached from sitting up straight, and my new three-inch Jimmy Choo heels were so uncomfortable I had slipped them off fourteen "thank you" speeches ago. A new pair of actors — restless young lovers from *The Young and the Restless* — came to the podium to announce the nominees for "Best Writing." *Finally.* This was my signal to get ready to leave; as soon as this award was handed to the winner, there would be a brief commercial break and I would be able to slip away. While Tommy was sweating, clasping and unclasping his hands as they recited the names of the five nominated shows and their head writers, I was squirming around in my seat. Jeremy realized I had a problem. "What's the matter?"

"I can't find my shoes," I whispered.

Jeremy immediately ducked down beneath the table, as though this was the important mission for which he had been waiting. He found my shoes and handed them to me just as I heard words for which I was completely unprepared:

". . . and the Emmy for Best Writing of a Daytime Drama goes to *Love of My Life* head writer Morgan Tyler."

"Morgan, that's you!" Tommy jumped up and pulled me with him. He pushed me toward the stage. "Go, go, GO!"

Barefoot, with my shoes in my hand, I ran. A team of associate writers were stampeding behind me toward their few seconds of on-camera glory. As we reached the stage, I let out a whoop of delight, impulsively tossing my three-hundred-dollar toe-squeezers high into the air. The audience laughed at the flying shoes and applauded the crazed writer who had just struck a blow for foot liberation. The presenting actors thrust a gleaming Emmy into my hands, then stepped back so I could face the podium microphone.

"Wow — I didn't write a speech," I said. "That's the truth. I've only had this job for two and a half years, so I never expected . . . actually, I voted for the *Days of Our Lives* writers."

Audience laughter gave me a moment to take a breath. I decided it was time to act like a grown-up.

"On behalf of our executive producer, Tommy Zenos, and our wonderful cast and team of writers, thank you," I said. "Miraculously, my name is going to be etched onto this award — if the engraver can pry it out of my hands — but two other names belong there as well. One is Harrison Landers, the brilliant man who preceded me as head writer. Harrison laid the foundation for so much that we're proud of in our show. The other person who should share this honor is Larry Romano, the actor for whom our 'Who Killed Jason Archer?' story was created. Thanks to Larry, 'Who Killed Jason Archer?' became a nationwide guessing game and put our show on the cover of *Time*."

I was watching the floor manager's signals and knew I had scant seconds left before I'd get the musical hook and be ushered offstage.

"*Love of My Life* began on television thirty years ago. It was born the same year I was," I said. "Larry was part of the original cast. He has been the most enduring — and endearing — villain in daytime drama, the tenderhearted bad guy women loved and men wanted to be. When Larry decided to retire, we wanted to give him a spectacular 'farewell party' of a story line. I hope we did."

The audience applauded warmly for popular Larry Romano. I hoped Harrison, in his seclusion, was watching on television, and knew that the award I was holding was for him, too.

A few minutes later I was standing in the semi-darkness of backstage, clutching my Emmy and waiting for the still photos to be taken. Onstage, another matched pair of gorgeous actors was reading the list of nominees for "Best Actress in a Daytime Drama." Because no one from our show was nominated in that category, I was silently rooting for the actress who plays "Vickie," the multiple-personality heroine of *One Life to Live*. Suddenly, a man grabbed me around the waist from behind. He yanked me tight against him with one arm as his other hand clasped one of my breasts.

"Oh, those luscious breasts," he whispered.

I couldn't see his face, but I recognized the voice, and the gall. It was the network's good-looking, golden-haired golden boy, Damon Radford, Vice President in Charge of Daytime Programming. Sweet young Jeremy's father.

"Let go of me, Damon."

"Don't worry, no one can see us back here."

There was no liquor on his breath, but I didn't expect there to be. He seldom drank alcohol because he liked to stay in control of any situation.

"Damon, I swear to God if you don't take your hands off me, I'll smash you in the face with this Emmy."

He believed me. He let go.

Neither of us ever mentioned the incident.

And now here it was, a late afternoon in October and Helen was staring at that same Emmy. The statue was on an eye-level shelf, nestled among my favorite books. "That award should have been mine," she was saying. "I would have won, but everybody made such a stink about that incest thing . . ." Helen had been the head writer on *Trauma Center* for nine years, but was fired for "that incest thing" as Tommy had predicted.

We were sitting in my cluttered little office with its bantam windows and peaked attic roof. Experienced at nesting in small spaces, I had managed to cram a desk, two chairs, a library table and three filing cabinets into the room. The obligatory television set was on top of one of the cabinets. Every surface was covered with bound scripts, loose script pages fastened together with color-coded clips, stacks of videocassettes and DVDs, copies of book-length long-term story documents and piles of reference materials. It was — and is — *organized* chaos; I know where everything is.

In spite of its modest size, my office has a great advantage — it's located in what was once a servant's room on the sixth floor of the Dakota, the same colorful old nineteenth-century apartment building at Seventy-Second Street and Central Park West where I live three floors below. I have a very short commute.

Helen turned her attention away from my Emmy and glanced out through one of the small windows overlooking the inner courtyard. The sun was going down and its last rays were casting El Greco–like elongated shadows against the courtyard walls. In an eerie way, the effect was beautiful, I thought.

"This building gives me the creeps," she said.

"A lot of *Rosemary's Baby* was shot at the Dakota," I replied, "but I don't believe the rumor it was a documentary."

Helen wasn't listening. She was studying the one photograph on my wall. It was a picture of a smiling man with a strong jaw and close-cropped dark hair who was in the driver's seat of a Land Rover. A young chimp was sitting on his lap, gazing intently out the windshield. Little chimp fingers clasped the steering wheel in a child's imitation of driving. She tapped one crimson fingernail on the glass that protected the photo and I flinched. "Please don't smudge the glass, Helen."

She indicated the man and asked, "Was that your husband?"

"Yes," I said. I was about to yank her hand away when she removed it.

"He was a hunk," she said.

*Oh yes, he was. That and so much more.*

Helen went back to scanning the room, and I took the opportunity to look at that precious photograph. It was one of the hundreds I had taken of him. I wondered what Ian would think if he could see me now . . .

"There's no place for my desk in here." Helen's voice drew me back from Africa, back from the past. "You'll have to rent another room for me," she said, frowning as she mentally calculated dimensions.

"No, Helen."

She ignored me.

I had agreed to "discuss" a possible scriptwriting job on *Love of My Life* only after enduring her weeks of intense lobbying. I finally gave in when she told me she was "fiftyish and desperate." I've been desperate, and in twenty-some years I'll be fiftyish, too. So here she was, but I was finding it difficult to have a discussion with her because she refused to listen; Helen was behaving as though conversation was a synonym for monologue.

"*Trauma Center*'s been on the air for forty-two years," she said, returning to her main theme. "Two hundred and sixty episodes a year times forty-two years adds up to — well, a *lot* of plots. So I created a romance between two characters who were brother and sister. I didn't know! It

16

was a secret, revealed twenty years ago, not even the *actors* remembered."

"It was bad luck the audience did."

"Those people need to get a life. I made one little mistake, and the bastard wouldn't give me another chance."

The "bastard" was my boss, Damon Radford. He used to be *our* boss, until he replaced Helen with Serena McCall, an actress who had previously played a beautiful but tormented neurosurgeon on *Trauma Center*.

"That son-of-a-bitch thinks with his prick," Helen said. "Serena can't write. She can't even spell."

"Other actors have crossed over to become writers for their shows," I reminded her. "Some of them came up with interesting stories because they understand the characters. Serena was on *Trauma Center* for seven years; she might turn out to be a good choi—"

"No, it has to be sex. She's figured out some disgusting new way to do it. Damon doesn't care if she ruins the show, not as long as he gets what he wants."

Helen nodded at the genealogy chart tacked up on the wall behind me. It stretched four feet long and traced the family trees of the two tentpole families on *Love of My Life*. It diagramed the relationships among family members and their assorted lovers, friends and enemies in the fictional town of Greendale, USA. "You're in trouble, too," she said, stabbing with a long red claw at two of the names on the chart. "Your 'Nicky' and 'Kira' romance hasn't caught on with the fans. It's so disappointing when that happens."

She turned to face me, smiling like a salesman about to close a deal. "I'll be a big help to you . . . Actually, we should be *co*–head writers. I'll make you look good, and nobody needs to know about it — you keep all the glory. Our little secret."

With every word out of her mouth, Helen Marshall was illustrating the old saying, "No good deed will go unpunished."

"No, Helen. We won't be co–head writers. We can't work together at all."

"Why not?"

"We don't like the same kind of stories."

That was the truth, but not the whole truth. The larger truth was she was a mean-spirited woman who never had a positive word to say about anyone, and I didn't want to have anything to do with her. Plus, whenever she came close to me, I smelled liquor on her breath.

"Tell you what — as a favor, just to help you out — I'll write scripts for the show. I can be your safety net, Morgy."

*Morgy. Yuck.* "My name is Morgan. There is no diminutive for it."

"How odd. What did your husband call you?"

*That's none of your business.* "We're fully staffed at the moment." I did not add the polite fiction I would call if the situation changed.

18

She smiled at me then.

It was the smile of a pervert offering candy to a child.

She leaned in close, and reflexively I drew back, repelled by her alcoholic breath. Helen didn't seem to notice I'd moved away from her. "What if I agree to split the fee with you?" she said.

"Absolutely not."

Her reaction was utter shock. I realized she'd never considered the possibility that I would turn her down.

"Helen, we don't have anything more to discuss," I said. "Now, please excuse me, I have to get back to work."

She left without saying good-bye. I knew I had made an enemy.

# 2

Two hours after Helen Marshall left, I finished writing *Love of My Life* Episode Number Seven Thousand, Nine Hundred and Six, printed out the pages for editing later and walked the three flights downstairs to my home.

My five-room co-op is on the Dakota's third floor. The living room, the den and the bedroom look out onto Central Park. The kitchen window faces the building's inner courtyard. My dining room, situated between the kitchen and the den, has no view. I've compensated with mural blowups of some of Ian's extraordinary wildlife photographs. It is my shrine to him.

John Lennon lived directly below my apartment, in a place three times the size. His widow lives there still. I've seen her from a distance, but I've never met her. Lennon was murdered outside this building when I was barely eight years old, when I had no idea where life was going to take me. How did a nice girl like me come to live upstairs above the ghost of John Lennon? It's a new twist on an old story that begins, "You see, I met this man . . ."

I was a nineteen-year-old sophomore theater major, attending Columbia on a scholarship and waiting tables weekends to cover living expenses. On the day that changed my life, a famous wildlife photographer and photo-journalist came to Columbia to give a lecture on endangered species. Ian Malcolm Angus Tyler was thirty-eight years old, not tall, but he had powerful arms. His dark hair was cut short, and he had the greenest eyes I had ever seen. He was even better looking in person than he was in the picture on the back of his book jacket.

He was an outdoors man. I was an indoors girl. He was on stage, standing at the podium, talking. I was in the fourth row of the auditorium, listening. We couldn't take our eyes off each other. After his lecture, we introduced ourselves, and then we were together almost every minute until we were married, exactly one week later. Before we had done anything more than kiss. Before we had seen each other naked.

We were married in a civil ceremony at City Hall. Ian's best man was a stranger he met in the hallway and lured into the judge's chambers with a ten-dollar bill. My maid of honor was my best friend from Columbia, Nancy Cummings. Impossibly blonde, impossibly slim and altogether dazzling, Nancy was so drop-dead stunning that I was afraid when Ian met her he wouldn't want me. "You're crazy," she said when I confided this to her. "We were sitting together when he gave his lecture. He never looked at anybody but you."

Nancy chose my wedding outfit — one of her designer dresses. Ivory silk, knee length, with a tight waist, high neck and long sleeves, it was the most beautiful dress I had ever worn. We were still letting it out in the bust and shortening the skirt moments before we had to leave to go to the ceremony. Two hours after Ian and I exchanged our vows, with grains of the organic brown rice Nancy threw at us still in our hair, we were on a plane to East Africa.

To his world.

I lost my virginity on a bedroll in the soft grasses of Tanzania, beneath the Southern Cross. Ian never called me Morgan; he called me Emma, after my favorite novel, Jane Austen's *Emma*. He taught me how to operate his cameras and trained me in the art of wildlife photography. He taught me how to move through the bush, holding my cameras without metal clinking against metal, without making sounds an animal wouldn't make. He taught me how to shoot rifles and revolvers. I was his wife, his protégée and his partner in adventure. He was fearless, and I would follow him anywhere.

We had almost six years together.

Two thousand and seventy-eight days of making love, making pictures and sometimes making waves with them when we recorded devastation or the results of corruption. Then one morning in the rough terrain near Lake Turkana in northern Kenya, our Land Rover blew a tire, spun out of control and crashed.

I was thrown out of the vehicle and suffered a shattered left wrist.

Ian was killed.

I came back to New York at the urging of Nancy Cummings. Although separated by half the globe, we had kept in close touch through e-mail. Still my best pal, she convinced me that the city was the finest place to repair my wrist and invited me to stay with her for as long as I needed. During the years I was in Africa, she had been busy, too — she had graduated from law school, passed the New York State bar exam and was now an associate in a large midtown law firm.

It took three surgeries and six months of intense physical therapy before I regained the use of my left hand and most of my dexterity. Experimenting, I found I could still operate my cameras, but I realized the passion I had felt for my work was missing. I could not imagine living what had been *our* life without Ian.

"I'm twenty-five," I told Nancy, "an ex-wildlife photographer with not quite two years of college, and my second language is Swahili. I've got to find a new way to make a living, but what am I qualified to do?"

"There must be somebody who'll appreciate that crazy résumé," she said. "But I can't think of who."

The answer appeared in, of all places, *TV Guide*.

Nancy saw a small article, got excited, waved

it in my face and started reading aloud: "The Global Broadcasting Network is looking for people with imagination and energy to be trained as soap opera head writers," she said. As she quickly scanned the whole piece, she told me, "They don't want writers with soap opera experience. No . . . it says they want 'fresh minds with fresh ideas.' They're especially interested in hearing from novelists, journalists and playwrights. You can submit writing samples to — blah, blah, blah — here's the network's address."

"I can't —"

"Of course you can! You're a playwright, Morgan. You wrote plays when we were at Columbia. One was produced off-Broadway."

"Waaaaaay off-Broadway," I said. "In New Jersey, in a forty-seat theater. Two performances, and they were free."

"You are a *produced* playwright," she insisted. "You don't have to volunteer *where*. Send them the play. If they like it, they won't care where it was produced. I'll make copies for you at the office. What can you lose except postage?"

They did like the play, or at least liked it well enough to pay me to write a sample "document," which they explained was six months' worth of story for the characters in one of their daytime dramas. "We don't refer to our dramas as 'soaps,' " I was told.

My instructions were to watch *Love of My Life* for a month, then stop watching. I was not to turn the show on again while I was writing. Instead, I was to pick up the story and carry it forward using my own imagination. I had to bring the stories they were telling to a conclusion, and then begin my own.

Before I began writing this audition piece, someone from the network delivered four large cardboard boxes to Nancy's apartment. They contained the personal histories of all the characters, sample story documents, sample scripts — even scale drawings for each of the one hundred and fifty-seven sets that were in various pieces in a warehouse, ready to be pulled out, assembled and dressed or re-dressed as needed.

I started creating romantic jeopardy and mystery stories for the show's characters.

It was a lot more fun than thinking about my own life.

For the first two years of my training in this "endless novel" form of storytelling, I wrote scripts and breakdowns under the guidance of head writer Harrison Landers. When he had a disabling stroke, I was quickly promoted to "acting head writer" to maintain the continuity of the show. Then Harrison fell into a coma.

I spent every evening at his bedside, reading to him, convinced he could hear me even if he couldn't respond. I adored Harrison. He was a sweet man, and he was more than a professional mentor to me. Sometimes I fantasized that he was the father I never had. He was in the coma for weeks; when he finally woke up, his mind was sharp, but he couldn't speak or walk. I wanted to keep visiting, but Harrison refused to let me see him. He barred everyone except his housekeeper, his doctor and the nurses who looked after him. After a few weeks of this, it became clear to the network he would not be able to return to the show, and I was officially given the head writer job. Tommy Zenos, the show's executive producer, told me Harrison had written a note urging I be named his successor.

*Love of My Life* was regularly in the top five in the ratings book when I took over. The show is now telling the stories I've created, and for the last year we've been in the top three. Success is exhilarating. And it's terrifying. I read a quote from some famous person who said, "The trouble with success is that you've got to keep on being a success." Of course, keeping our show in the top three is not the only problem I have.

Another is dealing with Damon Radford.

Damon should have his picture on the cover of every manual about sexual harassment, with a red circle around it and a red slash running diagonally across. His piggish behavior toward me has always varied from mild to outrageous, but he's not worried I'll bring charges against him; he's careful to spring his traps when no one else is around. With no witnesses it would be my word against his, and as Global Broadcasting Network's Vice President in Charge of Daytime Programming, he's in the power position.

It would be easier if I was writing one of the daytime dramas on ABC, CBS or NBC. The heads of daytime programming on those networks are based three thousand miles away in Los Angeles. It's my bad luck that Damon is the personal protégé of Winston Yarborough, Chairman of the Board. Mr. Yarborough wanted Damon's office close to his own, for ease in consulting on a variety of projects, so Damon was allowed to make New York his home and travel to Los Angeles twice a month.

Ironically, post-Helen, I was glad "Damon the demon" was in New York; I needed his agreement to an important story change I'd decided to make.

# 3

Ideas for future *Love* episodes kept churning in my brain. I'd finished editing but couldn't fall asleep, so I gave up trying. I got up and turned on the Home Shopping Network to see if my favorite designer, Terry Lewis, had figured out something new to do with suede. Head writers on daytime dramas make a lot of money, but it's hard to find time to spend it. I buy all my clothes in the middle of the night from fashion shows on Home Shopping and QVC.

Just as I was falling asleep at last, the phone rang. I checked the glowing red numbers on the face of my clock radio — ten minutes after three. I picked up the receiver and mumbled a less than gracious "hello."

"Morgan, Rick Spencer here." I heard distress in his voice. Rick Spencer is an ambitious young network executive who works directly under Damon Radford. He's so eternally fawning to our boss I once joked to Harrison that Rick was playing "Eve Harrington" to Damon's "Margo Channing." Harrison reminded me "Eve" ended up helpless in the power of "Addison DeWitt," Damon's personal hero in the movie.

"Rick, what's the matter?" I asked, and sat up.

"There's been an accident. Damon, and Cybelle Carter —"

Cybelle was currently the most popular actress on *Love of My Life*. The fact that she was with Damon Radford was a shock, but I wasn't in the backstage gossip loop.

"What happened?"

"Damon took her to a Broadway musical she wanted to see, then they went to that new comedy club — Bellylaughs — on Sixty-Third and Columbus. They were crossing the street and a car struck them both. A speeder. Hit and run."

"Oh my God." I was standing up and pulling off my pajama bottoms. "How are they?"

"It's bad, but they'll live. Damon wants you to get over here ASAP. Metropolitan Hospital. Seventh floor — East."

Seven East is the celebrity wing, complete with first-rate doctors on call twenty-four–seven and security guards the size of NFL linebackers. "I'll be right there," I said as I pulled my Bruce Lee T-shirt over my head. I threw on the nearest pair of black jeans, ankle boots and a dark green Terry Lewis suede blazer and was out of the apartment in five minutes. I wasn't worried about Damon. My concern was for Cybelle, personally, and for the show. Cybelle's role, "Kira," was on the front burner right now. She had four big emotional scenes scheduled to tape tomorrow.

Today.

★ ★ ★

Rick Spencer is so young looking that I always expect to see a retainer when he opens his mouth. I dislike Rick, and I have found it difficult to look at him ever since a night at Damon's apartment several months ago, when he helped to humiliate another human being. Fortunately, Tommy Zenos has most of the contact with "Little Ricky." Next to Rick was Nathan Hughes, the network's Chief of Public Relations. Nathan is perfect casting visually, with his silver hair, high forehead and dignified bearing of an ambassador. His manner was professionally cool and enigmatic, but I could tell the wheels in his mind were turning at warp speed, planning to spin this story to reflect glory on Damon and Cybelle should anything sordid come to light. I like Nathan because he's good to the people who work for him.

The third man to greet me as I exited the elevator to Seven East was Johnny Isaac, Cybelle's agent. Somewhere in his forties, he's short, shaves his well-shaped head, is wiry and tough as stainless steel. According to the *Page 6* gossip column in the *New York Post*, he's also a self-appointed gladiator in charge of protecting her from bad men. Somehow Cybelle had slipped his leash and spent at least this evening with the worst of the bad.

"You've got a lot of rewriting to do quick," Rick said, instead of hello. He was trying to as-

30

sume command of the situation, but instead of sounding authoritative he just sounded petulant.

"I've been thinking about that since you called, Rick. I'll work it out."

On my way over, I wondered what Cybelle was doing out so late the night before such a heavy tape day, but there really wasn't time to speculate. I had a lot of revising to do if the show had to tape around her for any length of time.

"Her right leg's broken," Johnny Isaac said, his voice a monotone. His face was immobile, his dark eyes impossible to read.

Rick added, "She's going to be in a cast for *six weeks.*"

"Look on the bright side, guys." I tried to lighten the mood. "If she'd gone home with Damon, she could have ended up in a cast for six *months.*"

Nathan whipped his head around so fast to see if anyone had overheard, I thought his neck might crack. "Don't say things like that!" he snapped.

My attempt at humor was in bad taste, I admit, but based on ugly truth. Damon was known in our tight little circle for physically abusing his women on occasion. Nathan Hughes managed to keep those episodes out of the gossip columns.

The bell over the main public elevator rang and two men got off.

The younger one was in his late thirties, over six feet tall and had a broad chest and well-muscled arms. He wore a pale blue shirt, with a dark blue tie. His gray tweed sports jacket was off-the-rack but well-cut, and he inhabited his clothes with ease. He had brown eyes with glints of amber. A mass of dark, Mediterranean hair covered his head and curled around his ears; he looked as though he was a week overdue for a haircut.

The older man was probably closer to fifty than forty. He had brown eyes, and what little was left of his hair was cut into a short fringe around the back of his head. No taller than five feet nine, this man weighed over two hundred pounds and looked like his favorite sport was eating. Sartorially speaking, he was a little more than rumpled, a little less than sloppy. The middle button on his dark brown jacket was missing, and his emerald green tie was knotted so ineptly it looked as though he had dressed in the dark.

I had written enough cop scenes to recognize plainclothes detectives when I saw them. Their arrival puzzled me; I had expected uniformed officers.

Nathan Hughes signaled the two men over with a wave and they headed in our direction. They flashed their badges as the older man introduced them both. "I'm Detective Flynn. This is Detective Phoenix. We're from the Twentieth Precinct. Homicide."

I felt my eyebrows shoot up toward my hairline. *Homicide?*

Nathan did the honors introducing our group, then he got right to his primary concern. Equating greater age with greater importance, he addressed the older man. "How can we keep this quiet, Detective Flynn?"

Detective Flynn took a moment while he squinted at us like a jeweler searching for flaws in suspicious-looking stones. "You can't," he said finally.

"Why are homicide detectives investigating a traffic accident?" I asked.

Detective Phoenix answered me. "The car that struck Mr. Radford and Ms. Carter didn't stop." He paused before he added, "We have a witness who says the vehicle speeded up and hit them deliberately."

I was stunned. "Somebody tried to kill him? I mean tried to kill *them?*"

My slip — assuming the target had to be Damon — did not go unnoticed. Five pairs of eyes were staring at me. I decided now was *not* the time to mention my personal fantasy of running Damon Radford over with heavy farm equipment.

"Does Mr. Radford have any enemies?" Detective Flynn asked.

I wanted to say, "Open the Manhattan telephone directory and start with A," but I kept silent.

Nathan did his diplomatic best. Assuming his

most avuncular tone, he said, "Damon Radford runs an important division of the Global Broadcasting Network. He's the head of daytime programming, and he's quite likely to be the next president of GBN."

That was news to me. Bad news. The more power Damon had, the more difficult he could make my life. On the other hand, perhaps that promotion would mean he would move to California?

"But enemies who might *kill* him?" Nathan managed to look incredulous. "Of course not."

His was a performance that deserved an Emmy.

"What about Ms. Carter?"

"Everybody loves Cybelle," I said. "She's sweet and unpretentious and undemanding." I did not add what I was thinking: *And if she's spending after-hours time with Damon, she must have an I.Q. no larger than her bra size.*

"Did your witness manage to get the car's license plate?" Rick asked.

"A partial. We're checking it out."

Detective Phoenix had been watching Johnny Isaac, who had yet to say a word to them. "Do you know anything that could help us, Mr. Isaac?"

"No."

I could tell the two detectives didn't believe him. I realized I didn't believe him either. I wondered what he knew, or suspected.

"Just for the record," Detective Flynn said ca-

34

sually as he opened his notebook, ready to write, "where were each of you earlier this evening?"

"Home," Rick replied. "Sleeping."

"Alone?"

"Yes, unfortunately." As he said this, the fingertips of Rick's right hand went up to his mouth and I saw he was biting his nails.

"Mr. Hughes?"

"Home."

"Alone?"

"No, I was with my wife."

"Mr. Isaac?"

"Home alone."

"Ms. Tyler?"

"Watching the Home Shopping Network. Alone."

Detective Phoenix couldn't suppress a tiny smile. "Did you buy anything?"

"Oh — you mean did I call up to buy something so my telephone records would prove I was home? No, I didn't. I didn't call anyone tonight."

Five men looked at me again. Phoenix looked with curiosity, Flynn with suspicion and Rick with bewilderment. From the expression on Nathan Hughes's face, it seemed as though he thought I might be the next problem he would have to solve. Johnny Isaac's reaction was the one that surprised me; he was watching me with amusement. It was the first unguarded expression I had seen on his face, and it told me that he was vulnerable under his tough-guy armor.

Suddenly my heart went out to him; in Beauty and the Beast stories, I've always been on the side of the Beast.

"I realize," I said to the detectives, "that a normal person probably wouldn't know a detail like that, but knowing that sort of thing is part of my job."

Detective Flynn was skeptical. "What kind of job is that?"

"I create stories for the daytime TV drama *Love of My Life.*"

"My wife watches that," Detective Flynn said. "She likes it — she keeps talking about some guy named 'Cody.' "

"So does my aunt," Detective Phoenix said.

This was shaping up to be a long night.

# 4

Detectives Flynn and Phoenix were still asking questions when a young doctor approached us saying, "Mr. Radford wants to see Mrs. Tyler."

I started to follow him.

Rick and Nathan started to follow me.

"No," the doctor said with a firmness I knew came from Damon, "he *insisted* that he see Mrs. Tyler first. After that he would like to see Mr. Hughes and Mr. Spencer, in that order."

In the corporate fast lane, your importance is determined by the order in which you are summoned to an audience with the king. Rick Spencer's face flushed red, embarrassed to be slighted in favor of a mere writer and a PR man. Detective Phoenix told the doctor, "Mr. Radford will see Detective Flynn and me immediately after he speaks to Mrs. Tyler." His tone of voice discouraged argument.

There have been people who struck me as plain when we first met, who then seemed to become more and more attractive as I got to know them. With Damon Radford that phenomenon worked in reverse. Slightly taller than medium height, slender and perfectly proportioned, with golden hair and intense brown eyes, when we were first introduced, I thought he was movie-star handsome. But day by day, encounter by encounter, he began to look as repulsive to me as the portrait Dorian Gray kept locked in his attic. The doctor opened the door to Damon's private room, then stood aside. I went in alone.

"There'll be dozens of changes to make on the fly," Damon said, signaling clearly that even with an I.V. drip in his left arm, his right arm in a sling, his right leg in a cast and his neck in a brace he was still in command. "With Tommy stuck up in Connecticut, you'll have to spend time at the studio."

"You're letting me near the actors?"

"I trust you," he said.

"Why?"

"If you could resist me, you can resist any-one."

"Damon, you've got an ego as big as Godzilla."

His eyes glittered like a hunter spotting game, and I realized he had mistaken my insult for "banter." He widened his mouth and showed his perfect white teeth, proving reptiles can smile. "I'm finally getting to you, aren't I?" he said. "If I'd known all it took was being hit by a car to rip off your widow's weeds and —"

"Nice," I said quickly, interrupting him. I gestured around the room. It was large and, with framed prints of Georgia O'Keeffe's flowers on the walls, as cheerful as a hospital room could be. He noticed I was looking at the prints and said, "I've got to get out of here before O'Keeffe gives me diabetes."

"I don't think the Prado's going to lend you their black Goyas," I quipped, mentioning the grimmest paintings I could think of. "Seriously, is there anything I can bring you?"

"You can bring your mouth over here and —"

"I'll take that as a no," I said and turned to leave.

"Morgan, wait. Have you seen Cybelle?"

"No, I haven't."

"She's next door," he said. "Go see her. Tell her we'll get her anything she needs. Personal maids to dress her, private duty nurses around the clock." He had dropped the compulsive lecher act and sounded sincere. "Tell her not to worry about anything. She's a nice girl, Morgan. She didn't deserve this."

I couldn't believe my ears. I had to be imagining it, but I thought I heard a note of real concern in his voice. *Concern for another human being? I must be hallucinating.* It's the lateness of the hour, I told myself as I left the room and headed next door. I'll be all right when I have some coffee.

Cybelle Carter's private room was not quite as large, but was also made cheerful by framed prints, mostly Monets. When I entered, the attending nurse pantomimed that the patient was asleep. With her eyes closed and her black hair framed by the white hospital pillow, Cybelle looked like Walt Disney's Snow White. We had met only once, a little more than a year earlier, when Tommy Zenos and I chose her to play "Kira." I had started to leave when her huge blue-violet eyes suddenly opened. In the soft, breathy, almost childlike voice her fans loved, she whispered, "Hi."

"I didn't mean to wake you."

"It's okay . . . You're Morgan Tyler. I love the stuff you write for me."

"Thank you." My eyes went to the cast on her leg and she began to cry. "Are you in pain, Cybelle?" I asked, nervously glancing at the nurse.

"I'm okay, but I'm just so sorry about the show, Morgan. Are you going to replace me now?"

"Of course not. We'll tape everybody else's scenes for the next few days. We'll tape yours later and edit them in."

"But I've got that beautiful dance scene. I love that scene." She struggled to sit.

"I figured out how to rewrite it," I said as I eased her back until she was lying in a comfortable position. "We'll have you in a gorgeous long dress, and the man will dance around you. It'll be very sensual."

She sighed in relief, then said something I could barely hear. I leaned closer. She repeated it. "He saved my life."

"Who?"

"Damon."

She saw the skeptical look on my face.

"He did," she insisted. "When he saw the car coming, he pulled me behind him so he got hurt the worst."

If she had told me Elvis was alive and under her hospital bed, I would have found it easier to believe. Then I remembered the message I was supposed to deliver. "Damon says not to worry about anything, Cybelle. We'll get you whatever help you need for as long as you need it. If there's anything you want that we don't think of, all you have to do is ask." I wasn't sure she heard me because she didn't respond. She was sinking into sleep as she whispered, "Damon saved my life. Please tell people. Nobody understands him . . ."

# 5

It was close to 5 A.M. when I finally got home.

I pulled off my ankle boots, exchanged the suede blazer for a comfortable old sweater and made a big pot of coffee. Because Tommy Zenos was in Connecticut for his uncle's funeral, it was my job to alert the director, Joe Niles, to the emergency changes in the day's taping schedule. Joe was our most frequently used director on the show's "director wheel." A well-known early-riser, and British, he answered the phone with a clipped, "Niles here."

"Cybelle's been in an accident," I said without preamble. "She and Damon were crossing the street last night and a car hit them. Damon has a broken leg and arm, and Cybelle has a broken right leg."

Joe was silent for a moment. He didn't react to the news about Damon and Cybelle being out together, so perhaps he knew about that, but then he surprised me by asking what struck me as an odd question. "Are they in pain?"

"It's manageable," I said, then I steered him back to business. "In place of the Kira and Nicky scenes, we'll tape tomorrow's Jeff and

Michelle. Their scenes use today's sets, and the actors already have their scripts."

"That works. I'll let them know."

"One more thing. I wrote a new scene for Link. I'd like you to tape it at the end of the day, after everybody else is gone."

"Ah, the plot thickens. Tell me all."

"I'll explain it later," I said.

"Good enough. I enjoy a mystery." I heard the scraping of a match. "The only thing I like about the French are their cigarettes," he said, and I heard him take a deep drag of one of his strong Gauloises.

It isn't very nice of me, but, frankly, I'm glad Joe smokes. I saw an example of his low character at the same time I'd discovered what kind of a jerk Rick Spencer really is. In my opinion, Joe Niles will deserve whatever his cigarette habit might do to him. When Tommy told me a couple of weeks ago that Joe's wife left him, without knowing the details of their split, or even knowing the woman, I was inclined to be on *her* side, not his. Joe interrupted my thoughts when he asked, "What other actors will you need in the new scene?"

"No one. Link will be all by himself."

"He'll love that. But he's not scheduled to work today."

"I'll call him."

After telling Joe I would see him in the studio later, I said a quick good-bye. He would call the rest of the production team. I poured a supersized mug of coffee and added my usual three packets of Sweet'N Low and half an inch of half-and-half. *Lots of cream and lots of sugar. You drink coffee the way children drink coffee,* Ian used to say. But there was no time for memories. I set to work reorganizing the scripts for the next few days.

An hour later I clicked "Send" on my computer and zapped the revised scripts into the production secretary's computer. She would now grab the baton and run the next lap in our creative relay race, printing out the new script pages, then copying and distributing them to all relevant parties. I reached for the show's personnel directory, found the number of Link Ramsey's apartment and dialed. The phone rang eight times before I heard a sleepy, "Hello."

"Hi. It's Morgan Tyler. Sorry to call so early, Link."

"You've decided to kill me off."

He was serious; it was every daytime actor's fear.

"Not today," I said. "Actually, I have something interesting in mind for you."

"Yeah?" He was fully awake now, his antennae quivering.

"Come into the studio late this afternoon to tape a new scene."

"You got it. Fax me the lines —"

"No lines."

Silence on his end. Then he surprised me.

"I hear my Cody's catching on with the fans."

"You think Cody is getting hot?" I stalled.

Even though the letters are addressed to them, actors don't get their fan mail until after the producers, the network and the head writer — *me* — read it. Sometimes that takes weeks. The official reason — in TV speak that means the official *lie* — is that it's a precaution, in case any of the letters are from dangerous nuts. The *truth* is we want to learn what the fans are feeling before the actors do. This way the actors can't, say, use a rise in popularity to try to sweeten their deals. Link was right, but it was too soon for him to know it.

"What gives you that idea?" I continued, sounding, I hoped, doubtful.

On the other end of the line, I heard Link Ramsey chortle. "There's no such thing as a well-kept secret anymore," he said, "just a friendly press. And the Internet."

"Who said that?"

"My publicist. What's cookin', Cookie? Come on, you can trust me."

Abraham Lincoln trusted an actor. Look what that got him.

"Call me 'Cookie' again and I *will* kill you off." Unfortunately, I *had* to trust Link. His co-operation was vital to what I had in mind to keep our ratings up. "Moreover, I'll make it happen *off*screen, so you won't get a death scene, or a memorial service with film clips of you."

"You're tough. Can I call you 'Cutie'?"

"Call me Morgan."

Then I told him what I was planning for Cody, the character he played.

When I finished, Link Ramsey was one happy actor.

I was downstairs and on my way out through the Dakota's courtyard when I was surprised to see Detective Phoenix. He was just entering the courtyard from the street.

"What's happened?" I asked, immediately thinking the worst.

He assured me he wasn't there to deliver bad news.

"Then why . . . ?"

"I'd like to get a look at the environment, at the studio where Ms. Carter works. And it's in the same building as Mr. Radford's office."

*He's been doing his homework.*

"If you're on your way over there, Mrs. Tyler, I'll drive you."

*And he has a nice smile.*

"It's only a few blocks, Detective. I like to walk."

He put his six-foot-something frame in gear to match my five-foot-six stride.

"Where's Detective Flynn?" I asked. "I thought partners investigated together."

"We're off duty."

The thought that he was walking beside me when he was off duty made me self-conscious. I tried to set myself at ease with humor. "You're a homicide detective. Aren't people killing people in your precinct this morning?"

"It's only seven-thirty."

*He has a nice voice.*

"The muggers have gone home to sleep and the murderers are still having their coffee."

*And a nice face.*

"Last night, when the doctor said Radford wanted to see 'Mrs. Tyler,' I thought you were married, but you said you were alone watching the Home Shopping Network, and later somebody mentioned that you'd lost your husband."

*Somebody mentioned.* The idea of being talked about made me angry.

"My husband is dead, Detective. I didn't misplace him."

"That sounds like it still hurts."

It did, but I wasn't going to discuss it. I decided to turn the tables and see how he liked someone prying into *his* life. "Did someone you loved ever die?" I asked.

"She only changed. I've seen too much of real death to use that word lightly." His beeper went off. He looked at it quickly, frowning. "Sorry. Gotta go. Maybe I can stop by the studio later." He hurried back to where his car was parked.

I was astonished to discover that I was just a little bit disappointed we weren't going to spend more time together.

47

# 6

*Love* is one of two daytime dramas taped in the studios located in the big gray building that is the New York City headquarters of the Global Broadcasting Network. The other is *Trauma Center*. Also taped at the GBN studios are a game show, a daytime talk show hosted by former movie star Kitty Leigh and the network's late-night comedy-variety hour. These five programs are the only ones that originate on the East Coast. The rest of the GBN schedule is taped or filmed in and around Los Angeles.

*Love of My Life*'s first scene of the day was supposed to go before the cameras at 8:30 A.M. It was a quarter to eight when I walked into the GBN building, to make sure that it did. We use two adjoining facilities, Studios 35 and 37, because each episode is an hour long. The first three of today's acts were to be taped in 37, while 35 was readied for afternoon use.

I took a quick look around and saw that the standard last-minute checks were being conducted to make sure the set doors worked, furniture was arranged properly and props were where they were supposed to be. When something doesn't work, or is supposed to be in place but isn't, the tape must be stopped and the problem corrected. That costs time, and time is expensive. More so than in any other part of a network's schedule, *money* is the real reason behind the "creative" decisions made in daytime television.

Joe Niles was already in the control booth when I arrived. Red-eyed and rumpled, with nicotine stains permanently embedded in his fingers, he looks overworked even when he's just returned from vacation. "Everybody knows about the accident," he said by way of greeting, "but I told them we put our contingency plan in motion."

"We don't have a contingency plan."

"People feel more secure when they hear four-syllable words like 'contingency.' It pretty much calmed everyone down."

"Define 'pretty much,' " I said. I could tell by looking at him that he was worried about something.

"It's Sean — that's no surprise, right? The argument scene between him and Nicky's father is first up, but Sean is coming unglued. Can you stick the little shit back together?"

I would solve the problem, but for the good of the show, *not* to make Joe's life easier. "Let me get my glue gun," I said.

"What if I got you a real gun?" Joe was only half joking. "I heard you shot tigers and elephants in Africa."

"*Lions* and elephants. There aren't any tigers

in Africa, Joe. And I never shot any living thing except with a camera."

He looked disappointed. I knew Sean O'Neil was a severe pain in his . . . TV monitor. Sean played Nicky, a young man from one of our show's two central families, the wealthy one. I had spent four months writing a poor girl–rich boy love story for Cybelle Carter's impecunious but angelic Kira, and Sean's affluent nice-guy Nicky.

Individually, Sean and Cybelle were likable in their roles.

Together they had no chemistry.

They were not exciting the fans and becoming the kick-ass Super Couple the show needed. Helen Marshall had been right about that. I didn't tell her when she said it, but I had already been plotting a major change in story line. So far, only three people knew about my plan: Tommy Zenos, Damon Radford and Link Ramsey, the actor I hoped was going to save us. Save *me*. Unless he or she has created the show, a head writer's job is secure only as long as the ratings are high.

Sean O'Neil wasn't in the makeup room, the coffee room, his dressing room or on the set rehearsing his lines. The floor manager told me he was in the bathroom, throwing up. I waited outside the door until he emerged. Privately, Joe Niles referred to Sean as "our pocket Adonis" because while Sean is head-turning handsome, he is not very tall. When he came out of the bathroom, I saw he was pale and tense, and patting at his perfect features with wet paper towels.

"Cybelle will be back to work in a few days. We can hide the cast on her leg."

"Huh?" He looked puzzled, then comprehension dawned.

I realized it wasn't Cybelle he was worried about.

"That's great," he said, too fast to be convincing. "Do you think I should send her some flowers?" He was making the offer, but his heart wasn't in it. Then tears began to spill from his arresting turquoise eyes.

Hoping to keep the morning's taping on schedule, I quickly slapped on my nurturing "Earth Mother" hat. "Tell me what's the matter, Sean," I said comfortingly. "Whatever it is, we can fix it."

He took a deep breath and told me the truth. "If Cybelle's out of commission, what's going to happen to *my* character? Maybe we should replace her. We could get that girl who *looks* like Cybelle, the one who just left *Trauma Center*. I heard she's available, and she's still in New York."

*It's lucky for this selfish jerk,* I thought, *that we can't do daytime drama without actors.*

"We're not replacing Cybelle," I said firmly. But he had just handed me an opportunity to drop a hint about the new story I was devising.

"I have something very exciting planned for

51

you, Sean. A hot, hot, *hot* development. Scenes that will make you the man to beat at the next Daytime Emmys."

As easily as they had appeared, Sean's tears dried up.

"Yeah? Tell me." He beamed his "Cutest Boy in the Senior Class" smile at me. I noticed he wore colored contact lenses.

"I don't have time right now, but I'll give you a hint, if you'll promise to keep it a secret. We can't let Cybelle or anyone else know about it."

"Oh, I promise, Morgan. You can trust me. I won't say anything to anybody."

"All I can tell you is I've been thinking Kira isn't good enough for Nicky."

He took the bait like a fish leaping into the angler's boat.

"You know, I've been feeling that too, but I didn't want to say anything. I wouldn't want to hurt Cybelle. You know, get her fired."

"Don't worry," I said. "I'll think of something for her to do."

I knew *exactly* what I was going to do with Cybelle, and I had lied to Sean. It was necessary, though, to get him into gear to do the job he was being paid for. Besides, I rationalized, it was not really a lie; I preferred to think of it as an anticipation of the truth.

Still, I didn't like lying.

I promised myself I was not going to do it again.

# 7

Since the day's taping was on track, I went to the hospital to check on Cybelle and Damon.

I met one of Cybelle's nurses in the corridor outside her room.

"That little short man, Mr. Isaac, he's been with her since last night," she said. "He slept next to her bed, on a cot he had us bring in for him."

The "nice me" was pleased Cybelle had such a devoted agent, but my cynical "evil twin" pegged Johnny Isaac's behavior as dangerously obsessive. It's a long and respected tradition in daytime drama that "evil twins" are smarter than their "nice" counterparts. Otherwise, why do so many of the "good" characters spend weeks, sometimes months, locked up in hidden basement cells while their evil look-alikes assume their identities, and even sleep with their unsuspecting lovers?

Hoping the nurse would tell me "no," I asked, "Can Mr. Radford have visitors?"

"A policeman's in there now," she said. "And there's a bunch of unhappy-looking people in the lounge waiting their turn."

"You should get one of those 'take a number' machines."

She shrugged. "You all are on your own. My shift is over." And she left.

I went down the hall and into the waiting room. The nurse was right. Damon's would-be visitors looked unhappy, in the manner that Tolstoy said, "Each unhappy family is unhappy in its own way."

In order of the grimness of their facial expressions, Teresa Radford was at the top of the list. I wondered if she was grim because Damon was badly hurt, or because he wasn't dead? The ex–Mrs. Radford had been movie star Teresa Gleason twenty years earlier when she married Damon, who was then a low man on the TV totem pole. Now deep in her forties, she was still lovely, and still had her trademark long red hair. She retained the bone structure the camera must have loved, but bitterness had hardened her mouth, and her eyes were puffy with fatigue.

Jeremy Radford, Teresa's and Damon's son, stood next to his mother. Jeremy always seemed older than fifteen to me. An inch taller than his father, and still growing, he was a good-looking young man. If Damon had a "best part of himself," it was Jeremy.

Standing closest to the lounge door, nervous as a racehorse waiting for the starter's gun to go off, was gorgeous, platinum-haired Serena McCall, former daytime diva, now the inexperienced head writer of *Trauma Center.* I amused myself imagining she took her position by the door so she could beat the other "concerned visitors" in a race to pay tribute to the patient.

I had not expected to see the other two people in the room. The first surprise was Tommy Zenos, apparently *not* in Connecticut for his uncle's funeral. Tommy was sweating and peeling the wrapper off a large-size Snickers bar. Several other crumpled and discarded Snickers wrappers were scattered on top of the end table next to him. His jacket was straining at the seams, and his yellow gold wristwatch had become so tight I knew he would have to go back to Piaget soon to have more links put in the band. Now, it wasn't strange that our show's executive producer had rushed back from his mourning family to rally the troops. Politically, it was smart. What was odd was that he hadn't called me as soon as he heard about the accident to find out what I was doing to cover Cybelle's absence from the studio. I was flattered he trusted me to handle the show, but I was curious about why he was off on a major chocolate binge. Tommy wasn't indulging himself in a few forbidden treats. He wasn't eating for pleasure; he was devouring candy like a drowning man grabbing at a life preserver. I wondered what could have happened to upset him so much.

The final unhappy face in the group belonged to Jay Terrill. It was a small, pointed face, with a twitching pink nose. Jay resembled a rodent, but he had none of a rodent's natural charm. He was staring at me in embarrassment, and he should have been embarrassed. Jay was one of my scriptwriters; he was supposed to be home writing. I remembered what Tommy called Jay behind his back: "the suck up." Several times recently I had seen him sucking up to Damon. Tommy had warned me Jay was after my job.

I said a warm "hi" to Tommy and Jeremy, a polite "hello" to Serena and Jay then I extended my hand to Damon's ex, whom I recognized from photographs and from having seen her movies.

"I'm Morgan Tyler, Mrs. Radford. I'm so sorry about what's happened."

What I meant was, *I'm sorry about what happened to Cybelle.*

She was gracious. "Please, call me Teresa," she said.

Tommy, the people-pleaser son of a daytime television legend — his father created three landmark dramas for ABC — felt he needed to elevate the quality of my sympathy. He identified me by job title. "Morgan's the head writer for *Love of My Life.*"

"I know," she said. Then, to me, she added: "I've been a fan for years. You've done a very good job keeping *heart* in the stories."

"Thank you. I've enjoyed your movies."

Any further mutual-admiration bonding was interrupted by the appearance in the doorway of Detective Phoenix. Serena, spotting an attractive man with no wedding ring on his finger, stood up straighter and aimed her breasts at him. "Hello," she said. "I'm Serena McCall."

"This is Detective Phoenix," I said, introducing them.

Serena extended her hand and he shook it briefly. I introduced the others in the room: Teresa Radford, Tommy Zenos, Jay Terrill and Damon's son, Jeremy Radford.

Jeremy spoke first. "How's Dad?" he asked Phoenix.

"The doctor just gave him a pain shot," Phoenix said. "He'll be asleep in a few minutes, but he wanted to see you, son."

Without another word, Jeremy hurried out of the lounge and down the corridor toward his father's room. Tommy, Jay and Serena, realizing they would not see the demon this morning, seemed relieved. Tommy had a question. "Did you find the person who hit them?"

"We found the car, Mr. Zenos."

"Call me Tommy."

Phoenix didn't call him anything. "The car was stolen, then abandoned after the incident," he said.

Serena, edging closer, unleashed her inner Marilyn Monroe and asked in a breathy voice, "What are you going to do now?"

That's what Serena *said,* but I got the feeling her real question was, *What are you doing for the rest of your life, you good-looking, employed, obviously straight man with a big gun?*

Phoenix's response to her spoken question

was to glance politely at Serena and them aim his answer to all of us in the room.

"There's nothing more we can do," he said. "Radford insists the witness was wrong when he said the car hit them intentionally. He's adamant that the event was an accident. Case closed."

Jay added his theory. "It was probably just a kid who stole a car to go joyriding, then when he hit somebody, he panicked and drove away."

Serena said what I was thinking, "Such a cliché. Is that how you would have plotted this story, Jay?"

He seemed to shrink into his rodent's body. He didn't reply, but from the glance he shot Serena, I would have advised her to stay out of any street where Jay Terrill had access to a car. Serena's cell phone rang and she turned her attention to it. All I could hear was her end of the conversation, but it sounded as though there was trouble on the *Trauma Center* set.

At this point, the party broke up.

Tommy, Jay and Serena left the lounge and headed toward the elevator. Teresa sat down again to wait for her son. I took the stairs.

Detective Phoenix caught up with me one flight down.

"Do you walk everywhere?" he asked.

"As much as I can. It helps me think."

"Uh, look, Mrs. Tyler —"

"Call me Morgan."

"Morgan. Since this isn't a criminal case anymore — what I'd like to say is that since we don't have any . . . professional . . . connection — would you have dinner with me tonight? With my aunt and me, at our home?"

"You live with your aunt?" I heard myself say, and realized it sounded judgmental and snobbish. He either didn't notice, or he overlooked it.

"Actually, she lives with me. You'll like Aunt Penny. She's a terrific lady, and she's a fan of your show."

*He must think I can't talk about anything else.*

"If you're off duty now," I said, "doesn't that mean you'll be back on duty tonight?"

"We're off until tomorrow. So . . . will you have dinner with us?"

# 8

I had not really slept since hearing about the accident, and had consumed little except a few quarts of strong coffee. I should have been stupid with exhaustion, but I wasn't. The new story pairing Kira with Cody had given me a shot of adrenaline.

I went from the hospital straight to my office, and started tinkering with it.

Physically, Link Ramsey was the opposite of Sean O'Neil. Sean was our fair-haired young prince, bleached blond hair and California surfer good looks. Link was our dark knight, hair the color of India ink, and mesmerizing ebony eyes set deep under wildly independent brows. His lips were full and sensual; when they curled upward on one side in his patented half smile, those lips suggested he knew secrets no nice girl should know. Sean was the young man a girl brought home to her parents. Link was that walk-on-the-wild-side a girl ran away to.

I knew it was right to put angelic Cybelle Carter and dangerous Link Ramsey together when I watched Link perform the no-dialogue scene I had written for him. It was a simple scene: Cody learns via a government telegram that the older brother he idolized, who brought up and protected him when they were orphaned, has been killed in the crash of his Marine Corps helicopter. Cody goes berserk with grief and wrecks his office, smashing and breaking things until finally he collapses in exhaustion.

Standing in the shadows behind the camera, I felt tears sliding down my cheeks. I was crying for Cody's pain. I was crying over a tragedy I had invented, for a character I had created.

And maybe some of those tears were for my own loss, too.

Watching, I realized I had put a lot of Ian into Cody.

Afterward, Link came over to where I was standing and hugged me. "That was a dynamite scene," he said.

"You were wonderful."

He released me from the hug and stepped back, but he took my hands in his, leaned in close and whispered, "You're gonna make me a star, Miss Morgan. I owe you. So . . . you got anybody you want killed?"

I laughed. "Not right this minute," I said as I took back my hands.

Link kissed me on the cheek and we said good night.

Why had I said "yes" when Detective Phoenix invited me to dinner?

Because I couldn't think of an excuse quickly enough?

Nope, that wasn't it. I am good at saying no, have become an expert at it in the last five years. The only men I know anymore are the men I work with, and they've all stopped asking me out.

Except Damon, the pig, who asks me *in*. To his bed.

Well, maybe it was because I was tired. I *was* running on adrenaline.

Since I had edited all afternoon, I had just enough time for a quick shower. How does one dress for dinner with a homicide detective and his aunt? Or the real question, how do I dress to express my lack of interest in having a second dinner with them? *With him.*

I put on a pair of plain black slacks and a loose black cashmere sweater. Much to the disapproval of my friend Nancy, I deliberately order my sweaters two sizes too large. She is convinced I'm trying to hide my body because I'm "stuck in widowhood." I argue with her, but to myself, I have to admit she is right.

I am afraid of being a single woman again.

I married so quickly I never learned *how* to date.

In my life, I've been intimate with only one man. It was wonderful beyond description, but everything I know about sex I learned from Ian. The thought of *being with* someone new scares me witless, so I don't think about it.

*Very adult, Morgan.*

I topped what Nancy calls my "unisex cat burglar outfit" with a pink suede blazer. I might look frumpy, but at least the pink will keep me from looking as though I'm attending a funeral. *Time to go.*

A cab pulled up as soon as I stepped outside, and a couple who lives on the fourth floor got out. We exchanged neighborly greetings as I took their place and gave the driver an address that was across Central Park. I had been startled to learn that Detective Phoenix lived on East Sixty-Eighth Street, between Madison and Park, but I'd tried not to show it. I had assumed he would live in Queens, or on Staten Island. That was where the New York cops on TV shows always lived. *He's a New York City homicide detective: how can he afford an East Side address?* As the cab accelerated, two possibilities occurred to me.

One: Phoenix is a cop on the take.

Two: He lives in the basement and moonlights as the super.

I hoped it was door number two. I prefer a man with dirty hands to one with sticky fingers. Why didn't I think to ask Detective Phoenix his first name? Why didn't he volunteer it? Maybe it's something awful, like . . . Fabio.

*Fabio Phoenix . . .*

No, parents couldn't be that cruel, could they?

I remembered reading about a Texas governor

63

named Hogg who named his daughter *Ima*. She should have shot him in some nonfatal but very painful place.

The cab pulled up in front of a well-maintained private town house, red brick with white trim. It was narrow, but four stories high. I thought the driver had made a mistake, but no, the brass numbers on the black lacquered front door matched the numbers on the piece of paper Detective Phoenix had given me.

I was afraid the answer was going to be sticky fingers instead of dirty hands.

*I'll make an excuse to go home early and never see him again.*

He opened the door almost as soon as I rang the bell. Instead of the jackets and ties he wore when he was being a detective, tonight he was wearing a soft yellow sweater and gray slacks. He was smiling at me.

"Hi," he said.

"Hi," I replied. *Brilliant dialogue, Morgan.*

He stepped aside for me to enter, then closed the door behind us and asked if I'd like him to take my jacket.

"No, thank you. I'm a little chilly." *At least I'm trying to be.*

He escorted me into the living room. It was comfortably furnished, with two deep, inviting couches flanking a wood-burning fireplace with a real fire in it. The walls were paneled in a rich old mahogany that gleamed from wax. There were fresh flowers in a vase on an end table.

"Why are you looking at my hands?" he asked.

*Caught.* I said the first thing that came into my mind. "I was trying to guess your first name."

"By looking at my hands?"

"You detect your way and I'll detect mine."

"My first name is Matt," he said.

*Matt . . .* Suddenly my throat felt dry. Why couldn't his name have been Fabio? Writers study names and their meanings. I knew that Matthew meant "gift of God."

*And Ian meant "God's gracious gift."*

He looked at me quizzically. Probably my face had betrayed my surprise.

We were interrupted by the appearance of a very attractive woman with quick movements and a bright smile. She could not have been more than five years older than Matt Phoenix — I put her age at forty-two or forty-three, tops. Her hair was the color of dark Godiva chocolate, her skin was soft and unlined and her lush figure was the kind that real men in the real world like. She was carrying a hot platter of something that thrust my salivary glands into overdrive.

"That smells like Heaven," I said.

"Stuffed mushrooms. Matthew said you'd probably be hungry." She put the platter down onto the coffee table. "Hi, I'm Penny Cavanaugh. Gosh, Morgan — you're as pretty as the girls in my stories."

65

Women who are serious viewers of daytime drama usually refer to their favorite programs not as shows, or soaps, but as their "stories."

Penny Cavanaugh — who didn't look like any "aunt" I had ever seen — was rearranging two of the pillows on the couch. "Come sit down," she said. I sat, and she sat next to me.

Detective Phoenix — Matt — asked what he could get us to drink. Penny opted for white wine.

"Something soft," I said. "If I have wine, I might fall asleep before dinner." I explained that I had not had more than two or three hours' sleep during the past two nights.

"That's awful. I'm a witch when I don't get enough sleep," Penny said. "Do you have insomnia?"

"No, I'm a good sleeper when given the chance. It's just that I've been on a heavy work schedule."

"I'm dying to know what's going to happen on *Love of My Life*," Penny said, "but I don't suppose you'll tell me, will you?"

I smiled at her as I replied, "Not even a hint."

"Would you take a bribe?" she asked, then glanced mischievously at Phoenix. "I guess I shouldn't ask that in front of the p-o-l-i-c-e."

"You know you wouldn't want her to tell you," Matt said as he handed Penny a glass of white wine and brought me a glass of orange juice. There was a teasing quality between them, which they both seemed to enjoy. They acted much more like brother and sister than like aunt and nephew.

I sipped at the juice. It tasted freshly squeezed, and it had the natural sugar that I needed to stay awake. "This is delicious," I said, nodding my appreciation. "At the studio, orange juice comes in boxes, from a machine."

"Penny doesn't allow anything that comes in a box in her kitchen," Matt said, with affection. "I used to joke that I was a prisoner of Martha Stewart."

"Poor you," Penny said with a smile, "forced to eat fresh food." She turned to me. "If he was alone, Matt would live on pizza."

"Don't knock pizza — it contains all the important food groups."

In his own home, Detective Phoenix — *Matt* — was relaxed and comfortable.

When dinner was ready, Penny refused to let me help her bring things to the dining table. Matt carried the heavy platters for her, then he pulled our chairs out and seated us before he took his own place at the table. Apparently, he was a well-brought-up homicide detective.

Penny was a wonderful cook. When I complimented her on the homemade ravioli, she told me that she had gone to cooking school two years earlier, where she learned to make pasta.

"The cooking teacher said she learned how to make fresh pasta from that wonderful actor, Danny Kaye; it's his own personal recipe. You'll

67

have to let me make you a soufflé next time. I earned a degree in soufflés," she added proudly.

"The diploma's hanging in the kitchen," Matt said.

"I flunked Indian curry, but, fortunately, that was an elective class. I just couldn't master clarified butter."

During dinner I also learned that Penny loved classic English novels, and poetry, especially John Donne, one of my favorites.

"The only living poet I like is Judith Viorst," she said. "She's so funny. Have you ever read her *How Did I Get to Be 40 and Other Atrocities?*"

"No, I haven't."

"You'll love her. She's so funny, and so smart about people. I think the book is out of print, but I'll try to find you a copy. I love going to old book stores."

Penny was delightful company, and was easy to be around. She had a great big laugh when she thought something was funny. I liked her, and not just because she thought I looked like an actress and was a devoted fan of my show. It wasn't only *Love of My Life* that she watched faithfully; she was virtually a human encyclopedia about the plots of several other shows.

"I'm so grateful to you people in television," she told me as she served dessert, which was homemade apple pie with a crust so light it fell apart when my fork touched it. "Your stories have got me through some rough times."

"Aunt Penny's a widow," Matt said.

She frowned at him, then turned to me. "That's not exactly true," she said. "I am, but not really."

I didn't know how to respond to that.

"Patrick's supposed to be dead," she explained, "but I know he's coming back to me."

*Uh-oh.*

I glanced at Matt and discovered he was watching me. He gave no clue as to what he was thinking, but I sensed that he was protective of her.

I decided to treat Penny's revelation as though it were sane.

"I don't understand," I said.

"Oh, I thought you would — you of all people."

"Well, I'd like to. What happened? To . . . Patrick?"

"He was killed in a plane crash seven years ago," Matt said. His voice was gentle.

"That's what they *told* us."

"But . . . you don't believe . . . them?"

"Of course not," she said. As evidence in support of her belief, Penny began to recount famous resurrections in popular daytime dramas. "Erica Kane's father came back from the dead. Both of Robert Scorpio's dead wives came back. Everybody thought Laura Spencer was dead, but she came back. Even Katherine Bell came back, and she died falling off a balcony right in front of everybody. That happened the night before she was going to marry hunky Stefan

Cassadine, who was really still in love with Laura Spencer, but he thought Laura was dead. And Dimitri's dead wife Angelique came back just as he was about to marry Natalie and make her a countess. Dimitri met Natalie when he found her trapped in an old well in the woods. Her rotten sister Janet threw Natalie down there so Janet could take over Natalie's identity and marry Trevor, the man Natalie loved. It all worked out because eventually Natalie did marry Trevor and Dimitri married Erica Kane." Penny took a breath. "So — that's why I work out five mornings a week, and why I won't get married again. I'd be a bigamist. I *know* that someday, when I least expect it — probably when I haven't got a thing in the refrigerator — Patrick's going to come back."

She was so matter-of-fact, and so sincere, that I wanted to believe her, even though I had no idea what to say. Penny, perfect hostess that she was, spared me embarrassment by changing the subject. "Would you like some peach ice cream with your pie, Morgan? I make it myself," she said, "with all fresh peaches."

# 9

Back in the living room after dinner, I had two cups of coffee, but it was obvious to Matt and Penny that I was beginning to fade.

"I better take you home," he said.

"Oh, no, I'll get a cab —"

"Not by yourself at this time of night."

*It's only eleven.*

I thought that, but I didn't say it.

I said good night to Penny, and told her how much I had enjoyed the evening.

"It was great meeting you," she said. "Let's do this again."

"I'd like that," I said, meaning it.

Outside it was a perfect mid-October night, cool enough to snuggle inside a sweater, but pleasant enough to enjoy walking. By silent mutual consent, Detective Phoenix and I ignored the cruising cabs and started walking west, toward the park.

"Penny's fun," I said. "And a fantastic cook."

"I'm glad you like her."

*How could I not like her?*

He had tossed the conversational ball into my side of the court. I took a whack. "I like her so much I want to think — I mean, is there any

71

possibility at all that . . . her husband might have survived?"

"No." He said it with authority, and for some reason that irritated me.

"I suppose you used your police contacts to find out —"

"I was just a rookie in uniform, but I did what I could. Penny and Patrick loved each other very much."

"Did you see the body?" I asked.

"The plane exploded over the ocean. Recovery wasn't possible."

"Are you sure he really got on the plane?"

"Penny saw him off."

"I never wrote one of those back-from-the-dead plots," I said. "Our show has a lot of romance and mystery, but I've stayed away from that story line. It's been done too often."

We reached Fifth Avenue, turned south, and walked along the low wall that borders Central Park on the East Side of Manhattan. There was something musical about the sounds of New York traffic in the crisp night air. "Penny worries me," he said. "This fantasy of hers gives her comfort, but it's keeping her from moving on with her life."

*Moving on with your life is highly overrated, Detective.*

We walked for a while in silence, enjoying the exercise, and the night, and the nippy air on our faces. When we reached Fifty-Ninth Street and Central Park South, we turned the corner and headed toward Central Park West. As we continued along the southern border of the park, he yanked me out of my private thoughts.

"Why don't you ask me what you want to know?"

"I don't know what you mean."

"Yes, you do. Writers lie for a living, but you don't have to lie to me."

I was silent; I didn't want to tell him what worried me.

"You wonder how a cop can own an East Side town house," he guessed.

*There it was.* "Yes, I do."

"And you're thinking the worst."

"Yes, I am."

"I thought so; I've had that reaction before."

*Before? How many women has he brought home to Aunt Penny?*

"Well, you're wrong," he said. "I'm not dirty, and I'm certainly not rich." He smiled at me. Ruefully. I realized that seldom have I seen a genuinely rueful smile.

"Actually, I'm almost house poor," he said. "Keeping the place up is like feeding a herd of elephants. I grew up in that house. Granddad made a lot of money by inventing something that everybody uses. When he died, he left all his money to charities, but he left the house to me."

"What did he invent?"

"I'm not going to tell you," he said. "You have to guess."

"Air conditioning?"

He shook his head. "That was a man named Carrier."

"Cardboard."

"Negative."

"Toilet paper?"

"Nope. Give up?"

"Absolutely not. I'll figure this out," I said.

"I bet you won't."

"For how much?"

"I don't gamble for money," he said. He thought for a moment and then suggested, "How about this, the loser buys the winner the pizza of his choice."

"Of *her* choice. It's a bet," I said.

Twenty minutes and five wrong guesses later we arrived at my building. It was nearly midnight and Seventy-Second Street was quiet. There wasn't even much traffic on Central Park West. With the quick, sharp eyes of a good cop, Matt checked to make sure no one was lurking in the nearby shadows, and that Frank, the Dakota's night security man, was at his post at the entrance to the courtyard. Then he turned his attention to me.

"I'll call you," he said.

"I'd like that."

There were a few moments of silence while we just looked at each other. His dark eyes were making me a little nervous, but in an exciting way.

"You have pretty hair," he said finally. "Marmalade . . ."

"Marmalade?"

"Your hair is the color of marmalade."

"Good night, Detective — Matt."

"Good night."

He didn't try to touch me, but he watched until I was safely inside the building.

Upstairs, I went right to the kitchen to see if I still had the jar of marmalade that came in the basket of goodies one of the show's sponsors sent to me last Christmas. Yes, there it was. Like tins of fruitcake, jars of marmalade might spend years unopened. I took it off the shelf and held it up to the light. Not a bad match; it *was* the same general blonde-red color of my hair. The man was observant. I wondered what else he had observed? I wondered just what he meant by "I'll call you." Was he really going to call me? Or was that just "man-speak"?

I wrote a scene last summer in which a mother translates what her daughter's boyfriend said by explaining to the girl the difference between "man-speak" and English. I fell asleep trying to figure out what it was Matt's grandfather had invented. "Something that everybody uses . . ."

# 10

The next afternoon Damon summoned me to a creative meeting at his apartment. We were scheduled to play the tape of the new scene I'd written for Link Ramsey, and to discuss the story line change I wanted to make in order to pair Link's character with Cybelle's. Earlier that morning, he had talked the doctors into releasing him, hired two male nurses to tend to his physical needs and arranged for his apartment to be equipped with the paraphernalia necessary for his recovery.

That much he told me when he called; it was my *guess* that the coffin filled with his native earth would be replaced temporarily by a hospital bed.

Damon lived on Central Park West, in a majestic old edifice just nine blocks north of the more eccentric building where I lived. Too close for my taste. Even if I strolled, it was only a few minutes away.

The butler showed me into the antique-filled living room. As fine as the individual pieces of furniture were, what took and held a visitor's eye were the six framed drawings from Picasso's autobiographical Vollard Suite. Several memorialized the erotic relationship of Picasso and Marie-Therese Walter, his model and mistress, the woman he called his *amour fou* — his mad love. The most striking drawing hung over the fireplace, where no one in the room could miss it. Titled "Rape IV," it was an example of Picasso using his genius to celebrate male violence.

Damon still wore a neck brace, and his right leg and right arm were immobilized in hard casts. Using a cane for balance, he was standing up near his gigantic television set. He turned when I came into the room, saw me looking at the drawing over the fireplace, and winked. I was relieved to see that the demon and I were not going to be alone. Tommy Zenos was there; he seemed even more nervous than he usually was around Damon. There were traces of powdered sugar on the front of his jacket. He was just putting a videotape into the VCR, and his eyes told me he was as relieved to see me as I was to see him. We exchanged quick greetings.

Then I asked Damon how he was feeling.

"Better than my enemies would prefer." He gestured for Tommy to push "Play" on the VCR.

It was the tape of the new scene I wrote for Link.

We watched it in silence. Three pillars of the temple waiting for lightning to strike. If possible, the scene was even more powerful on the screen than it had been when I watched it being taped live in the studio. Tommy was as moved as I had been. When it was over, there was the hush a dramatic writer dreams about, the stillness that means an audience has been totally caught up in what they've seen.

Damon was the first to emerge from the spell.

"Your boy broke a lot of props," he said. "I should take the cost out of your pay."

Tommy was usually too timid around Damon to say anything that wasn't an echo of the daytime chief's pronouncements. Not today. He didn't even look at Damon before he spoke to me. "You were right and I was wrong," he conceded. "I didn't think it would work — turning Cody into Kira's love interest."

Damon was not going to be ignored. "Just because Cody raped Kira doesn't make him unredeemable. Most women want to be raped by the right man."

That was just too disgusting to ignore. "Damon, you are a cockroach," I said.

Tommy gasped. "Morgan didn't mean that —"

"Yes, I did."

"Shut up, Tommy," Damon said.

Damon wasn't offended that I called him a cockroach. In my experience, it was impossible to offend him. I steered us back to the business at hand, as though I hadn't heard what Damon had said, and as though I hadn't said what I'd just said. "The people out there —" I gestured toward his terrace, at the America beyond the railing that encircled his balcony. "Most of the people in our audience don't take rape lightly."

"Then you have a big problem, Morgan."

*And when I solve it, you'll say "we" did a great job.* "If I had *known* the audience would go crazy for Link Ramsey," I said, "I wouldn't have made him Kira's rapist." I paused. I didn't look at Tommy, but I was giving him a chance to tell Damon the truth; it was Tommy who *insisted* I make Cody her rapist.

But Tommy did not speak up, and that was his big mistake of the day.

Damon turned on our producer. "You fat scum, Tommy, letting Morgan take the blame. You're a snot-nosed, overweight nothing, an empty suit with a producer title that you couldn't earn, but that you have — for the moment — only because your father is one of the few creative geniuses in Daytime. You're living proof that talent skips a generation."

Tommy was pale as death and shaking. I knew that he was petrified of authority figures, starting with his tyrant father. He was too wounded now to defend himself.

It made me sick to my stomach to witness Damon's cruelty to people who were too afraid to fight back, or to tell him to take his job and shove it wherever it would hurt the most. But I had learned a long time ago that I couldn't stop Damon when he was in one of his demon-moods.

I wanted to help Tommy regain a shred of his

79

dignity, so I said, "We should be grateful, Damon. Tommy's the one who found Link Ramsey in that off-Broadway play and signed him up. Now that we realize the audience isn't responding to a Kira and Nicky romance, we've got the solution right in our own cast."

Damon indicated the tape. "How do you plan to use this scene?"

"We can't undo the fact that Cody raped Kira," I said, "but we *can* brainwash the audience into forgetting. I want Joe to partly reshoot the rape like this: We edit our new Cody scene so it's at the beginning of the sequence. Then we see Kira in the doorway. I'd like a new shot of Kira, reacting in shock to what Cody's done to his office. I talked to Cybelle's doctor this morning — we can shoot her from the waist up. The idea is that Cody's assault on Kira is not the act of a rapist at all, but instead it's a primitive, mindless loss of control, in reaction to his grief over the death of his brother."

Damon looked skeptical.

Tommy, sick with humiliation, was staring at Damon's balcony as though he wanted to leap over it.

"We'll reshoot Kira's face during the assault," I said. "We can use a body double for full length when they're on the floor. Our reshot scene won't look as violent. It will look more as though Cody surprised Kira by grabbing her, but that she realized something awful must have happened and she responded to his need —"

"A sympathy fuck," Damon said.

"I wouldn't phrase it that way. *Then* we take our new scene and play it over and over and over again as a flashback. Kira will think about it, and we'll play that flashback. Then Cody will think about it and we'll run that flashback. Cody will confess it to a priest, and we'll play that flashback. Our *new* flashback. We'll brainwash the audience into thinking that what they saw was not as terrible as they thought it was at first."

" 'The big lie' . . ." Damon smiled with perverse satisfaction. He seemed to be comparing me favorably to Joseph Goebbels, Hitler's architect of propaganda, whose theory was that if you told people the same lie often enough, it would become their truth. "Okay, do it," he said finally.

Damon continued to ignore Tommy Zenos. "But if this *doesn't* work, if Cody and Kira don't become our Super Couple . . ." His voice became as soft as a viper's hiss. "Then I'll just have to punish you. Won't I, Morgan?"

I managed to get out of his apartment before I succumbed to temptation and pushed Damon over his own balcony.

Late that night I had been asleep for less than an hour when the phone rang. It was Joe Niles.

"Morgan — Damon's been murdered. Somebody pushed him over his balcony."

# 11

Police cars had closed off the street at Damon's corner, and a combination of yellow tape and uniformed officers blocked access to the building. A small crowd of "civilians" had gathered, whispering to each other. Considerate — trying not to wake the dead. The first person I recognized was Matt Phoenix. As I came closer, I saw he was talking to Joe Niles and taking notes.

Matt looked up and saw me.

"What are *you* doing here?" His tone was professional.

"I telephoned her," Joe said.

"Why?" It sounded like an accusation. Where was the gentle voice that told me I had pretty hair?

Joe's feet were surrounded by half-smoked cigarette butts. "Why did I call Morgan? I — I just . . . just thought . . . she should know . . ." he stammered. It sounded lame, even to me.

"Who did you call first, Mr. Niles — the police or Mrs. Tyler?"

That *was* an accusation. Detective Phoenix, who wasn't "Matt" to me now, was browbeating Joe. In spite of my distaste for our director, I thought Phoenix was treating him badly, without a good reason.

"I called nine-one-one. Then I called Morgan."

"Who else did you call?"

Joe hesitated, taking time to wipe the perspiration from his forehead and neck, although it was a chilly night.

"Who else did you call? We can find out from your phone records."

"Bloody hell, I am not stalling," Joe protested. "I just saw a friend of mine smashed to pieces on the bricks. That has left me more than a bit shaken." He took a breath. "I also informed the network people I thought should know. Rick Spencer and Nathan Hughes."

"Rick works with Damon," I said. "Nathan's head of public relations. You met them both at the hospital the other night."

"I remember."

"Rick said he was going to call Mr. Yarborough," Joe said. Then he added, "Winston Yarborough, the chairman of the network."

"Just the next of kin, huh."

*Detective Phoenix is a sarcastic bastard,* I thought, then realized, "Ohmigod — Jeremy." I looked at Joe. "Has anyone told Damon's son? Or Jeremy's mother? They shouldn't find out on the news."

Joe shook his head. "Not I."

Phoenix aimed a professional frown at me. "Who did you tell?"

"No one — I didn't know what happened, so I came right over." Now *my* explanation sounded lame. Why did I rush to Damon's? Did I want to make sure he was truly dead? "What *did* happen?"

Before he could reply, the medical examiner's van arrived.

"Stick around," Phoenix told us. "I have some more questions." He strode off to meet the medical examiner. Detective Flynn emerged from the side of the building and joined him at the van. Then Phoenix and Flynn led the medical examiner toward the patio, which was enclosed by a thick wall of foliage and out of sight from the street.

"What happened, Joe? Quick, before he comes back and arrests us."

"That's not funny."

"Lots of things aren't funny," I said. "Can you tell me what happened?"

"It was damned awful, Morgan. I found his body."

I have seen a dead human being, and I know the experience has a profound impact. If someone else had been in this situation, I would have tried to comfort that person, but I couldn't bring myself to comfort a pig like Joe Niles. He was on his own.

"He was lying in the middle of the brick patio below the balconies. You can't see it from the street —"

"I know. Why did you go around to the patio?

Actually, why did you come to Damon's this time of night?"

"He called me earlier, while I was having dinner. Said he had something important to discuss, and I was to be here at 1 A.M. I was early, so I decided to go around to the patio to have a smoke. He doesn't allow smoking in his apartment."

One A.M. was a strange time for Damon to schedule a meeting. He was well known for getting up at six o'clock every morning so he could telephone Los Angeles, where it was three o'clock. He liked to fling questions at his underlings when they were asleep, when they were most likely to make mistakes in their answers. I had never heard of his scheduling a meeting for later than the dinner hour. Damon liked to be finished with his business day by ten o'clock at night so that he could enjoy his personal life. But maybe that vile personal life was the reason he had wanted Joe to come over.

"Did you see him fall?" I asked.

"The detective just asked me that when you got here. No, thank God. He was already lying there . . . so much blood . . . and his face, it was all mashed . . ." He shuddered at the memory. "I walked onto the patio, struck a match to light my cigarette — God, I almost tripped over him."

"When you called, you said someone pushed him over the balcony. How do you know that's what happened?"

"Well, how else could it? You've been up to his apartment. The railing's more than waist high. He couldn't have climbed over with casts on his arm and leg. So I just assumed . . ." His voice trailed off.

"Did you tell that to Detective Phoenix?"

"Yes." He saw me frown. "Christ, he'll suspect me, won't he? If it happened the way I thought it did. He could think I knew because I killed him."

"Joe, I can't believe anybody would think that, just because you made a good guess — if you did. We don't know that. We really don't know anything at all."

Twenty minutes later, Detectives Phoenix and Flynn came back into view, followed by the medical examiner. They were accompanied by two men carrying a body bag on a stretcher. The detectives went over to the building's entrance to question the doorman, but I couldn't take my eyes off that stretcher as the medical examiner supervised its loading into the back of his official van. Damon Radford, heir apparent to the kingdom of the Global Broadcasting Network, was now only a lifeless object. When I turned away, I noticed Joe was staring at the covered body, too. There was a look very much like *relief* on his face. As I watched him watching Damon's remains disappear into the medical examiner's van, I remembered something Joe told Phoenix earlier that had struck me as odd.

What he said was "I just saw *a friend of mine* smashed to pieces on the bricks."

Joe Niles referring to Damon as a "friend" was typical. Behind Damon's back, Joe had expressed his absolute dislike of our boss. Maybe I was being too literal; in the entertainment business people frequently use the word "friend" to describe any relationship from the barest acquaintance to implacable hatred. The two words that are most abused in this profession are "friend" and "love." Still, I could not help wondering if Joe was lying to Phoenix to make it appear that he had no reason to kill Damon?

If, indeed, Damon actually had been murdered.

Or did Joe and Damon have a personal relationship unknown to the rest of us worker bees involved in putting *Love of My Life* on the air?

If Damon had been murdered, I wasn't particularly hoping for the killer's apprehension. It was likely that whoever had been up in the penthouse with Damon last had a very good reason to want him dead. Still, as someone who creates plots for a living, including murder mysteries, I was curious to find out the who, and the why.

The detectives finished questioning the doorman and returned to where Joe and I were standing. I had a question for them.

"Who's upstairs in Damon's apartment?"

"Forensics — the crime scene team."

"Nobody else?"

"No. Should there be?"

"Damon hired male nurses to be with him on eight-hour shifts. Where is the one who should be on duty now?"

"The doorman said he left with Radford's doctor, about nine-thirty. He said Radford didn't have any other visitors tonight."

"He wouldn't necessarily know. He couldn't have seen anyone who went up or came down by way of the service elevator."

"Service elevator?"

"Each wing has a service elevator that stops at the kitchen door of each apartment. It's for deliveries, but if you're in a hurry, it's quicker than going down the front way."

Three men were looking at me, but not the way a woman likes to be looked at.

"Good lord, Morgan," Joe Niles said, "how many times have you been to Damon's?"

"My best friend, Nancy Cummings, lives in this building. Ten E. I stayed with her for several months, when I first came back from Africa."

We heard the roar of a motor and the screeching of brakes as the first TV news truck arrived. A camera-ready news reporter hopped out, followed by her live-on-the-scene broadcast crew.

I aimed a defiant look at Detectives Phoenix and Flynn. "I'm going to tell Jeremy about his father," I said. "He loved Damon. It's going to be terrible for him, but maybe a little easier if he hears it from somebody who's not a stranger."

Flynn nodded to Phoenix. "I hate the noti-
fying-the-next-of-kin part of the job. You go
with her, Matt."

"Where does the boy live?" Phoenix asked
me.

"On East Seventy-Seventh Street."

"I'll drive you," he said.

# 12

Phoenix opened the front passenger door of a dark sedan and I got in. Until I saw the two-way radio hook-up, and the red bubble light balanced on top of the dashboard, I wouldn't have known it was an unmarked police vehicle. As I fastened my seat belt, I thought about the surprising turn my life had taken.

Because someone had *tried* to kill Damon, I met Matt Phoenix, the first man to interest me since I came back to New York. And now, because someone had *succeeded* in killing my horrible boss, I would not get to know this detective with the mysterious grandfather and the terrific aunt. Phoenix was investigating Damon's murder, and I was on the list of people who might be the killer.

My life had become a daytime drama.

While I was musing on the thin line between life and art, Phoenix had climbed into the driver's seat, fastened his own safety belt and put the car in motion. I looked at his strong profile and decided his was a face I might like to photograph.

"What's the number on East Seventy-Seventh?" he asked.

"Three forty-five."

"So you know the address without looking it up," he said. From the tone of his voice, it sounded as though he had judged me and found me guilty of something.

"What is the matter with you?" I asked. "Everything you've said to me tonight sounds like an accusation."

"Sorry. I didn't mean it that way."

"Did you lose your charm pills?"

That forced a smile to his lips; his tone softened. "I wish you hadn't come to the scene when Niles phoned you," he said.

"Why not?"

"You're calling attention to yourself. Why did you come?"

"Joe and Tommy Zenos and I work together as a team. Whenever there's a problem, we come to each other's aid."

"Niles called *you*, he didn't call Zenos. Why not?"

"Tommy is a good producer. He's smart and efficient, he knows when to delegate and he has a good eye for spotting talent," I said, "but when it comes to real life, Tommy tends to go to pieces in a crisis."

"Look, Morgan, I don't think you killed Radford, so let's get you out of the line of fire. Tell me where you were tonight."

"Home alone all evening, editing scripts. Rewriting behind a new writer who hasn't got some of the voices right yet."

"Voices?"

"When writers create dialogue for established characters, we have to craft their lines in the particular way those characters — those actors — speak. Use the words and phrases, or style of speech that are their . . . their verbal *fingerprints*, I guess you'd say. For example, one of our characters never uses contractions when he speaks. Another one seldom finishes a sentence. Somebody can be a good writer, but not necessarily have a good 'ear' for individual nuances." I realized I'd been rattling on and took a breath. "That was a long answer to a short question."

"You have a nice voice; I like to hear you talk."

At that moment, he sounded as though the detective part of him had gone off duty. It felt like I was sitting beside the man who walked me home after dinner and told me I have nice hair. "Matt, will you tell me what happened to Damon — at least what you know."

"That's not much. Yet. We think the railing was too high for Radford to go over by himself — not with casts on one arm and one leg. But it wasn't the fall that killed him."

I was stunned. "Then what — ?"

"There's a bullet hole in Radford's head."


Teresa Gleason Radford and her son occupy a twelve-room apartment in a fine old residential building on East Seventy-Seventh. One of the best in a sea of concrete bests. "I've been here

92

once before," I said as we walked into the lobby, "to take Jeremy home after the last Emmy Awards because Damon had 'things to do,' as he put it."

Matt showed his badge to the man at the security desk and said that Detective Phoenix and Mrs. Tyler were here to see Mrs. Radford.

The security man's eyes widened. "Did something happen?" he asked.

"Please ring Mrs. Radford's apartment for us."

He picked up the house phone and dialed. After a few seconds someone answered and he announced our presence. He listened, mumbled "Yes, ma'am," and replaced the receiver. "She says to come up. Apartment Fourteen B."

As Matt pushed the elevator button, he said, "I've never understood why so many buildings refuse to admit they have a thirteenth floor. No matter what they call it, the floor above twelve *is* thirteen."

"Maybe they think the Bad Luck Fairy can't count."

It was not one of my wittiest responses, but it was nearly 3 A.M. on yet another night when I hadn't had enough sleep.

Teresa was standing in the entrance to Fourteen B when we got off the elevator. Either she slept in her eye makeup or she had the fastest hand in the East with a mascara wand. And her abundant red hair was freshly brushed. She looked tired, but even two hours before dawn she was a beautiful woman. At the hospital, and now, in her foyer, whatever illumination there was caught the perfect contours of her face in just the right way. Directors of photography must have loved lighting Teresa Gleason.

"Detective Phoenix . . . and Morgan. Good morning."

She ushered us into an enormous living room, decorated in country French antiques and fabrics. As she guided us toward a seating area, the heavy silk of her caftan made a soft, swishing noise. It was the only sound in the room. She gestured for us to sit, but we both chose to stand.

"Has something happened?" she asked.

I felt as though I was third row center in a Broadway theater, watching her play the young Queen Victoria. *Has something happened?*

"We have some bad news, Mrs. Radford," Matt began. "Your husband —"

"My former husband." Her icy tone was like a slap in his face. Matt's eyes narrowed at her.

"Your *former* husband," he said. "Damon Radford is dead."

I wasn't surprised Matt had omitted the traditional "I'm sorry for your loss."

I said, "We didn't want you and Jeremy to hear this from the news."

"That was very thoughtful of you, Morgan. I'll tell Jeremy when —"

"I'm awake, Mom."

He had come into the living room through an archway to our left. He was wearing pajama bottoms and a NY Knicks T-shirt, and his hair was sleep-rumpled. He looked apprehensive as he asked, "What's going on?"

I thought Teresa was going to say something, but she didn't.

His eyes shifted from his mother to me. "What's happened, Morgan?"

"It's your dad," I said. I was aching with sadness for this boy who loved a man he had never really known. But maybe it was better that Jeremy didn't know the kind of man his father really was. I reached out for his hand as I said, "I'm so sorry to have to tell you this —"

Teresa finished the sentence for me. "He's dead." Her voice was devoid of emotion. I wondered why she hadn't said, "Your father is dead."

Jeremy's eyes filled with tears. He didn't go to his mother for comfort; instead, he stood up straighter, as though good posture would help ease his pain. He ignored the tears that began to course down his cheeks.

Teresa became all business. "I don't understand this," she said. "At the hospital they told us Damon was going to be all right. Did he have some internal injuries? Did the doctors commit malpractice . . ."

"Mom!" Jeremy's voice was sharp.

Teresa responded to his rebuke. She tried to sound as though she cared, but it was not one of her better performances. "Why did he die?" she asked.

Matt was terse. "He fell from his balcony."

Teresa gasped. One soft, creamy hand flew to her throat.

Jeremy's eyes widened in shock. "How'd that happen? He couldn't even walk."

"We're investigating," Matt told him. Then he added, in a gentle voice, and to Jeremy alone: "I'm sorry for your loss."

The boy nodded at Matt, then said to me, "Thanks for coming over, Morgan. I appreciate it." At that moment, he sounded more like a man than a boy.

"The kid's got a crush on you."

"I don't think so."

"Oh, yeah. We sensitive guys can spot these things." He meant for me to smile at that, and I did. We were back in the car, and he was driving me home.

"I suppose he *likes* me," I said. "And if he does, it's because I've spent time with him at the network functions his father brought him to. He would take Jeremy to a table, and then leave him surrounded by strangers for most of the evening. Jeremy and I seemed to gravitate to each other — two almost outsiders."

"I'd like to hear about that."

"Not now." *Maybe not ever.*

"Then tell me about Jeremy."

"Well, for example, at the last Emmy Awards, I was by myself, no date, so Jeremy and I were seated next to each other at the table. No one else was paying any attention to him, so I asked him some casual questions about himself. He didn't stop talking for twenty minutes. I really enjoyed hearing about his friends and his school. I also got the feeling there weren't many people who listened to him."

"What do you think of his mother?"

"I feel sorry for her."

"Why?"

"She looks so fragile. I've seen some of her old movies on television — she was a different person then. Not just younger, but so *physical.* Teresa Gleason made adventure pictures, and knockabout romantic comedies — she was gorgeous, but she swung from ropes, swam under water, rode horses bareback — she was 'one of the boys.' Teresa *Radford* seems so timid."

"Tell me about the people who worked — or played — with Radford. Which of them do you think might have had a reason to want him dead?"

"Oh, no, I'm not going to spread gossip. You're not going to use me to get information that might damage innocent people."

"I'm only asking you to tell me what you know —"

"I'll walk home the rest of the way," I said, grabbing the door handle.

"We're three blocks from your place. You'll stay put until we get there." He sounded as angry as I felt.

I stayed put. We didn't say another word to each other.

When we reached Seventy-Second Street and Central Park West, I yanked open the door and got out as fast as I could. He hadn't completely stopped the car. I headed straight toward the entrance to my building and didn't look back. I was already inside the courtyard when I heard Phoenix gun his motor and drive away.

# 13

"Morgan — do you know what's happened?" Nancy was excited, but I could hear a note of concern in her voice, too. It was a quarter to seven in the morning.

"About Damon." I had just awakened, after less than three hours of sleep. "Yes." I was pouring coffee into a mug the size of a large flower-pot. "I was there this morning, right after they found his body."

"And you didn't come up to see *me?*"

"It was almost two o'clock —"

"Jesus, Morgan, I wouldn't mind being woken up to hear about a murder in my own building."

"Have the police said it was a murder?" I asked.

"Oh, come on — all the morning news shows are saying it. But how is this going to affect your job?"

*That's what she's worried about.* "I don't think it should. The show's ratings are high."

"So far, so good then. Now, when's the funeral? I want to go with you."

"I don't know anything about a funeral. And why would you want to go?"

"To see who's there, of course. Maybe I can spot the killer."

"You changed your name to Nancy *Drew?*"

"I'll ignore the sarcasm, grumpy, because I probably called before you've had your coffee. Just tell me this, if Damon was a character on your show, and all the others who might have killed him were characters too, who would *you* choose to be the murderer?"

"Can't do it. I like the people who might be suspects more than I liked the victim."

"You've got to stop telling the truth like that, Morgan. The police will think you did it. I'll bet right now everybody else is talking about how much they *adored* Damon, what a *wonderful* man, what a *terrible* tragedy — yada, yada puke."

"I'll let you know when I find out about the funeral."

**TV KINGPIN SLAIN** screamed the *New York Post.* **TV HONCHO CANCELLED** bellowed the *Daily News.* Both papers had pages of photographs, provocative stills of Teresa from her movies, Damon and Teresa's wedding picture, and shots of some of the models and actresses Damon was known to have dated since their divorce. *The New York Times,* with typical restraint, reported the few known facts of the police investigation on page fifteen. The story was accompanied by a headshot of Damon. It was the same picture used in Global Broadcasting's most recent Annual Report. Nathan Hughes's office probably gave it to the *Times*. The photograph wasn't retouched; staring at it, I had to admit he actually had looked like a younger Robert Redford, or an older Brad Pitt.

*The Wall Street Journal* wondered if Damon Radford's death would have a negative effect on Global's stock price. No photographs.

"Murder in the Penthouse" was the lead story on GBN's nationally syndicated TV show *Entertainment News*. Similar stories topped news magazines on the other broadcast and cable networks. I imagined Damon — wherever he was now — furious it had taken his death to make him the biggest star on television.

The TV in my office played in the background all morning as I worked furiously to revise several weeks' worth of scripts. I had to create places into which we could insert the counterfeit flashbacks of the reshot rape scene, and revise those same scripts to incorporate the changing relationship between Kira and Nicky, and Kira and Cody. It would be faster to do this myself than to explain what I wanted to one of my staff writers. Cybelle said she loved the dance scene I wrote for her. With my new plan, I was keeping the dance, but it would be Link Ramsey who would be in the scene with her, not Sean O'Neil. And I had to come up with a new story for Sean's character, Nicky.

A little after twelve noon, Tommy Zenos surprised me by showing up at my office. He was toting an expensive wicker picnic basket. Although he had taken the elevator, he was huffing, puffing and sweating as though he had walked up all six flights. "I . . . brought us . . . lunch," he said between labored breaths. He opened the top of the basket and took out cutlery and cloth napkins.

I leaned over and looked at what else the basket contained. The top item was fresh Iranian caviar. He opened it and spread some for me on a thin cracker. It was *delicious*. As soon as I swallowed, I said, "This is quite a treat, Tommy."

"Beware of Greeks bearing gifts," he joked. But I knew it wasn't really a joke; he was much too nervous. I realized that this picnic basket had come with strings attached, strings as thick as coaxial cables.

"What's this gift going to cost me?"

"Morgan, you're not going to tell anybody — *anybody at all* — about what happened up at Damon's that day, are you?" It was more of a plea than a question.

"There's nothing to tell. We watched the tape of Link's new scene. If Damon hadn't just got out of the hospital, we would have watched the tape in his office."

"Thank you, Morgan."

"There's nothing to thank me for."

"The police might not understand," he said.

"I mean, Damon said horrible things like that all the time, to everybody. You know that. Everybody knows that."

"Tommy —"

"It didn't mean anything, what he said. Just words. I wouldn't kill Damon because of that. Not that anybody said I did. Kill him, I mean."

Tommy Zenos didn't know how to take "yes" for an answer.

"Damon liked the new scene, Tommy, and he told us to go ahead with the story changes we want to make. I don't remember anything else he might have said."

He looked as though the governor had just called and told the warden to put the lethal injection needle away.

"Morgan . . ." He was stretching my name out so it sounded as though it had more than two syllables. "I'd . . . I'd like you to get more involved on the production side of the show, work with me *closer*. I think you'd make a fine co–executive producer. I mean, I've thought that for a long time, but even more. Now, I mean."

*He was trying to bribe me!* Even though I liked him, I wanted to rub his caviar in his face. I might have, except that I like fresh caviar, and until today I hadn't had any in years. Not since my first wedding anniversary, on a moonlit night in Mombassa. Out of respect for the caviar, I controlled my temper. "No," I said.

"No — what?"

"I don't want to become co–executive producer that way, Tommy. You don't have to pay me, because you didn't buy anything from me."

"I mean it, Morgan. I can use your help . . . when the police are gone and all this is over."

I put the jar of fresh black caviar back in its place, wiped my hands on a napkin and folded the wicker lid back down, closing the basket. I swiveled away from Tommy and faced my computer again.

"I have to get back to work," I said.

As soon as the medical examiner released Damon's body, Teresa Radford took charge of making arrangements for the funeral. When I learned the details of the service, I called Nancy at her office.

"Do you still want to see Damon sent on his way to 'the other side'?"

"After everything you've told me about him, I wouldn't miss it."

"There's an official 'to be admitted' list. I'll have your name put on it. Eleven o'clock Friday morning, at the Frank E. Campbell Funeral Chapel, on Madison at Eighty-First Street."

"Funeral home to the stars. Good choice," she said.

# 14

By ten-thirty Friday morning a crowd had formed in the street outside the Frank E. Campbell Funeral Chapel, gawking at the celebrities who were going in. As I made my way through the crush toward the entrance, I heard someone say, "Will you look at the size of this crowd?" I remembered reading about a Hollywood wit who, when he saw the immense turnout for the funeral of the despised head of one of the studios, made the famous crack, "Well, give the public what it wants and you can't keep them away."

I gave my name to one of the two black-suited men who flanked the entrance. He checked it off on his clipboard and I was admitted into the packed chapel.

A gleaming brass casket, framed by huge arrangements of Casablanca lilies in black ceramic urns, rested on a low platform at the front of the chapel. The casket was closed. The Global Broadcasting Network's official photograph of Damon, his face twice the size it had been in life, rested on a brass easel next to the casket.

I was in the right place. So was Damon.

Nancy had arrived early and saved me a seat. Over the years enough men have complimented me so that I know I'm all right in the looks department, but next to Nancy Cummings I usually feel like furniture. This morning, wearing a gray Prada ensemble that perfectly accentuated her slender curves, and clutching a red lizard Ferragamo bag, she looked even more gorgeous than usual. She stood up to let me into the row and towered six inches over me, instead of her usual three. I looked down and saw she was wearing new Manolo Blahnik stiletto pumps. When five-foot-nine-inch Nancy wears three-inch heels and someone asks her how tall she is, she smiles and replies, "I'm five feet twelve."

All around us, people were speaking to each other in hushed tones, while at the same time their eyes scanned the chapel to see who else was there. As I sat down, I saw that Nancy, too, was assessing the celebrity quotient under Frank E. Campbell's roof.

"Do you know who's here?" she whispered.

"Who?"

"Everybody who's important on your network," Nancy said.

That was not much of an exaggeration. I had expected to see everyone connected to *Love of My Life* in attendance, and the *Trauma Center* folks, and the rest of the daytime schedule over which Damon had direct control. What surprised me was how many of the creators, producers and stars of shows on the prime-time and late-night schedules were there; I wouldn't have thought they would have had much contact with the head of daytime programming. Helen Marshall was also among those present. She was dressed all in black and held a black lace handkerchief close to her pale face, prepared to cry for the man who had fired her.

In the row behind Helen, I could see Cybelle Carter, who looked as though she was in pain. She was in a wheelchair, parked at the end of her row. Johnny Isaac was directing the foot traffic around her, making sure no one bumped into her, or jarred her chair in the narrowed aisle. Farther back I was astonished — and thrilled — to see Harrison Landers, the man who trained me. Tears of happiness filled my eyes and threatened to overflow at the sight of him, out in public at last. His complexion had the ruddy glow of health, and his wiry gray hair was still thick, still cut military short. With his bright hazel eyes and broad shoulders, I thought again, as I had when we worked together, that he must have been one of the best-looking Marines in Vietnam. He still had the broad shoulders, but now he was in a wheelchair, too, his paralyzed legs covered by a blanket.

Unlike Cybelle's chair, a temporary convenience that had to be propelled manually, Harrison's was an electric model. Someone had affixed the Rolls-Royce *Spirit of Ecstasy* hood ornament to the right armrest, just in front of the hand controls. Harrison's "Rolls" was parked several rows behind Cybelle's "compact," on the opposite side of the aisle.

My joy that Harrison was well enough to leave his apartment was total, but I was surprised he hadn't let me know how much improved he was. I thought he was still bedridden from the stroke he had suffered three years ago. *The stroke that had followed his terrible fight with Damon.* I wanted to go over to him, to tell him how much I missed him. I wanted to make plans to see him, but with this crowd, under these circumstances, I realized that wasn't possible. So I smiled and made the "phone call" gesture with my hands. Harrison smiled in response, and nodded to me. It was a start.

The eulogies began. Hypocrisy on parade.

The first to speak was Father John Collins. He introduced himself as Damon's priest.

*Damon had a priest?*

"I'd like to have been a fly on the wall of that confessional," Nancy whispered.

Father Collins praised Damon as a long-time supporter of the Catholic Youth Athletic Center. "He insisted that his generous contributions be anonymous."

"But I'll bet they were tax deductible," Nancy whispered.

*"Shhhhh."*

The next speaker came in the person of a delicate little woman with silver hair who appeared to be in her seventies. Father Collins introduced her as Elizabeth Radford, Damon's mother. In the five years I had worked in daytime, I had never heard any reference to Damon's parents. He might have sprung fully formed from the head of Zeus for all we knew.

Mrs. Radford's voice was soft, with a distinctly Southern accent. Without the aid of the podium microphone her words would not have carried past the first row. "Damon was a wonderful son," she said. "He treated me like a queen. My husband, his father, died when he was only five years old. I wasn't well, and I didn't have any family . . . I had to put Damon in foster homes . . . for seven years . . . I didn't see him again until he was twelve years old . . . but he always treated me like a queen . . ."

My God, a child whose father died, exiled by his mother to foster homes for seven years. It gave me a new image of Damon. A helpless little boy was a Damon I never knew, and now never would.

Mrs. Radford was followed by Winston Yarborough, the network's founder and chairman of the board. Yarborough lauded Damon's "mastery of the television medium," recounting a story that had become legend.

"One day almost twenty-five years ago," he said, "I received a letter from a communications major in his junior year at the University of Missouri. A young man I'd never heard of named Damon Radford. He sent me his twenty-page thesis on Global Broadcasting, pointing out the network's weaknesses and including a plan to improve our ratings and our overall level of audience satisfaction. I was astounded at the clarity of his thinking, and the freshness of his ideas. Most of all, I was impressed with the initiative he displayed by putting so much work into his detailed assessment of our company. At first, I admit, his paper made me angry because he attacked some of my most cherished strategies. But when I calmed down and thought about it, I realized this young man had an extraordinary mind. I contacted him by telephone and we talked for two hours. As soon as his college year ended — he was a *junior* — I brought him to New York for a weekend. By the end of that weekend, I had arranged for his transfer to UCLA, and started him off with a part-time job at our affiliate station in Los Angeles."

Winston Yarborough's voice broke. I realized that he really had cared about Damon. *Had he ever seen the Damon I knew?*

Yarborough took a sip water from a glass on the podium and went on to his conclusion. "Damon's rise in our company has been well-documented. Suffice it to say I had great faith in Damon. He was my protégé, my highly regarded colleague, and it had been my plan to make him my successor when I retired. I loved him like a son."

Neither Teresa nor Jeremy spoke.

For me, the biggest surprise of the service was the appearance of the woman who rose from her seat with the family and came forward

110

to close the program. Her back had been turned to me and I had not recognized her until that moment. It was Kitty Leigh, the petite, blonde, doll-like former child star with the spectacular singing voice and the sensation-filled personal life. After many public ups and downs in her career, she was currently hosting a daytime talk show for the network. Kitty's gaudy personal life, full of ruthless men who damaged her, could have supplied daytime drama material for several years.

"This was Damon's favorite song," she said.

Without accompaniment, she began to sing Irving Berlin's "There's No Business Like Show Business." But she sang it in a way I'm sure Mr. Berlin never envisioned. Kitty turned into a love song what Berlin had written as a rousing anthem for the Broadway show *Annie Get Your Gun*. (Under the circumstances, there was a touch of irony in the choice, I thought.) Instead of belting out the lyrics, Kitty caressed them. She transformed the song, just as years ago Barbra Streisand's sensuous reinterpretation of "Happy Days Are Here Again" put a new spin on that old political campaign tune.

Kitty was fabulous. She held the chapel spellbound. When she finished the last note of the line "Let's go on with the show . . ." there was a moment of silence, then the chapel burst into an inappropriate round of applause. I couldn't fully concentrate on her performance, though. I was recalling a scene I'd witnessed four months

111

earlier at Damon's apartment. He had forced Kitty to degrade herself in front of his guests. Rick Spencer and Joe Niles were present; their behavior that night is the cause of my deep dislike of the two of them.

Based on what Damon did to Kitty, I thought that of all the people at Campbell's, she had the most powerful reason to want him dead.

As soon as the funeral service was over, Nancy left to go back to her office. I had to go through the receiving line to pay my respects to the three surviving members of Damon's family.

When I reached Jeremy, I hugged him.

"I'm so sorry about your father."

"Thanks," he said. "You've been great."

I told Jeremy the truth; I *was* sorry that his father was dead. My deeper regret was that Damon had been his father. At least the Damon I knew. Perhaps there was another Damon — or perhaps there might have been another, a different, Damon, had it not been for whatever happened to him during those seven years he was in foster homes. When it was my turn, I said something polite to Teresa. She said something polite in return.

I had been watching Elizabeth Radford while I waited to express my condolences to her. I suppose I was searching her face for some trace of Damon. It was there, in the cheekbones. She didn't have Damon's vitality. Up close I could see that she was tired, and that her eyes were dull with grief. Her replies to expressions of sympathy were perfunctory, her handshake mechanical. A little old lady wind-up doll.

Finally it was my turn to speak to her.

"Hello, Mrs. Radford. I'm Morgan Tyler. I —"

Her eyes suddenly came alive and she embraced me. "Oh, my *dear*. I'm *so happy* to meet *you*," she said.

Gently, I disengaged myself and asked, "Why?"

"Damon told me so much about you. But he said I wouldn't be able to meet you until the wedding."

I was sure she was confused. She was certainly confusing me.

"What wedding?"

"Your wedding to my son! I know it was supposed to be a secret, but that can't matter now." She embraced me again and she began to cry. As awkward as it was, there was nothing I could do except hold her comfortingly.

I was so astonished by what she said I didn't think about who else might have heard her. Then I glanced up and saw Teresa and Jeremy staring at me. Teresa was steaming with fury. Jeremy looked betrayed. As carefully as I could, I disengaged myself from the elderly woman for the second time.

"That isn't true," I said to the three Radfords. "Damon and I weren't going to be married. There's some misunderstanding."

"Why are you denying it?" Mrs. Radford

113

looked as though I had slapped her. "My son loved you."

Teresa glared at me, then put one arm around her former mother-in-law. "Come with me, Mother Radford. I think you should lie down now," she said as she led the grieving woman away.

"Jeremy, it isn't true," I said, reaching out to him.

He stepped back, dodging my touch. "I thought you were my friend." His eyes were filling with fresh tears of shock and pain. "But you weren't."

He turned and hurried away, following his mother and grandmother.

In death, Damon had managed to strike one more painful blow.

# 15

Detectives Phoenix and Flynn were waiting for me as I left the Frank E. Campbell Funeral Chapel. I hadn't heard from Phoenix since I refused to tell tales on my colleagues and stormed out of his car without saying good night. The first thing I thought when I saw him was, *Now what?* What I actually said was, "Yes?"

"Ms. Tyler," said Detective Flynn, "there are a few questions we'd like to ask you."

"Are you taking me down to your station?"

"How about we buy you a cup of coffee around the corner?" Phoenix said.

I wanted to tell him where he should shove that cup, but I restrained myself. The truth was I needed to sit down and I needed some coffee. What I did not need was another surprise. Damon's mother had thrown me for a loop.

At least Phoenix and Flynn were known quantities.

We settled into a curved imitation leatherette booth in the back, where it was quiet, with me sandwiched between the two detectives. Phoenix was a big man measuring north to south; Flynn was more than ample going east to west. A smiling waitress approached with an order pad. She asked us what we would like to have in a manner that suggested she really wanted to know. I enjoy being around people who like doing what they do, and this woman's genuine smile lifted my spirits.

"Three coffees," Flynn told her.

"Separate checks," I said.

Phoenix told his partner, "She's joking, G.G."

I looked at Detective Flynn, who was built like two sides of beef. "Your mother named you Gigi?"

"It's G.G. Two initials. For George Gordon," Flynn said.

"His mother liked poetry," Phoenix added.

"George Gordon, Lord Byron," I said. Suddenly I felt a little uncomfortable because I was showing off. Then I realized Phoenix was showing off, too. I wondered if he was showing off for me.

The waitress returned with our coffee and began distributing the cups.

Flynn looked from his partner to me, and back to his partner, and then addressed both of us. "If you two are through talking about whatever the hell you're talking about, can we discuss the murder?"

"I didn't hear anything," the waitress said as she scurried away.

Phoenix bypassed the sugar bowl and pushed the container of Sweet'N Low toward me. Flynn eyed his partner with suspicion.

"You know how she takes her coffee?"

"Lucky guess," I said. I emptied two packets into my cup. "What do you want to ask me?"

Detective Flynn took his little notebook out of a jacket pocket, but Phoenix was the one who began their coffee shop interrogation.

"According to the folks at your network," Phoenix said, "*nobody* had a motive for killing Radford. But everybody has a theory."

"Theories are flowing like my wife's mascara when she watches a Disney movie." Flynn's tone was affectionate; it was the first thing about him I liked.

"We want to run a few of those theories by you," Phoenix said. "For what you can add. Or subtract."

"Okay," I said.

"We heard Radford had big gambling debts," Phoenix said.

"Damon didn't gamble."

"It was a drug killing," Flynn said.

"Damon didn't take drugs."

"Jealous husband?" Phoenix asked.

"He didn't go after married women."

"Plenty of single women, though," Flynn said.

"From what we've heard," Phoenix said.

"And read," Flynn added.

"How long have you two been partners?" I asked them.

They answered simultaneously:

"Five years." (Flynn)

"Six years." (Phoenix)

117

"You two sound like a married couple," I observed.

"Hey!" said Flynn. "What are you saying here?"

"I'm joking, G.G.," I said. "May I call you by your initials?"

Detective Flynn looked as though he didn't know what to make of me. I had that same trouble myself sometimes. Phoenix got the interrogation back on track. "Two of the people we've talked to say they think you killed Radford," he said.

"Oh, great. His mother says I was going to marry him. Other people say I killed him. Is everybody in New York going crazy?"

"So . . . you were going to marry Radford," Phoenix says slowly.

"You should have told us that!" Flynn says, annoyed.

"No, I wasn't going to marry him," I say, exasperated, and then I actually shudder at the thought. "His mother must have confused me with somebody else."

"Who?"

"I don't know," I said. "Who accused me of killing him?"

"We can't tell you that."

"Why not?" I was getting angry. "I'm allowed to face my accusers."

"That's at trial," Flynn said. "We don't have to tell you anything at this stage of the investigation."

"That's a pretty damn unfair investigation. Do I need a lawyer?"

"You're not under arrest." (Phoenix)

"Did you kill him?" (Flynn)

"No, I did NOT. Do I have to print cards stating that?"

Phoenix studied me for a moment. "It was Helen Marshall and Jay Terrill," he said. "They're the ones who said they think you killed Radford."

"They wish I had," I snapped. "Helen's a competitor and Jay works as a scriptwriter for me. They both want my job."

I tried to look casual, but what Phoenix just told me hurt like hell.

I had hired Jay, and tried to help him master our craft, as Harrison had helped me. Now I find out he told the police I murdered Damon. As for Helen . . . I wanted to go somewhere and scream. I picked up my bag. "If you're not going to throw me in jail, I'm going back to my office."

"Are you Morgan Tyler?" A voice broke in.

I hadn't seen this stranger in heavy black-rimmed glasses approach our booth.

"Yes?"

He shoved an envelope into my hand. "Have a nice day," he said, hurrying away.

The envelope had my name on it, and bore the name and return address of an entertainment law firm known to handle some of television's heavyweights. Phoenix and Flynn watched me open the envelope. Phoenix looked concerned. "What is it?"

"I'm supposed to be at this law office tomorrow morning at ten o'clock," I said, scanning the letter. I looked up. "For the reading of Damon's will. Why in the world would they want *me* there?"

"As far as I know," Phoenix said, "the only people who are invited to the reading of a will are the beneficiaries."

Flynn's eyebrows went up and he looked at me with fresh suspicion.

"If Damon left me anything," I said, "it's probably a basket full of cobras."

"You'll find out tomorrow," Flynn said.

His tone of voice made the statement sound like a threat.

# 16

After we left the coffee shop, Phoenix and Flynn dropped me back at the Dakota. I didn't stop at my apartment; instead I took the stairs directly up to the sixth floor. I admit I use work the way other people use drink or drugs. I take my mind off my own troubles by creating havoc in the lives of my characters.

The phone was ringing as I unlocked the door.

I hurried inside, dropped my handbag and snatched up the receiver. "Hello?"

"Morgan? It's Penny Cavanaugh. Remember? Matt's nutty Aunt Penny?"

"This is a nice surprise." I sat down and let out a deep sigh. "Truthfully, Penny, you're the only nice surprise I've had today."

"That's too bad. When I have a day I'd like to rip out of the calendar, I cook. Actually, I do that when I've had a good day, too."

"I can roast things over a fire in the ground, but the only thing I know how to make indoors, on a stove, is scrambled eggs."

"I'd like to ask you to come over for dinner tonight, but Matt's acting like a bear. He growled that I can't invite you because you're a suspect in his murder investigation."

121

"He's barred me from your house?" I managed to keep my voice level, but I was gripping the receiver the way I would like to have been gripping Detective Phoenix's neck.

"I don't think you killed that man, Morgan. But if you did, I know you must have had a good reason."

I wished Penny Cavanaugh was *my* aunt. I needed a loyal Aunt Penny more than Matt Phoenix did. "Penny, I have an idea. I'll take you out to dinner at a restaurant. The good detective didn't say you and I couldn't go out together, did he?"

"No, he didn't think to close that loophole," she said. There was a note of sly humor in her voice.

"How about tonight?" I said.

"Tonight is fine. Matt can make his own dinner. He won't like it, but that'll teach him not to act like my father."

"Where would you like to go?"

"I read about a restaurant up on Ninety-Sixth and Broadway," she said. "It's a Cuban place. They say the food is great."

"Cuban sounds perfect."

We agreed we'd meet at seven-thirty, and hung up.

For the next six hours, unless Detective Phoenix decided to break down the door and arrest me, I was going to work on a new love story for the character of Jillian. Harrison Landers cast the actress who plays Jillian six years ago, when she was just fifteen. The audience had watched her develop into an ethereal beauty. Jillian's last story line culminated in her barely escaping death at the hands of a maniac. After all of that drama, I rested the character for a while. Now enough time had passed for her to be in one of the front burner stories again.

She was perfect for the story of love and jeopardy I had in mind.

I turned on the computer and began to outline the scene in which shy, frightened young Jillian Lowell meets Gareth Anthony, the older mystery man who will become "the love of her life."

By six o'clock I had outlined some three months' worth of scenes.

Things would not go smoothly for Jillian and Gareth. Both would first deny and then resist their attraction to one another. Jillian was terrified of making another mistake; the last man she trusted, the sweet-faced but homicidal Michael, had almost killed her. Gareth did not want to fall in love with Jillian, because he was hiding a tormenting and dangerous secret from his past. The outline would be filled in with dialogue by the scriptwriters I'd assign, and the resulting scenes folded into episodes that would play out over the next several months.

As a general rule, breakdowns — outlines of episodes — are done six weeks in advance of air. Scripts are written four weeks in advance (to give me time to do any rewriting that may be necessary) and episodes are taped two weeks before the air-date. Actors get their scripts a day or two before they are scheduled to work.

In hour-long daytime dramas, there are usually three main stories going at once, involving characters that span a range of ages. Something for everybody in the audience is the theory. One story would be in the early stages of its development, another further along, and the third story would be intensifying toward one of its dramatic peaks.

We plan those peaks to occur during November, February and May.

These are the months when all of the shows on television, whether entertainment or news, throw maximum excitement at the audience in order to attract the highest possible number of viewers. The higher the ratings, the more the networks and the local stations can charge advertisers for commercials, because commercial time is sold to advertisers based on the number of viewers each program attracts during these months.

If planning stories according to the calendar isn't complicated enough, we also have to design episodes to honor contractual obligations to the actors. That means if an actor is being paid on the basis of three performances a week, the head writer has to be sure that the actor is used that often; otherwise money is being wasted.

Fortunately for us writers, honoring actor

contracts doesn't mean that the actor has to appear rigidly each week on this schedule. The total episodes for which he is paid are calculated over a thirteen-week cycle, which makes the planning of story episodes a little easier. As Harrison Landers explained it to me, the job of a daytime drama's head writer is part creativity and part geometry.

I had another hour before it would be time to leave to meet Penny.

I wanted to spend it getting Jillian and Gareth to let down their defenses and admit how they feel about each other. In my outline, Jillian had arrived at Gareth's office late at night, unexpectedly, to deliver a gift she had made as a surprise for him. But Jillian is the one who gets the surprise when, hearing her behind him, Gareth reflexively whirls around and levels a Glock 19 pistol at her:

The expression of shock, of horror, on Jillian's face stabs Gareth in the heart. He pulls her into his arms, caresses her, murmurs that he is sorry, he didn't realize she was there, that when he heard someone behind him his old Marine training just took over.

Jillian tells Gareth to stop lying to her. What she just saw was not his old Marine training. It's time he told her the truth. She trusts him, why won't he trust her?

All right, he will tell her the truth, but not here. Gareth puts the pistol in the pocket of his jacket, closes his safe and replaces the panel that conceals the door to the secret room. As they are leaving the office, Gareth brushes against a large, heavily wrapped and padded object. What is it?

Jillian forgot; that's the reason she's here in Gareth's office tonight. It's a surprise and she wanted to hang it on the wall before he returned.

Gareth tears open the wrapping paper to find an extraordinary, poster-sized photograph that Jillian took of one of Gareth's favorite rare stamps, the beautiful 1882 one-cent Dolly Madison. Jillian's had it enlarged and framed like a painting.

Gareth is more than pleased; he's touched at what Jillian did for him. What was his response? He nearly shot her. He can't bear that thought. He takes her hand and promises that he will tell her everything. He'll confide in her where they met, on the grounds of his partially restored imported castle outside of town.

Alone together in the quiet beauty of the park-like setting, Gareth tells Jillian the truth about himself. Most of it. He tells her about The Club, and about the fact that he was an espionage agent from his final year at the Sorbonne until shortly before he came to Greendale, to begin a new life.

Although he gives her no details that could endanger anyone else, he tells her that he's been called back into service for one last important assignment, one that he cannot refuse. He does not tell her why he cannot refuse, that he is being forced back into that dark world by blackmail, the same way he forced his superior to let him out of it.

He tells Jillian that he has now put his life in her hands by telling her this, and that her own life will be in danger if anyone ever discovers what she knows. Her protection, and his, depends upon Jillian's ability to keep silent.

Can she do that? Can she keep Gareth's secret no matter what anyone in her family, or in town, might say about him? Can she hold her tongue and keep her head no matter how angry she may become at what she feels are unfair comments about Gareth? Does she realize that she is in love with a man she cannot defend, because to do so would endanger his life?

Gareth tells Jillian that the best thing she could do for herself would be to leave him now. Jillian should go and never look back. Gareth will leave Greendale; she need never see him again. All she has to do is say the word.

Jillian touches his face with one soft hand.

If that speech is a proposal of marriage, she whispers, then her answer is "yes."

For a moment, Gareth is speechless. Then he smiles at her and replies that such a question, phrased in that way and posed to a gentleman, can have only one answer.

Gareth tells Jillian that he wants her in his life more than he has ever wanted anyone. He wants her formally, legally, conventionally and forever. But would she consider marrying in secret, and keeping their marriage a secret until it is safe to go public with their relationship? It will mean eloping, without family, with none of the beautiful trappings that Jillian deserves to have on her wedding day. Is Jillian sure that marrying Gareth is what she wants to do, really, under these difficult circumstances?

Yes, she is sure.

Gareth tells her that he will find a place where a couple can marry without anyone knowing. However, there is one formality he must take care of before he can make those plans.

What is that?

Gareth takes one of her hands in both of his. Will Miss Lowell do Mr. Anthony the great honor of becoming his wife some forty-eight hours from now? Yes, she will. And they kiss. And kiss . . .

*God, I love this stuff!*

At six-thirty I had to shut down the computer, because I was planning to walk to the Cuban restaurant. Two long blocks west to Broadway and then twenty-four blocks of normal length north would work out the kinks in my legs and back that came from sitting and writing for hours.

# 17

The name of the Cuban restaurant on Broadway and Ninety-Sixth was El Malecon. As I approached, I saw that the last four letters of the red neon sign above the entrance had burned out, leaving it just "El Mal" — the bad.

I hoped that wasn't an omen.

I was a few minutes early. While I waited outside for Penny, I studied the menu posted on El Mal's smoked-glass front window and tried to remember my high school Spanish. I was still in *Aperitivos* and had gotten as far as *Camarones al Ajillo* $5.95, when Penny Cavanaugh's cab pulled up and she got out. She looked great in a brown wool pants suit with a soft beige sweater and a necklace of amber beads the color of wild honey. Next to her, my black leather motorcycle-chic jacket and baggy pants made me feel like a hoodlum.

She gave my outfit a discreet glance.

"You look . . . trendy," she said.

"I was going for dangerous."

"Mission accomplished," she said.

Inside the restaurant, we saw that El Malecon was about two-thirds full. The decor was no-frills cozy: red shades on the wall lights, sawdust on the floor, tables set with red plastic cloths and white paper napkins. Enticing odors were coming from the kitchen. We were greeted by a smiling young man wearing tight pants, two-inch lifts in his shoes and too much styling gel in his hair. He showed us to a table by the window and pulled the chairs out for us.

"I am Miguel, your host. I will return," he promised.

Penny put her handbag down between her chair and the wall and looked out at Broadway's passing parade. There wasn't much to satisfy her curiosity. Only a few of society's mobile misfits were on the street, and vehicle traffic was relatively light. Miguel returned with a large pitcher of red wine with chunks of fresh fruit cut up in it.

"We didn't order anything yet," I said.

"Sangria, for the ladies' first visit. From us."

"Thank you."

"That's so nice," Penny said, giving him a smile.

Miguel reeled off the specials. We chose the two entrees he seemed most enthusiastic about. He grinned with pleasure. "Now, you ladies, we start with *Camarones* — shrimps in garlic over mashed plantains. One order for two is enough. It will make you happy."

He hurried away to make us happy.

Penny edged her seat closer to the table and leaned in toward me. She lowered her voice and said, "There's something I've been dying to ask you, Morgan. If you don't mind."

"You can ask me anything."

"On *Love of My Life* — do those people in the story know what's going to happen? In the story?"

"No. We're very careful not to let the actors know the future for their characters. Each new turn of events is a surprise to them."

She gave a sigh of relief. "That's just like life," she said. She sat back in her chair, relaxed again.

"We try to make the story lines more exciting than life," I said. "I read an interview with Elmore Leonard where somebody asked him why he thought the books he wrote were so popular. He said, 'It's because I leave out the parts that people skip.' That's what we try to do — leave out the parts that people skip."

Miguel returned with our *Aperitivos*, which he divided onto two plates. He beamed as we tasted the dish and expressed our approval. Glowing with pride, he bounced away to greet two new customers who had just come in the door.

When we were alone again, Penny said, "I heard Matt talking to G.G. — that's his partner."

"Yes, I've met Detective Flynn," I said. My tone made it clear I had not been charmed by the encounter.

"Oh," she said with a reassuring smile, "he's actually a lot nicer than he seems the first nine or ten times you're with him. And he has a terrific wife. I'm sure you'll meet her. Anyway, Matt and G.G. were talking about you. People at your company have been telling them things you said about that dead man. Before he died, I mean. They're saying you didn't like him very much."

"I didn't like him at all, Penny."

"Maybe you shouldn't be so honest about that. G.G. thinks you killed him."

"What does Detective Phoenix think?" I restrained myself from telling her the negative feelings I was having at this moment about her nephew.

"He wouldn't tell me. He didn't like it that I was listening. All he said was they were investigating other people, too."

*Too. Other people, too.* "That's a dose of reality," I said.

"I hope I didn't upset you." She sounded concerned.

"It was good that you told me, Penny. I've been working so hard I guess I haven't been taking the spot I'm in seriously enough."

"I know how to perk you up. Come to the shop tomorrow and I'll give you a complimentary deluxe European facial."

"Facial?"

"I give facials at Natasha's on Madison."

I'd never been there, but I'd heard about Natasha's. It's an expensive day spa where the working rich and the idle rich go to have their troubles steamed, exfoliated and massaged away.

"We have a lot of celebrity clients," Penny said. "We do some of the actresses on *All My Children* and *One Life to Live*. And your Jillian, and Mrs. Lowell, and Kira from *Love of My Life* — and that movie star who has the talk show on your station. She's one of my favorite regulars."

"Kitty Leigh?"

Penny leaned in close to me again and lowered her voice. "We're not supposed to talk about our clients — and I'd never say anything bad — but oh, what an awful life she's had." Her eyes were large and dark with sympathy for Kitty. "She told me about that disgusting old man at the movie studio when she was a little girl who used to . . . you know . . . *do things* to her. And about her first husband who got her hooked on drugs, and her second husband who stole all her money and the agent who ruined her movie career. And about the famous married author who broke her heart. And she's had to go through most of that on the front pages of the supermarket papers. *Last* week she said that my facials are keeping her sane now that she's in television . . ."

It was after ten-thirty and we were full of good Cuban food, Sangria and wine-soaked fruit when I paid the check. Penny tried to pay half, but I reminded her that dinner was my treat. Miguel hurried to open the door for us, and said he hoped we would come again. I told him we would. There wasn't much traffic and only a few pedestrians were on Broadway when we stepped out into the chilly night. A panhandler whose heart didn't seem to be in his work sat on the sidewalk, leaning back against the outside wall of El Mal, drinking designer coffee out of a tall plastic personal mug. When he spotted Penny coming out of the restaurant, he started to get up, but I met his eyes with an uninviting scowl and he slumped back down again.

Nearby, two thin young men with matching leather jackets and matching platinum blond hair were walking a pair of identical white standard poodles. Across the street a middle-aged couple was in a heated argument as they bought an armload of magazines at the newsstand. Penny had been watching the two blond men with the poodles and said to me, "It doesn't look like a dangerous neighborhood, but I don't think you should walk home alone. I'll drop you off." Nodding agreement, I stepped into the street, scanning Broadway for an empty cab. Half a block away one was coming toward us. I waved my hand at it, but I was too late.

A chubby man had darted into the street, flapping one arm frantically and jumping up and down. The cab stopped for him. Because the man was carrying a doctor's medical bag, I didn't mind losing the cab to him. I wanted to think he was on his way to save a life. Penny joined me in the street. Neither of us saw another vacant cab. I turned away from Penny, assessing our chances of catching one on this spot. They weren't good.

"Let's walk down a couple of blocks," I said. "I think we'll have —"

Suddenly Penny screamed.

Simultaneously, I heard the roar of an accelerating engine. I whirled around and was momentarily blinded by the high beams of a car that was rocketing toward us! The primal instinct for self-preservation took over. My body went into action faster than my mind processed thought. I shoved Penny into the narrow space between two parked cars, and hurled myself after her.

Penny stumbled into the curb and fell backward onto the sidewalk.

I landed hard against the fender of a parked car.

The speeding car roared over the spot where only seconds ago I'd been standing, and I felt a powerful whoosh of air in my face as it tore a five-foot gash along the side of the vehicle parked in front of me. My heart was thumping, my pulse was racing and somewhere in my mind I knew I was going to have one huge purple bruise on my hip, but adrenaline was pumping through my veins so fast I couldn't feel any pain. I turned to check on Penny and saw that the panhandler was helping her to her feet. She was able to stand up, but she was shaky, and her eyes were dilated with fear. She was gripping her purse with both hands, her knuckles white, her fingers welded to the leather. I took a deep breath, trying to force my pulse to slow as I asked her if she was okay.

She nodded her head. "What about you?" she asked. Color was coming back into her face.

"I'm fine," I lied.

Penny brushed off her derriere, which was covered with dirt where she'd landed on the sidewalk. "I split my slacks in the back. It's just in the seam, I can fix it," she said. Then, joking, she added. "I dented my dignity."

The panhandler indicated Penny and said to me, "I spilled my coffee helping her up."

"Thank you," I said. I reached into my handbag, grabbed a bill and pushed it into his hand. I thought I gave him a five, but from his wide-eyed reaction and effusive mumbles of appreciation, it might have been a twenty. I didn't care. He hurried away and Penny was looking at me with an expression of concern. "Are you *sure* you're all right?"

"I'm indestructible," I said. Pure bravado. Or wishful thinking.

"Could you see the license plate?" Penny asked.

"No, the car was going too fast."

That was the truth, but only part of it. I *had* caught a glimpse of the driver. Whoever it was had been wearing a mask. Our nearly being run over had been a deliberate act.

"There's a cab," Penny said.

She wrenched one hand away from the iron grip she had on her purse and signaled. The cab swerved to a stop for us and we got in. Penny collapsed in relief against the back seat.

"Central Park West and Seventy-Second Street," I told the driver, "and then through the park to East Sixty-Eighth."

We didn't talk on the way to the Dakota; we were both still too shaken for idle conversation. I used the time to try to make some sense out of what had happened there in the street in front of El Mal. It was unlikely anyone would try to kill Penny Cavanaugh, cosmetologist to the stars.

That meant the intended target had to be me.

But *why?* Who could possibly want me dead?

The cab stopped at the corner of Seventy-Second and Central Park West, and I said good night to Penny. "I'll call you tomorrow about the facial," she said. "You'll love it. It'll take all your cares away."

I doubted that.

# 18

As I was getting ready to go to bed, I debated whether I should call Detective Phoenix and tell him that I was almost murdered. Would he believe me? While I was imagining both sides of the argument, the phone rang. I was halfway out of my slacks as I picked up the receiver.

"Are you crazy?" demanded the furious voice on the other end of the line.

"That depends on who's asking."

"This is Matt Phoenix. What's the idea of almost getting Aunt Penny killed?"

"I can't believe that's what she told you!"

"Of course she didn't put it that way."

"That's because she's *nice*."

Silence. Then, "I'm sorry." He sighed. "It's late, I was worried. In my job I don't see many happy endings."

"This probably isn't the best time to tell you, but the driver who almost ran us down? He was wearing a ski mask. Penny doesn't know that, I didn't want to worry her."

"Yes, she does know that. She told me and she's worried about *you*. You didn't get the license number — not even a partial?"

"No."

Phoenix was silent for a moment, then, "Do you want me to get a uniform to come over and stay with you?"

"Absolutely not. I'm in my own home, the doors are locked and I'd like to go to bed. Unless you have something else to say."

"Until we sort this out, be careful where you go and who you're with."

"God, Phoenix, you are irritating! I don't need a father," I said.

"You need somebody."

"No, I don't! I can take care of myself. Always have." I took a breath and got my temper under control. I didn't want to fight with Phoenix because I liked Penny. And I kind of liked him, too. *Maybe. A little.* "Okay, I give in," I said. "I will be careful. I promise."

"Good. Penny doesn't want anything bad to happen to you." After a moment's pause, he added: "Neither do I."

"Yeah, you just want to win our pizza bet."

I heard him chuckle. "The bet's on time-out until this case is over, but I haven't forgotten it. Take care of yourself."

"Good night," I said.

As I replaced the receiver, I knew I was too keyed up to sleep. I slipped a robe on over my Bruce Lee T-shirt and satin pajama bottoms and went upstairs to my office. As usual, I ignored the elevator and took the stairs. The three flights were dark, but I was used to that. When I was struck by the urge to write in the middle of the night, I always carried a flashlight in addition to my keys.

Inside my office, I clicked on the lights and turned on the computer.

Back to the story of Jillian and Gareth.

Gareth makes arrangements for the secret wedding ceremony. Instead of using one of the planes in the fleet owned by his company, Heartland Air, he hires a small plane in Chicago, for cash. He knows that for a man in his business there is safety in being unpredictable.

Gareth flies Jillian to a rustic little town in Nevada. As Jillian discovers, they have come to a perfectly preserved ghost town. The spunky old woman who owns the town is waiting for them at the end of the crude air strip, with her horse and carriage, which are decorated for the occasion.

Gareth helps Jillian into the carriage and the woman drives them to the chapel in the center of the town's one street. They are met on the front steps by the woman's husband and by the Justice of the Peace, whom Gareth has imported from the nearest city.

Jillian gasps when they enter the little chapel. It is filled with tiers of white roses and illuminated by the light from dozens of tall white candles. Jillian whispers that this is the most beautiful sight she has ever seen. Gareth agrees, but he is looking at Jillian, not at the exquisitely decorated chapel.

Jillian and Gareth are married in a romantic ceremony, with the spunky western lady and her husband as their witnesses. This wedding might be an elopement, but Gareth has made sure that there is nothing quick or ugly about it. Jillian and Gareth exchange their vows in a setting so perfect that they will cherish the memory for the rest of their lives.

After they are pronounced husband and wife, and kiss, they toast their future with the champagne Gareth also thought to provide.

The western lady tells Jillian that she is a very lucky girl to have found a man who loves her so much that he will perform miracles, like having hundreds of perfect white roses trucked into a desert ghost town. For this one day, for Jillian, Gareth brought the dead town back to life.

The new Mr. and Mrs. Gareth Anthony arrive back in Greendale that evening, to spend their wedding night in the habitable part of Gareth's castle.

When they reach the castle, Jillian discovers that Gareth has been busy here, too. The rooms are filled with white roses. White roses everywhere. Gareth tells her that white roses are her flower. For the rest of her life, wherever she is, and wherever he may be, when she receives white roses they will be from Gareth.

A superb cold supper is waiting for them. Champagne is on ice and music plays on the newly installed stereo system. Gareth says that he considered hiring violinists, and blind-folding them, but couldn't figure out how to get them back to town after dinner without leaving Jillian, so he opted for recorded music. He hopes she doesn't mind. She does not.

He extends his hand. She takes it, and they dance. Alone in the candlelight, surrounded by white roses, lost in the joy of their love.

Dinner remains untouched; the ice sur-rounding the champagne melts into a pool.

Jillian Lowell becomes Mrs. Gareth An-thony in the complete sense of that title. This is the most wonderful night of her life, and of Gareth's. He knows, as Jillian does not, that he must leave her in the morning.

If Gareth can pull off the dangerous assign-ment he has been forced to accept, he will re-turn to Jillian in a few days. If.

I paused, my fingers hovering just above the keyboard. If I was killed, or arrested for Damon's murder, Gareth might not survive to return to Jillian.

Whoever replaced me at *Love* could decide to kill him off.

I had to find a way to get out of the mess I was in.

# 19

The reading of Damon's will was scheduled for 10 A.M. at the law offices of Bristol, Cotton, Carroll and Seligman, located at Three Seventy-Five Park Avenue, on the twenty-ninth floor of one of the most famous landmark buildings in the city. The Seagram Building is positioned way back from the street on the rear portion of its five-million-dollar lot. Set on bronze-faced pillars, the thirty-eight story façade is made up of alternating bands of bronze plating and a shade of tinted glass called, appropriately, whisky brown. A full one-third of the space in front of the entrance is taken up by a pink travertine plaza with twin fountain pools flanked by trees. The building and plaza were designed by the world-famous architect Mies van der Rohe to be an oasis in Manhattan's concrete desert.

New York City officials were enraged when it was completed.

They complained that the expansive, open plaza was wasted space.

The real issue at hand was that the plaza could *not* be taxed in the way that enclosed spaces used for business or living *could* be. City officials became creative themselves. They slapped the Seagram Building with the charge of being "excessively prestigious" and imposed a taxation valuation nearly double per square meter than what was required of contemporary skyscrapers nearby.

I crossed the plaza and walked through the building to the elevators.

It was five minutes to ten when I arrived at Bristol, Cotton, Carroll and Seligman.

"I'm Morgan Tyler," I told the receptionist. "I have a ten o'clock appointment with Mr. Seligman."

"He'll be right with you. Please have a seat with those gentlemen."

I turned in the direction she indicated — and came face to face with Detectives Phoenix and Flynn.

"Good morning, gentlemen."

"Hello." (Phoenix)

"How's it goin'?" (Flynn)

"Why don't *you* tell *me* how it's going?"

The appearance of a young man with light brown hair, and the heavily muscled torso of a serious weightlifter, interrupted our sparkling repartee. He extended a hand the size of a catcher's mitt in welcome.

"I'm Leo Seligman, Damon's attorney. You must be Morgan Tyler."

"Yes."

He looked at the two detectives, who were bracketing me like bookends.

"And you gentlemen are . . . ?"

144

"Detectives Phoenix and Flynn, Twentieth Squad, investigating the murder of Damon Radford. We'd like to be present at the reading of the will."

"Well, I have no objection. Do you, Ms. Tyler?"

"Me? No, why should I mind?"

"Let's go to my office, then. The others are waiting."

The others turned out to be Damon's butler, Damon's housekeeper, Teresa and Jeremy. The latter two looked surprised to see me, and not pleased. Neither of them spoke to me, nor did they acknowledge the presence of the two detectives.

Leo Seligman made sure that we all had chairs. His secretary offered us coffee, tea or soft drinks. There were no takers, so she slipped into a seat and prepared to take notes. Seligman took his place behind his desk and began the proceedings by making sure we all knew who we were, and why we were in his office.

"Where's Mrs. Elizabeth Radford?"

"I'm here representing Mother Radford," Teresa said. "She didn't feel up to coming herself."

"Quite understandable," Seligman said. He picked up a legal document. "As some of you know, I've been Damon Radford's personal attorney for the past six years. This is his last will and testament. It was revised by Damon and signed by him two weeks before his death."

Seligman then proceeded to explain the terms of the will. Damon forgave anyone who owed him money. He left ten thousand dollars to his housekeeper, and twenty-five thousand dollars to his butler. Their faces reflected disappointment at the size of their bequests.

"Damon left a one-million-dollar trust fund to provide for the care and comfort of his mother, Elizabeth Radford, for the duration of her life," Seligman told us. "Upon her death, whatever remains in the trust will go to his son, Jeremy."

Seligman began reading from the will.

"My former wife, Teresa Radford, was well provided for by the terms of our divorce agreement, so I intentionally make no monetary bequest to her here. However, if she wishes, she may have any or all of the books in my library." Seligman paused. It was a theatrical moment. Then, sure that he had the breathless attention of his audience, he went on.

"The bulk of my estate — exclusive of the aforementioned bequests, and including all artworks, stocks, bonds, other investments, royalties, insurance policies and my ten-room apartment at Eighty-First Street and Central Park West and its content — is to be liquidated and divided in the following manner. One half in trust to my son, Jeremy Radford. The principal will be dispersed in three increments, when Jeremy reaches the ages of twenty-five, thirty and thirty-five. Until then, he is to receive the income from the trust, for his benefit and in amounts to be determined by the executor."

Teresa interrupted. "Who is the executor?"

"I am," said Seligman. "And if for any reason I am unable to fulfill that obligation, one of my law partners will assume the duty. If for some reason that becomes impractical or impossible, the Bank of Manhattan will assume the responsibilities of executor."

Jeremy asked, "How much money are we talking about?"

"Depending upon market fluctuations at time of asset liquidation, your half of the estate will amount to between seven and eight million dollars."

Detective Flynn jumped right in, "Who gets the rest?"

Seligman rebuked Flynn with a scowl, then resumed reading aloud. "The other half of my estate is to go in total and without restrictions to the woman I love and plan to marry, Morgan L. Tyler of One West Seventy-Second Street in this city."

"You lying little bitch!" Teresa yelled.

"There has to be some mistake," I said.

"No mistake," Seligman assured me. "You've just become a wealthy young woman, Ms. Tyler."

*What I've become is a woman with a powerful motive to murder. Thanks a lot, Damon.*

"There's one more clause." Leo Seligman wasn't finished. He resumed reading from the will, "If Morgan L. Tyler, or Morgan Tyler Radford, if that is her name at the time, dies within six months after my death, it shall be deemed for the purpose of this will that she preceded me in death. In that event, the remainder of my estate shall go to my son, Jeremy."

# 20

The atmosphere in Leo Seligman's office was colder than inside a meat locker.

I couldn't leave quickly enough.

Detectives Phoenix and Flynn caught up with me at the elevator. "We need to have a talk," Phoenix said. I stuck my hands straight out in front of me, wrists together.

"I'm a size seven and a quarter in handcuffs," I said.

"How do you know that?" Flynn asked, raising a brow.

"She's kidding." With a gentleness that surprised me, Phoenix used one of his large hands to push mine back down. "But we really do need to have another talk," he said.

We settled ourselves in a booth at a coffee shop on Lexington Avenue, around the corner from the Seagram. The waitress put cups in front of us, filled them and departed.

"This is our second date, guys. Is it my turn to pay?"

"Why do you try to turn everything into a joke?" Phoenix asked.

"Because when I cry, my mascara runs."

Flynn snorted. "Just like my wife."

"Look, I swear to you — both of you — I had no idea what was in Damon's will. We had nothing remotely like a romantic relationship."

"You two never even kissed?" (Flynn)

"Not with my cooperation."

"So he was after you." (Phoenix)

"Now and then. Never with any success. But striking out with me didn't bother him. His date book was always full."

"You expect us to believe that?" Flynn asked. "We just heard him leave you at least seven million dollars."

"No, I don't expect you to believe me, but it's the truth."

"You make up plots for a living," Phoenix said, picking up the ball. "Think about this. If you and Radford were not going to get married, then why would he put you in his will? What possible reason could he have?"

"He had no reason whatsoever. He knew I despised him. I'm sure he wouldn't want me to have his money." I stopped talking as I realized something that hadn't occurred to me.

Phoenix caught the expression on my face. "What are you thinking?"

I didn't want to tell the truth about what I was thinking, not yet. First I needed some information, so I tried to get it by bluffing.

"I'm amazed you consider me a suspect," I said. "I couldn't possibly have murdered Damon, and you should know that."

Flynn got hot. I had impugned his detective-hood. "Yeah? And just how should we know that?"

"I have an alibi."

"Who? Who's your alibi?"

"Alexander Graham Bell," I said. "Think about it. Joe Niles called me a few minutes after one in the morning. I was home. I couldn't have shot Damon, pushed him over his balcony just before Joe found him, and got home in time to answer Joe's call."

"You had plenty of time," Flynn said.

"Not even if I flew."

"You could have crawled and still had plenty of time."

"Radford didn't go over the balcony just before Niles got there," Phoenix said. "According to the medical examiner, Radford was killed sometime between eleven P.M. and midnight. His body couldn't be seen from the street because of the hedge enclosing the patio. It was Niles's assumption that Damon crashed just before he got there. And, initially, it was ours."

"Wrong-o," said Detective Flynn.

*The probable time of death. That's what I was hoping they'd tell me.*

"So," I said, "I've just lost an alibi — and gained a motive."

"You can help yourself," Phoenix said. "Send us in another direction."

"I have *no idea* who killed him. I can't just sic you on somebody."

151

"You mean you won't."

"Okay, guys," I said. "No more jokes. Just how much trouble am I in here?"

"Take my advice," Flynn said. "Don't make any long-term plans."

I walked back to West Seventy-Second Street, thinking about what had occurred to me at the coffee shop.

Damon's money.

There was one word in Damon's will that nagged at me because I didn't know what its relevance was. In the general description of his assets — stocks and bonds and real property — I had heard the word "royalties." As far as I knew, Damon had never written a published book, or a produced screenplay or songs, invented something or done anything for which one might collect royalties.

Finding out what royalties he received might lead me to the source of his fortune.

And that just might provide a clue as to who murdered him.

# 21

When I reached the Dakota, I found Jay Terrill (the rodent) waiting for me by the reception desk. I hadn't spoken to him directly since I learned he told Detectives Phoenix and Flynn he thought I was a murderer. Jay was shifting his weight from one foot to the other and clutching a ten-by-thirteen envelope to his chest. When he saw me, he flashed a big fake smile. "Hey, Morgan!"

"Jay."

I gave my attention, and a genuine smile, to Alice, the motherly woman who is the Dakota's first line of defense. "Do I have any mail?" I asked, leaning across her desk.

"Just the usual ton, sweetie." She handed me the pile the postman had left.

"Thanks, Alice." I turned to Jay, nodded at the envelope he was squeezing. "Is that the script?"

"A day early." He handed it to me. There were sweat marks on the outside of the envelope where his fingers had left impressions. "You have the new breakdown for me?"

"Not yet."

That was what he was afraid of. If I didn't give

him a new breakdown, that meant he wasn't getting a script assignment for next week. I decided to let him worry for a while.

"Uh, Morgan, can we go up to the office and talk?"

"Some other time. I'll call you about the script."

Now he was really sweating. "Well, let me walk you to the elevator."

"I take the stairs." I started walking and allowed him to follow me. When we were alone in the cool interior of the building at the foot of the polished wood stairs next to the elevator, he launched into his plea.

"Please, Morgan, don't be mad. The cops made me tell them —"

"They *made* you tell them you think I killed Damon? How did they do that, Jay? Electric shocks?"

"You're upset, I don't blame you, really."

"That's generous of you, Jay."

"Look, those cops tricked me! They got me all tangled up — I didn't know what I was saying! Are you going to fire me because I made one little mistake? You've got to know I'd never get you in trouble intentionally."

*And the check is in the mail, and I'll respect you in the morning.*

"I'm not going to fire you, Jay. I'm going to give you a chance to prove how valuable you are to the show."

"Oh, I will. I'll prove it."

He was so eager that for a moment I hated myself for what I was about to do.

But only for a moment.

"I'm going to give you script assignments for the next eight weeks —"

"Great! Oh, Morgan, you won't be sorry."

"Tuesday shows."

He looked as though I'd struck him. I would have liked to, except I don't believe in hitting.

"Tuesday . . . ?"

"The next *eight* Tuesdays, Jay."

In our business, Tuesday episodes are the ones writers like least. They are devoted almost entirely to recapping — letting the audience know what happened previously, in case they missed the much more important Thursday, Friday and Monday episodes.

"I'll get the breakdowns over to you by messenger."

"Yeah, okay," he said, looking furious.

"I'll call you about this," I said, indicating the script he'd given me, "when I've read it." Then I started up the stairs. I didn't look back.

When Harrison Landers was training me, he said most daytime writers hated two things worse than having a root canal. The first was writing Tuesday episodes, and the second was writing breakdowns, the synopsized layouts of daily episodes. At the time, I decided I was going to love both of those assignments, was going to do them with every ounce of ability I had. I was determined to be the best breakdown writer and the best Tuesday scriptwriter Harrison ever had. I don't know if I became the best, but I was the most cheerful and the most enthusiastic.

Miraculously, I really did come to enjoy what others considered drudgery.

The nighttime dramas frequently start with brief clips from earlier episodes and a voice over that intones, "Previously on *NYPD Blue*" or "Previously on *ER* . . ." Those scene snippets fill in details the audience needs to know. But "prime-time" dramas produce only twenty-two, twenty-four or twenty-six hour-long episodes a year. We produce two hundred and sixty episodes for that same year. With a five-days-a-week show, film clips won't do it.

A Tuesday-writer's task is to create scenes in which characters recount recent events to each other. There's an art to turning what is "old news" to the daily viewer into lively scenes that can be enjoyed whether a viewer knows what has happened or not. The technique I used often involved having characters argue about what they had been doing, or about what other characters had been doing. To make the recaps entertaining, I injected comedy whenever possible. Sometimes I used confessional scenes, or fantasy scenes of "what I *should* have said."

Harrison enjoyed my Tuesday scripts because he didn't have to rewrite them. He was generous with his praise, and he let me know the actors looked forward to Tuesday scripts that had my name on them. Damon noticed the ratings for our Tuesday shows had improved, learned about my work from Harrison and used a compliment to me as a tool to berate other writers. That made me about as popular as a rash. I remember thinking at the time that life is just high school all over again, only with bigger bills to pay.

Harrison . . . I've missed him very much.

When I saw him at Damon's funeral, it was the first time I'd seen him in more than two years, since he banned all visitors. He'd sent me a brief note, telling me he did not want his friends and colleagues to see him helpless. Harrison had been such a vigorous, physical man. It was terrible for him suddenly to find himself a prisoner in his own body. Even though he wouldn't allow me to visit, I sent him notes at least once a week. I sent him anything I could think of that might make him smile. I kept it up, hoping that one day he would respond. Only two weeks ago I'd sent him a book of his favorite hilariously eerie Charles Addams cartoons, but, as usual, there had been no response.

As soon as I entered my apartment, I put Jay's script and my pile of mail down on the bedside table and checked for telephone messages. The first was from Penny. "My five o'clock appointment cancelled. If you can come over then, I'll give you that complimentary Deluxe European guaranteed-to-banish-all-cares facial. I'll keep the spot open until I hear from you." She left the number of Natasha's on Madison.

When Penny answered her line, I said, "Hi, it's Morgan. Thank you. I need my cares banished. Be there at five."

"Wonderful. I think I can promise you'll be glad you came."

The next call I made was to Harrison Landers. His answering machine picked up. I left a message telling him I'd missed him, and asking if I could come to visit soon. Before I finished the sentence, he picked up the phone.

"Doll, it's good to hear from you. Of course you can come over. How about tomorrow?"

"Perfect. Can I take you out to lunch?"

There was a momentary pause. "It's not easy for me to get out." Then, "Why don't you come here, I'll order something —"

"No, I'll bring lunch. What would you like — as if I didn't know."

"Thin crust, double cheese and —"

I finished with him: "Pepperoni."

For that moment, he sounded like the old Harrison Landers.

"Oh, Morgan. I'm in the same building, but I've got a ground-floor apartment now. One B."

I had one more call to make before I could get to work on Jay's script. I looked up a phone number and punched it into the keypad. "Good afternoon. Bristol, Cotton, Carroll and Seligman," said the melodic voice at the other end of the line.

"This is Morgan Tyler. Mr. Seligman, please."

Leo Seligman came on the line almost immediately. His voice was warm and cheerful. "What can I do for you, Ms. Tyler?"

"I have a question. When you were reading Damon's will, you mentioned that part of his estate came from royalties. What are the royalties from?"

Silence . . . then a heavy sigh that sounded like a rebuke. When Leo Seligman spoke again, his voice was guarded, and distinctly less warm.

"I'm afraid I can't give you that information, Ms. Tyler. You are not eligible to claim the estate for six months."

"I'm not trying to claim it," I said. "I just want to know the source of Damon's royalties."

"Until you are eligible as an heir, that information is privileged communication and therefore not available to you."

"Thank you."

"Don't hesitate to call again, Ms. Tyler, anytime you have a question."

He had just told me he wouldn't answer the only question I wanted an answer to, but there was no touch of irony in his voice. Which led me to the conclusion that Leo Seligman did not understand the concept of irony. I finished reading Jay's script, made notes for revisions, placed calls to the other scriptwriters to check on their assignments and scheduled my two breakdown writers to come to a meeting at four o'clock the next afternoon.

At last it was time to leave for Natasha's.

Natasha's — or "The palace of perfect skin" as it's known in the social columns — is located on Madison Avenue, between Fifty-Fourth and Fifty-Fifth Streets, behind a pale blue door. The lobby is decorated in the same shade of pale blue, accented by gold leaf and crystal. Penny, her hair pulled up into a ponytail and wearing a smock so white it was nearly blinding, stood by the reception desk, making a notation in the blue and gold appointment book.

She smiled when she saw me. "Hi. Let's get you started."

She took my hand, led me to a dressing room and handed me a pale blue robe.

"Take off your clothes and put this on. Then come to my room, it's right next door. You can leave your clothes here, but bring your bag." She lowered her voice to a whisper, "One of our clients who's here this afternoon has a . . . *little problem*. We try not to put temptation in her way."

As I exchanged my clothes for the soft jersey robe, I began to feel myself relax. I needed this coming hour of steaming and creaming and being masqued and moisturized. Barefoot and wrapped in the flimsy robe, I went into Penny's private treatment room and closed the door behind me. The light was invitingly dim. It was so dim it took me a moment to realize Penny was not alone.

Standing beside her was Detective Matt Phoenix.

He looked as surprised to see me as I was to see him.

# 22

"What is *he* doing here?"

"Penny." His tone was accusatory. "You said you needed to talk about something important." With a nod in my direction he demanded: "So why is *she* here?"

"So you didn't know I'd be here?" I asked.

"No. Or I wouldn't be here."

"Matt, don't be rude." Penny turned to me. "And Morgan, don't get mad. I called you both. I know during a murder investigation you two aren't supposed to be alone together —"

"I feel as though I've missed an episode," I interrupted. "*Why* did you trick us both? And why am I in this robe?"

"You're here undercover?" Phoenix winked at me.

"That's not a very good joke," I said, "but it's the first I've heard you make."

"Are you implying I have no sense of humor?"

"I'm saying I haven't seen evidence of it."

"*Evidence.* That's why I brought you two here," Penny said.

Phoenix turned to her. "Explain," he said.

"Until you solve the case, we — the three of

us — can't have a simple friendship. So, I thought of a way to move things along faster."

"Oh, I want to hear this."

"Don't be sarcastic, Detective. *I'd* like to hear your idea, Penny."

"Thank you." She smiled, then continued, "The two of you should work together. Share information. Morgan already knows all the people you and G.G. are talking to, Matt. She could recognize some clue you might miss."

"Thanks for your faith in me, Penny," he said, his voice dripping with sarcasm.

"You forgot to have lunch, didn't you?" Penny turned to me. "Matt's so crabby when he misses a meal. He's been like that ever since he was a little boy."

I didn't want to think of Matt Phoenix as a little boy. I wanted to get us back to the safe subject of violent death. I turned to Phoenix. "As an act of good faith, will you answer one question for me?"

"If I can."

"Is there anyone, of the people you've talked to, who has an absolutely airtight alibi for the time frame of Damon's murder?"

"Nathan Hughes, the PR man, and that vice president, Rick Spencer, were with Mr. and Mrs. Yarborough at a dinner party the Yarboroughs gave. Ten people swore Hughes and Spencer didn't leave the Yarborough home in Greenwich, Connecticut, until one o'clock in the morning. Before he found the body, Joe

Niles was at an English pub called The Fox and Hounds, on Lexington and Sixty-Fifth. We found three people who swore he was playing pool with them until close to twelve-thirty. Cybelle Carter and Johnny Isaac were together at her place, with a nurse. Teresa Radford and her son say they were together. I don't put much stock in a mother and her son providing alibis for each other. Or an agent and his client, except that Mrs. Radford, Jeremy and Ms. Carter lack any motive we've been able to discover. The nurse doesn't think Isaac left Ms. Carter's, but she admits she fell asleep for a while. Isaac is apparently obsessed with Ms. Carter. He hasn't made any secret about hating the victim, but neither have you, Morgan."

"Look, I thought of something on the way home today. It's an area I think you should explore."

"What area?"

"Damon's money. He was a poor boy. How did he amass millions of dollars? I'm going to look into it, too."

"No. I don't want you looking into anything. You'll just get in the way."

"You've got one hell of a nerve!"

"I agree with you," Penny said. "You're not very diplomatic, Matt."

Phoenix realized he'd lost ground with both of us and tried to recover it. "What I *mean* is, this is a murder investigation. It's a job for professionals. Someone out there killed a man and could kill again. Someone already tried to kill *you*. I want you out of the line of fire."

"And I want you to stop speaking to me in that condescending tone."

"Okay, I'll stop condescending and you'll stay out of my investigation. Deal?"

"You're the professional," I said with a bright smile on my face.

I hoped it would blind him to the fact I had not agreed to his deal.

"Now, if that's settled . . ." I turned to Penny. "Is the offer of a facial still good?"

I left Natasha's more relaxed than I can remember feeling. Ever.

Including the stress-erasing hour spent at the tips of Penny's expert fingers, I've had a total of three facials in my life. The first was a present from Nancy, the day before my wedding. The second was also a present from Nancy, when I came back to New York after almost six years in the jungles of East Africa. Before I left Natasha's, I bought Nancy a gift certificate.

It was after seven o'clock, dark and, when I stepped outside, cool. In spite of the chill I decided to walk, for a few blocks at least. I was living a mystery story, and I needed to figure out, or find out, some answers. First, why had Damon left me *millions* of dollars? Astonishingly, I was an heiress. Sort of. I had to live for the next six months to collect the money. Which I wasn't sure I would accept when the time came. If I died in the next six months, the money would go to Jeremy. I did not believe for a moment that Jeremy would consider killing me, but I wasn't so sure about Teresa . . .

"Follow the money," Deep Throat told Bob Woodward in *All the President's Men* more than thirty years ago. It was still excellent advice. I was getting cold, and hungry. I spotted an empty cab, flagged it down and gave the driver my address.

I saw a tall man coming out of the Dakota as I was getting out of the cab. Broad shoulders, athletic build, about forty. Very good posture. His hand was raised to signal my cab, but he lowered it.

"Are you Morgan Tyler?" he asked.

*Oh great.* "Yes." *What now?*

"I just left a note for you at the desk. I'm Kevin Chet Thompson."

The name was vaguely familiar; so was his face.

Kevin Chet Thompson, whoever he was, had the thick, curly hair of Michelangelo's statue of David. He also had large features, just regular enough to be attractive and just irregular enough to make him something better than handsome. *Interesting.* I had the feeling I had seen him on television. On *Oprah*? Maybe. I was pretty sure it hadn't been on *America's Most Wanted.*

He waved my cab on its way.

"Why did you leave me a note?" I asked.

He noticed I was shivering. "You're cold," he said. "Shall we go up to your place where we can talk?"

"No!" It came out more forcefully than I meant it to. "Look," I said, "I've had a long day. Whatever this is about, you can call me at GBN tomorrow. Now, if you'll excuse me . . ."

Chagrinned, he said, "That was stupid. Of course you're not going to invite me in. You haven't the slightest idea who I am, have you?"

I hate people who make me guess who they are and what they want. "You're from Publishers Clearinghouse," I said, "and you're here with my ten-million-dollar check."

He laughed. "I don't have ten million dollars with me, but I'm carrying enough to buy you dinner. Are you hungry? Is there a place near here that you like?"

*Food. It would be nice not to cook.* "I'll go get your note, read it and then maybe we'll talk. Wait here." He nodded and I went into our reception office.

Frank Gerber, our night man at reception (who was a former professional wrestler, known in the ring as "Frank N. Steen"), handed me the note. "The guy just left," Frank said.

"He's still outside." I tore open the envelope and scanned the note.

"Is he giving you trouble?" Frank asked. He came around from behind the desk, ready to leave his post for me.

"Not yet," I said. "I'll scream if I need you."

The note introduced the stranger as Kevin Chet Thompson, said that he'd been asked by a publisher to write a biography of Kitty Leigh and that he wanted to talk to me about daytime television. His handwriting was better than mine.

Shoving his note into my pocket, I went back outside and faced him.

"You have picture I.D.?" I asked.

Grinning at me with an expression somewhere between amusement and respect, he took his wallet from an inside jacket pocket and handed it to me. It was elegant butterscotch leather from Hermès, so soft that holding it in my hand was a sensual pleasure. I opened it to his driver's license. The name was Kevin C. Thompson, and his face matched the photo. I wanted to ask how he managed to have an *attractive* picture taken at the DMV, but I restrained myself, closed the wallet, and handed it back to him.

"There's a deli down Seventy-Second," I said. "In the middle of the next block."

"Sounds good to me." As we started walking west, he took off his jacket. He was wearing an Irish cable-knit fisherman's sweater underneath. "Here," he said.

Before I could respond, he draped his jacket around my shoulders.

It was so big on me it almost reached my knees.

I wasn't cold anymore.

# 23

Ben Frankel's popular deli restaurant, called Mr. Ben's, has been on West Seventy-Second Street between Columbus and Broadway for more than sixty years. A small sign in the front window states it has not changed ownership in six decades. The interior is simple and unembellished — tables and chairs in front, booths in the back, lights in the ceiling. While there is nothing that could pass for *décor*, it is always immaculate, and the food is wonderful. Most of the regulars who keep the cooks and the waiters and waitresses hopping from seven in the morning through an early dinner hour had gone home when we got there.

We wouldn't have any trouble getting a table.

Inside, in strong light, I saw that my mysterious escort had thick reddish-brown hair and dark green eyes. His fisherman's sweater was the color of Devonshire cream. I took all that in at a glance, so he wouldn't think I was staring at him. I removed his jacket — dark green cashmere, lined in brown silk — from around my shoulders and handed it back to him.

Mr. Ben was bustling over to meet us. Small and compact, with courtly manners and shining silver hair, he had to be over 90, but he still greeted those who came into his restaurant with a welcoming smile, clean and crisp paper menus and a bad joke of the day. I ate here alone, or picked up takeout, twice a week. Mr. Ben thought a young single woman was a crime against nature, but after a few polite refusals, he stopped trying to fix me up with his grandsons.

"Do you know what the definition of a lawyer is?" Mr. Ben asked me.

"No, what?"

"A lawyer is a Jewish boy who can't stand the sight of blood."

I laughed, which pleased Mr. Ben.

Kevin Chet Thompson laughed, too. His kindness pleased me.

Mr. Ben showed us to one of the relatively private maroon leather booths at the back. He handed us menus, and winked at me, grinning, with an almost imperceptible nod in Kevin Chet Thompson's direction. I held my tongue.

"What would you lovely people like to drink?"

"Coffee," I said. "Extra caffeine."

"Coffee," Kevin Chet Thompson said. "As strong as you can make it."

Mr. Ben signaled the nearest waitress, who brought us two coffees, and extra Sweet'N Low. Then he looked at me. "Turkey breast, maybe? Or stuffed derma? Today the derma is a poem."

"I'll take the derma," I said.

"How's the brisket?"

"So tender you won't need a knife," Mr. Ben said.

"Sold," said my dinner companion.

Mr. Ben nodded approval, took back the menus and left to give our orders to the kitchen. From across the table, I looked up to find Kevin Chet Thompson staring at me as I put two packets of Sweet'N Low into my coffee cup.

"What?"

"I was three rows behind you at Damon Radford's funeral," he said. "You were sitting with a gorgeous blonde who looks like a super-model."

Nancy *is* gorgeous, and she *does* look like a supermodel. She's also as generous as she is beautiful, and I've never had a better friend. But Kevin Chet Thompson saying she was gorgeous annoyed me.

"Her name is Nancy Cummings, and she's a lawyer," I said. "With Newton, Donovan, Lipton and Klein." That was enough information for him to be able to call her.

"That's more than I wanted to know," he said.

"What *do* you want? You said you're writing a biography of Kitty Leigh."

"No, I said I'd been *asked* to write her biography. I haven't decided if I'm going to do it. I prefer to write about crime."

My brain suddenly made the proper connections. "*That's* who you are. I read your biography of Earl Rogers, and your book on that cold case investigation, *Murder in Vermont*." I stopped because realization smacked me in the face. "Oh, my God." I rose halfway up out of my seat.

"Don't go — let me explain."

I eased back down into the booth. "If you thought I was going to leave, you haven't tasted Mr. Ben's stuffed derma." I sighed. "What do you really want from me?"

"Not what you're thinking," he said. "Not exactly."

" 'Not exactly' is classic man-speak. Tell me in English."

"My publisher wants me to do Kitty Leigh's biography. Movie star bios aren't my thing, but with all of the drama in her life, I agreed to think about it. I met her, talked to her for a few hours. She said she's willing to cooperate, even though I was clear that if I wrote the book, it wouldn't be one of those 'authorized' white-wash jobs. I'd find out everything about her son's suicide, her times in rehab, the disappearance of her stepdaughter, all that."

I wondered if he knew what Damon did to Kitty.

"Before I decided whether or not I would do the bio, Damon Radford was murdered. *That* interested me a lot more, so I went to his funeral. I saw Kitty's performance, realized she must have had some kind of relationship with him. And I saw you there . . ."

He smiled at me again. The self-protective

part of me wanted him to stop. The leap-before-I-look part of me enjoyed it.

One of Mr. Ben's waitresses brought us our orders. Kevin Chet Thompson thanked her. I liked that, but I couldn't help wondering if he was *really* charming, or if he was *being* charming because he wanted something from me.

"Looks great," he said.

"Tastes better."

Mr. Ben came over to watch as each of us took a bite of our respective derma and brisket. The food was every bit as good as promised, and we praised it sincerely. With a satisfied smile on his face, the proud old man left to go make sure other diners were happy with their meals.

"Alone at last," Kevin Chet Thompson said.

"But we're not alone."

He looked up from his brisket, glanced over at Mr. Ben then asked, "Is he coming back to have dessert with us?"

"I meant Damon is at this table with us. Isn't he?"

"Here's the situation," he said. "I'm considering writing a book about the murder of a man who seemed to have everything, including somebody who wanted to kill him. You're part of the story."

"A very small part," I said.

"A very important part."

"Because I'm a suspect?" I asked.

"Because he left you half of his estate."

"How do you know that?"

"Wills are a matter of public record."

"You're lying to me. That's not how you know because the will isn't public record yet. There are a lot of odd bits I've had to learn in order to write a show with accuracy, and at what point wills are made public happens to be one of them. Damon's won't be available to examine for another couple of days. So, who told you about me? Was it his lawyer, Seligman? The truth."

"I know Teresa Radford socially," he admitted. "I went to see her, to talk about her ex-husband, and she told me about the will."

"If you and I are going to talk about anything — or even finish dinner together — I want you to promise not to lie to me again. And a lie of omission is just as bad as far as I'm concerned. It's not only dishonest, it's insulting."

"You're tough," he said.

"I'm waiting for your promise."

"I promise not to lie to you again. And I'm sorry."

"I can just imagine what Teresa told you about me," I said. I put my fork down and sat back against the upholstered booth. "She thinks Damon and I were having a secret romance." I sat up straight and looked him directly in the eyes. "Damon and I absolutely were *not* romantically involved."

"But you must have been important to him, or why would he have —"

"I don't expect you to believe me," I said. "No

one else seems to. But the truth is I haven't the slightest idea why Damon put me in his will. He knew I despised him."

He thought about that for a few bites, then said, "If we can figure out why he left you the money, it might lead us to the person who killed him."

*We? Us?*

"Did Teresa tell you about *all* of the terms of the will?" I asked. "I mean, do you know that my so-called inheritance comes with a string attached? More like a garrote."

"I like that word, garrote."

"I did too, until I felt this one around my neck. I don't know if I'm going to take the money, but I have to live for the next six months to be eligible to collect."

I didn't add that someone had already tried to run me down in the street, before I even knew about the will. I realized that other than Nancy Cummings, and Penny Cavanaugh, and maybe Penny's irritating nephew, I had no idea who in this world I could trust. I didn't know this man sitting across from me . . .

"What are you thinking?"

"If the situation I'm in was a story line on *Love of My Life*, the continuing character — me — wouldn't know whether the new character who just entered the story — that's you — was going to turn out to be a good guy or a bad guy."

"Say you were writing this — how does your lady decide?"

"Time decides," I said. "The year before last I created a murder story that became a big hit with the fans and was all over the media."

"I remember reading about it. That was yours? 'Who Killed Jack . . . somebody?' "

" 'Who killed Jason Archer?' The character of Archer was a longtime villain on the show. When the actor told us he didn't want to sign a new contract, we decided to give him a fantastic send-off story. Not even the actors could figure out which of the characters murdered him. Only the producer and I knew. But when the identity of the killer was finally revealed, it was a different character than the one I had originally planned. I made the change, and then, of course, I had to change the motive. The first actor chosen as the killer had become too popular with the audience. We couldn't waste that asset, so a less popular cast member took the fall."

"Convicted by a jury of the fans." He was smiling at me.

"Life is tough," I said. "On screen and off."

"Statistically speaking, if a homicide isn't solved in the first forty-eight hours — and this one hasn't been — there's a good chance it won't be. The murder rate keeps rising, but the number of cops stays the same. Work with me, Morgan. With what you already know and what I can dig up, we have a better chance than the police of finding out who killed Radford. I'd like to prove you didn't do it."

"Why? You don't even know me."

"Call it instinct," he said.

"Are you going to write a book about Damon's murder?"

"Truth? I haven't decided yet. But finding out who did it and writing the book aren't necessarily a package deal," he said. "I need to think about whether I want to give a year of my life to poking into Damon Radford's secrets."

"I need to think about this, too."

"Tell you what — let me take you to dinner tomorrow night. You can give me your answer then. If you say 'yes,' I'll buy you two desserts."

# 24

As soon as I got home, I Googled Kevin Chet Thompson.

I found quite a bit of information.

He earned a doctorate in psychology from Georgetown University at the age of twenty-four. His specialty was criminal psychology. Kevin Chet Thompson, Ph.D., spent two years as an instructor at the Virginia State Police Academy, teaching how to analyze the criminal mind. He was an advisor to jails and to parole boards. He's licensed to practice in Virginia, New York and Connecticut, but began easing out of private practice eight years ago when he started writing. He's had five books published. Three were true crime stories. Two of the cases he documented were solved by the information he uncovered. His other books were biographies of famous — some would say infamous — criminal defense attorneys. I had read the book about Earl Rogers, a fascinating, complicated man and attorney, brilliant but flawed. The book was very well written. The other biography was of a San Francisco criminal lawyer, named Jake Erlich. To defend someone accused of murder, Erlich charged "everything" the defendant had. If a potential client protested that "everything" was too much, Erlich was supposed to have replied, "What is the rest of your life worth to you?"

There was, however, no personal information on Kevin Chet Thompson.

I closed out of Google, clicked onto Amazon and looked up his most recent book to check out the flap copy. There wasn't much about the author, just his photograph, a headshot cropped tight, and the information that "Thompson is a criminal psychologist and lives in Greenwich, Connecticut." No mention of wife, children, or dogs.

I shut down the computer and called Nancy.

"I need to talk to you," I said, "but I don't want to go to your building for a while."

"I'll come over there. Get out the Oreos and pour the milk."

Nancy arrived at my door wearing ivory silk pajamas and low-heeled Fendi slippers. It was the kind of outfit she could sleep in or, with the addition of evening shoes and jewelry, wear out to a black-tie party. Over her pajamas she'd thrown a fake fur coat that was such a good imitation of golden sable, a real live sable might need to take a closer look.

She draped the coat over the back of a sofa in the living room and followed me into the bedroom. We climbed onto my queen-size bed, where I'd already set up a tray table with the milk and cookies. As Nancy separated the two halves of an Oreo, I filled her in on my extraordinary day. I told her all about the terms of Damon's will, my surprise visit with Detective Phoenix at Natasha's house of skin and my dinner with Kevin Chet Thompson.

"First thing tomorrow," she said, "I'm going to set you up with one of our tax attorneys so he can start protecting as much of your money as possible from the IRS."

"It's not *my* money. When the six months are up, I probably won't accept it. I'll let Jeremy have it."

Nancy stopped nibbling on the single Oreo she would allow herself. She looked at me, horrified. "That's ridiculous. *Of course* you'll take the money. That boy already has so much money it'll probably ruin his life. It's too late for a few million dollars to ruin yours."

"Thanks."

"What I mean is, you're already a grown-up. Right now you earn a good living, but there's no such thing as job security for a writer! What the IRS doesn't take, falling ratings can make vanish, poof. This co-op is a good investment, but what other investments do you have?"

"None."

"That's got to change," Nancy said.

"Talking about Damon's money feels ghoulish. You know what a hostile relationship we had. Why would he leave me half of his estate?"

"I admit it's bizarre. Maybe he really did love

you, secretly. But, as the man said, 'Frankly, my dear, I don't give a damn.' Money is freedom, Morgan. The way I see it, I have six months to persuade you not to be an idiot. Tomorrow is not too soon to see a tax attorney. Now, let's talk about something more important. Men."

"Men are more important than the fact that I'm suspected of murdering Damon?"

"Oh, that. We have criminal lawyers at Newton, too. I know the best one. I want you to meet him anyway. His name is Arnold Rose." Nancy's cheeks were getting pinker, and her eyes were brighter than I had ever seen them.

I jumped to the nearest conclusion. "At last, you're in love. That's so wonderful! I want *details*."

"I'm not in love . . . not exactly. I'm not sure . . . Maybe it's just deep *like*." Then Nancy absolutely stunned me — by taking an unprecedented second Oreo. "I'll tell you about him some other night." She was going to stop talking, but then she couldn't stop herself. "He's incredible, Morgan. He's the most brilliant man I've ever met. His depositions read like great novels."

"You read his depositions? For pleasure?" This revelation definitely called for another Oreo, so I reached for it.

"I swear, Arnold asks the most incisive questions. He absolutely nails the people he's after when he's grilling them. I've never admired a man as much as I admire him." She finished her milk and extended her glass to me. "May I have some more? Just half a glass." As she waited, she said, "You know, I think I've finally figured out the right type of man for me."

I poured more milk. "What type is that?"

"A workaholic overachiever who needs me."

She said that without a trace of irony; she was utterly sincere. I had never seen Nancy Cummings so vulnerable. Silently, I prayed that this Arnold Rose was worthy of her. "Have you two . . ." I gestured delicately with my Oreo. "Are you two . . . ?"

Normally, the last word I would use to describe Nancy would be *shy*, but her eyes went down and she studied the interior of her glass of milk as she confided, "We have. We are. And he's wonderful there, too." She lifted her eyes and I saw that they had gone dreamy with erotic memory. Then she firmly shut the door on those thoughts. "I'm not rushing into anything," she assured me. "Now, let's go back to the exciting part of your day where two separate attractive men want you to work with them to solve a murder."

"That's not precisely how it is," I said. "Detective Phoenix wants me to stay out of his way. 'Out of the line of fire,' as he put it."

"That's gallant."

"That's Neanderthal." I reached for my fourth Oreo. Nancy was still nibbling on the first half of her second.

"Did you agree, to stay out of the way?"

"Nanceeee, you know me better than that."

She smiled. "So you just made him *think* you agreed," she said.

"Men don't listen between the lines, like we do."

"Lucky for us. Okay — when this is all over, when somebody has solved the case, which one of these men do you want to keep?"

"Neither of them is mine to keep."

"Come on, they're interested in you. How could they not be? You're pretty and you're funny, and when they get to know you, they'll find out that you'd step in front of a bullet for somebody you loved. But let's hope that's not going to be necessary."

"Let's hope," I said.

I reached across the bed for the handbag I had carried today, took out the envelope from Natasha's and handed it to Nancy.

"What's this?"

"A gift certificate for something that's almost as good as sex."

She raised her perfectly arched eyebrows at me. "Can you remember back that far?" she asked.

"It's only been —"

"It's been too long," Nancy said. "In America, widows aren't supposed to throw themselves on their husbands' funeral pyres." She opened the envelope and smiled with delight. " 'Deluxe European Facial.' I've been meaning to try Natasha's. This is terrific, thanks. Who's Penny Cavanaugh?"

183

I gave Nancy the *Reader's Digest* version of Penny. I told the part about her being Detective Phoenix's aunt, but I left out Penny's belief that her dead husband was going to come back to her because so many spouses come back from the dead in her favorite daytime dramas.

Nancy finished the plain half of her second Oreo and gave the frosted half a contemplative lick. "I used to think, before I met Arnold, that it would be fabulous if a man was something we could order from QVC," she said. "All a woman would have to do is dial that eight hundred number and tell the operator 'I'll have the tan one with the dark brown hair, and the Harvard background. Oh? You have that item in petite, average or tall? I'll take the tall. Yes, you can put that on my Visa.' "

I laughed, and almost knocked over the milk.

"It's nice to hear you laugh," Nancy said.

"It felt good. For a moment I forgot that, thanks to Damon, I've got bigger problems than I've created for the characters on *Love*."

"I'm afraid you do."

"Nancy, I can't just leave my fate in the hands of homicide detectives and crime writers. It's a *job* to them, but it's my *life*. I've got to find out who killed Damon."

"We can hire a private detective. Our firm uses an excellent —"

"No. No private detectives. No strangers. I've been thinking about this, and I've got a plan."

"Don't do anything nutsy."

"I'm going to use what I do for a living, what I do when I'm trying to come up with a new plot for the show," I said. "Explore the back stories of the main characters, make a list of the people who had reason to hate Damon. I'm sure the answer to who killed him is somewhere in those relationships."

# 25

The first thing I did after I'd had my morning coffee was phone Nathan Hughes's office at GBN. His secretary answered.

"Good morning, GBN Publicity."

"Hi, Gloria, it's Morgan Tyler."

"Good morning, Mrs. Tyler. I'm afraid he's not in yet. May I take a message?"

As always, Gloria's voice was warm and comforting, which made me think she must have been very good at her former profession, social secretary to the wife of America's Vice President. It was Harrison's opinion that Gloria, having experienced the legendary back-stabbing in high-level politics, had the best preparation of any of us to work for a television network.

"I don't need to talk to him," I said. "You could help me, if it's not too much trouble."

"What is it?"

"Can you fax me the guest list for Mr. Radford's funeral service?"

"It's no trouble at all. The list is on my desk. What's your fax number?"

I gave it to her. "You're terrific, Gloria. That was all I wanted. You don't even have to tell Nathan I called, I'm sure he's busy."

Within a few minutes my fax machine did its beeping and whirring routine and pages of names came sliding out. I would look at the list, see if anyone seemed out of place. It was four single-spaced pages long, so I put it aside to study later. I had two scripts to edit before my lunch date.

Harrison Landers has lived in his stately old building on West Sixty-Fifth Street for twenty years. For most of that time he had an art-filled apartment on the tenth floor, facing Central Park. His housekeeper, Agata, a motherly Italian woman, greeted me warmly when I rang the bell of his new apartment at the rear of the building. Although I had called her once a month to ask about Harrison, I hadn't seen Agata for almost two years, since Harrison refused to let me visit him. She was a little thinner, and her face had more worry creases, but her personality was as kind as ever. No one could have looked after Harrison with more devotion than Agata. Her smile widened when she saw that I was carrying a flat box from what had been Harrison's and my favorite neighborhood pizza parlor.

"He will be so glad to have a Poppa Gino's again," she said.

"How's he doing?"

"He has his good days and his bad days." She lowered her voice to a whisper as she confided, "He's happier when the lady comes here. She make him feel good."

"A nurse?"

"No nurse — a *lady*."

The way she said it made me think the *lady* was making Harrison "feel good" by techniques that did not require a medical license. There wasn't time to ask anything else; Harrison pushed open an interior door and whizzed into the hall in his electric wheelchair. His thick gray hair looked freshly cut, and his face was smooth-shaven. He wore a navy blue wool cardigan over a pale blue cashmere sweater. A navy blue blanket covered his legs.

"I thought I heard your sweet voice, Doll," he said.

"Don't try to con me. You smelled the pizza."

"Guilty, but come here and give me a hug," he commanded.

"Yes, sir, Major Landers, sir," I replied, affectionately using the rank he'd had in Vietnam. I handed the pizza box to Agata and leaned over to embrace Harrison. I was surprised at how hard his upper body felt.

"Wow," I said. "I leave you alone and you turn into Mr. Muscles."

"Yeah, from the waist up."

There was an unmistakable note of bitterness in his voice, though he tried to conceal it with humor. "I missed you, Doll," he said. Then he drew back, adjusted the controls on his motorized chair to make a turn and started rolling down the hall. "Follow me to my lair."

"*Now* you're making the naughty suggestions," I joked. "You *must* have worked at NBC."

This comment made him laugh. It referred to a daytime drama called *Another World* that had run on NBC for decades until it was cancelled in the late 90s. Harrison had written for it until he was hired away to be head writer on *Love*. Before Harrison wrote for *Another World*, the show had a story line that featured a young woman accused of murder, who, when she was acquitted, married her lawyer, a much older man. The girl who played the role, a good actress named Susan Trustman, told Harrison that NBC made her and the actor who played her husband on the show sleep in twin beds — until his character was hit by a car and paralyzed from the waist down. The day he came home from the "hospital" in a wheelchair, the network moved a double bed into their set.

"Don't let these wheels fool you," he chuckled.

Glancing around, I recognized most of the comfortable furniture, and his collection of pre-Columbian art. "Your things fit very well in your new place."

"Everything fits well except me." He patted the sides of his wheelchair. "I'm a problem wherever I go, which is why I stay here ninety-nine point nine nine nine percent of the time. I'll only go out to celebrate a national holiday, like Damon Radford's funeral." His tone was biting. He tried to smile, to soften the remark, but there was not even a glint of humor in his eyes.

189

Agata came in just then with small plates and napkins, balanced on the pizza box. Harrison always insisted pizza had to be eaten out of the box, but he conceded on the subject of napkins. She set us up at the game table in the living room, which opened out onto a walled garden. At this time of year, it was all wall and no garden. I decided that the next time I came over, I would bring things that would bloom in October.

"Thank you, Agata," he said. The housekeeper adjusted a pillow at the small of his back to give him maximum comfort, then she smiled at us and withdrew.

"You look wonderful," I told him. I meant it.

"Physical therapy turned me into a workout junkie. Now I've got a great-looking body, from the waist up. You win some, you lose some." He reached out and pulled a chair over to the table for me. I sat, lifted a slice out of the box, put it on a plate and handed it to him, then took one for myself.

"Hmmmm. It's just as good as I remember," he said. He saw the look of surprise on my face and answered the question before I could ask it. "We used to have pizza together. It was our treat. I didn't want to have it by myself."

That touched me, but I knew Harrison didn't like to — as he called it — "wallow in sentiment," so I responded with a joke. "So you *haven't* been cheating on me by eating pizza with other women?"

"Nope, I've been 'true to you in my fashion,' Doll. Hand me another slice."

"I've missed you . . ."

"For a long time I missed myself."

As I separated the biggest piece from the warm pie for him, I asked what I most wanted to know. "With some more therapy, will you be able to walk?"

"Not a chance." He took a bite and chewed. I thought it was until he could be sure his voice didn't betray emotion. He swallowed, touched his lips with a napkin and said, " 'Fraid I won't be able to run that marathon I never intended to run, or take my dog out for a walk — if I had a dog. I can't even use a walk-in closet. I've got a wheel-in, with all low racks." He gave me a funny, Groucho Marx, eyebrow-wagging leer. "But you can tell anybody who asks that I'm hell on wheels."

I laughed, and we ate more pizza. "Have you been watching our show?"

"Never miss it. You're doing a great job, Doll. I'm proud of you."

His praise was more satisfying to me than the Emmy on my shelf.

"Do you feel like working?" I asked. "No marathons to run — we sit down to write. What about you and me being the co–head writers?"

That suggestion stopped him with a slice of pizza halfway to his mouth. He put it back down on the plate before he answered.

"That's a step down for you," he said softly.

Even though he was keeping his voice resolutely unemotional, I knew him well enough to think he was pleased with the suggestion. I pressed my case. "I wouldn't have this job if it wasn't for you. I'd love it if we could work together again."

"I appreciate what you're trying to do —"

"I'm trying to help myself by collaborating with the most talented man in the field," I said.

"Too late, Sweet Face. I'm already working."

"You are?" That was the last thing I expected to hear. "Where? You returning to daytime is big news, and I didn't hear —"

"You didn't hear because it's a secret. I'm only telling you because of what you were willing to give up for me. I'm helping Serena McCall," he said.

"You're writing *Trauma Center*?" I was stunned.

"Serena and I are writing it together. She gets the credit, we share the money."

I wondered if Serena was "the lady" Agata referred to. Then I remembered him telling me once, that when he worked he "looked but didn't touch," and I had no reason not to believe him. Not only had he always treated me like a colleague, but he didn't follow up on any of the opportunities Tommy Zenos told me he could have, with actresses on the show.

"That's wonderful," I said, "if that's what you want. I'll start watching the show. But why keep it a secret?"

He looked at me. A steady look. His rigid face

was meant to mask his feelings, but I knew what he was communicating.

"It was Damon's idea? Is that why he gave her the job, to get you?"

"No, Serena got the job the old-fashioned way, she fucked him for it. Then she came to me for help. She told me Damon was all for my working with her, with certain conditions. One of them was that my involvement be a secret."

"Doesn't anyone else know?"

"The producer knows, and whoever cuts the checks. But as far as everybody else connected to the show is concerned, I might as well still be in that coma — or dead."

"That's terrible," I said. "What other conditions are there?"

"Don't you know?" His voice had grown suddenly cold.

"How could *I* know?" I asked.

"I assumed you knew about the arrangement because you and Damon were — God, how could you let yourself become his —"

"Harrison! I wasn't Damon's *anything*. What makes you think that?" I felt sick to my stomach suddenly.

"I agreed to see you today because I wanted to get a look. I'm surprised his corruption of you doesn't show on your face yet."

"Corruption — ?"

"The bastard said you two were going to get married. He left you his money. What the *hell* am I supposed to think?" His jaw was rigid.

"Who told you I was involved with Damon?" I asked.

"Serena," he said, his voice flat. "She brought me champagne to celebrate. She said she was relieved she didn't have to be in his bed anymore because you were there now."

"But I wasn't!"

"One of you is lying."

I was so angry at Serena that if she had come into the room, I would have slugged her. "Do you really think *I'm* the one who's lying?" I asked, incredulous.

Harrison answered my question with silence. He pushed the half-eaten pizza away from him. The gesture signaled he was pushing me away, too. "I don't see why Serena would lie," he said. "And Damon's will speaks for itself."

I stood up.

Now I was as angry at Harrison as I was at Serena.

"I thought you knew me," I said. My tone was so sharp it startled him and he looked up. "We spent so much time together, you should know what kind of person I am."

"People change." He turned away and gazed out into his garden, where nothing was blooming. "When you think about it," he said, "maybe you'll realize you broke my heart. Now I'd like you to go."

I started to leave.

I had my hand on the doorknob. I loved Harrison like a father, and I was devastated. I had just lost him for the second time. But then I stopped and turned around. Harrison was still staring out into his gray stone garden. His back was to me.

"No," I said firmly.

He turned his head just enough so that I saw his face in profile.

"What do you mean — 'no'?"

"I mean no-I'm-not-leaving." I raised my voice, made it a little singsong, almost childish. "And you can't make me," I said.

He spun his chair around to look at me. "I don't believe this."

"Believe it, Harrison. You're stuck in that chair." I began dancing around the room in quick little steps, as though I was dodging him. "But I can run around your furniture, duck into your closets, climb over your sofas." I was smiling as I said this. He looked confused. He hadn't expected this reaction and didn't know how to respond to it.

"I'll call the police," he said, rolling toward the telephone.

I was faster; I sprinted to the phone table and held the instrument high over my head. "I can rip the plug out of the wall before you can call," I said.

"*What's wrong with you?*"

"You're not going to end our friendship because I'm not going to allow it. You mean too much to me, Harrison. So, I've decided to stay right here in your apartment until I convince

195

you I wasn't involved with Damon. I'll call Tommy and tell him to send my work over here. I'll call my friend Nancy and have her bring me some clothes. If Agata won't cook for me, I'll order in on my cell phone. And I'm going to follow you from room to room and keep talking until I make you believe me."

"That's your plan, is it?"

"That's my plan," I said as I put his telephone back on the table.

He rolled closer to me. He wasn't smiling.

"Come here," he said. Before I knew what was happening, his left hand shot out and he grabbed my right arm in a powerful grip. He pulled me down close to him so that my face was inches away from his. Just for a second I thought he was going to hit me. But then he kissed me. On the cheek.

His voice was soft. "You're crazy, you know that?"

"Of course I am, or why would I want to be here with you?"

"I love you, Doll . . ." Gently, he put his hand in my hair and gave a hunk of it an affectionate tug. "I'm sorry I believed Serena," he said. "The thought of you with that . . . slime . . . it made me a little nuts." He let go of my hair and put his hands in his lap.

I touched the back of his head lightly, just for a moment.

"I'm going to force myself to take a chari-table attitude about Serena," I said. "Other-

196

wise I might give in to my primitive instincts, and I'm already suspected of one murder. Maybe she was in love with Damon and he used her, then dumped her. It wouldn't be the first time he — hey, how did you know Damon left me money?"

"Serena told me."

"How did *she* know?"

"You'll have to ask her. Now forget about Serena," Harrison said. "Are we all right again?"

"Of course we are. We always will be." I hugged him, then I stood up and uttered a line that used to be one of our running jokes, "You're my second-favorite man."

He blew a kiss at me. "Yeah, yeah, always the runner-up. Call me 'Mr. Congeniality.' Now go make somebody else's life a living hell before I forget that you're too old for me," he joked.

Out on the street I smiled at the bumper-to-bumper New York City weekday traffic. I even smiled at strangers who passed me on the sidewalk.

I had my treasured friend Harrison back.

Walking up Central Park West, I turned a new mystery over in my mind. *How had Serena McCall known what was in Damon's will?* She hadn't been at the reading, and it was yet to be made public. I thought about this puzzle, as I would a plot point for one of my story lines. If Serena was a character on *Love of My Life*, how would I

197

be able to explain the fact that she knew the contents of a will when she shouldn't have . . .

*How . . . how . . . ?* Then an idea occurred to me.

I took out my cell phone and had the operator connect me with Leo Seligman's office. When he came on the line, I got right to the point.

"Who were the witnesses to Damon's will?" I asked.

"I'm sorry, Mrs. Tyler," he replied. From the tone of his voice, he was walking that tightrope between being firm with me, and being cordial enough to make me want to be his client if I did inherit. "I'm sorry that I can't tell you anything for six months, until you are eligible to inherit."

"Then just confirm something for me. Was Serena McCall one of the witnesses to Damon's will? You don't have to answer in words," I said into the phone. "Just nod your head there on the other end of the line."

Silence. I think I confused him.

"I was joking," I said. "If Serena was one of the witnesses, just grunt."

He didn't grunt; he gave in. "Yes," he said. "She was."

"Thank you."

Disconnecting, I let Leo Seligman off the line and off the hook.

I pictured the scene: Damon telling Serena he was through with her because he and I were going to be married. To prove the lie, he signed a new will in front of her, letting her see that he was leaving half of his fortune to me. He even made her sign the will as a witness. Thinking this scene through, playing all the emotional strings, just as I would if I were creating it, I realized it was probably at this moment that Damon called his mother. He must have done it in front of Serena, or why would he have told his mother at all? So Damon telephoned her, and let Serena hear Elizabeth Radford's voice. Then Damon lied to his mother, telling her that he loved me, and about our impending marriage. He would have done this just so Serena would have the pain of hearing the call. To him, it was all a big, cruel joke.

I believed this scenario for two reasons.

The first was that I knew Damon's penchant for cruelty to people who were unlucky enough to love him. The second — and for me this was the most convincing — was because Damon *had not expected to die.* Sherlock Holmes put it something like this: "When every other possibility has been eliminated, the one that remains, however unlikely, will be the answer."

For the time being, I was going to keep this theory to myself.

# 26

Kevin Chet Thompson said he would pick me up in front of the Dakota at eight o'clock. He arrived at the wheel of a new Range Rover. The sight of it gave me a jolt; it's the civilized version of the old Land Rovers Ian and I drove all over Africa. *Why couldn't this criminal psychologist have come in a cab? Or on the bus?*

From the driver's side, he leaned across and opened the passenger door for me, but I didn't get in. My hesitation puzzled him. "What's the matter?"

"You have a Range Rover," I said. *That's great, Morgan, state the obvious.*

"I thought you'd like it. You're not one of those people who think anything bigger than a Geo Metro is a crime against the environment, are you?"

"No, I'm not."

I got into the passenger seat. Automatically, I reached down to the side of the seat, to feel for the rough patch on the frayed old leather. I had mended the cut in the leather myself, with duct tape. But of course it wasn't there.

Kevin Chet Thompson started the motor and pulled out into traffic.

"I'm all in favor of our hostage-like dependence on foreign oil," I said. He laughed, but I realized how harsh what I had said sounded. Why was I acting like this? Was it possible that riding in a Range Rover was making me feel disloyal to Ian? What was the matter with me? I glanced sideways at Kevin Chet Thompson and discovered he was looking at me quizzically.

"Are we having our first fight?" he asked.

"Not yet," I said. Then I smiled in an attempt to make up for my acerbic remark. "Where are we going?"

"To Elaine's, if that's okay with you."

"I've read about it, but I've never been there," I said.

"Good. I'll be the first. To take you to Elaine's."

Elaine Kaufman, the "Elaine" who was famously partial to writers at her Second Avenue saloon, greeted Kevin Chet Thompson as though she was especially partial to *him*. He responded to her enthusiastic greeting by saying he had missed her, too. Then he introduced me. Elaine said she was happy to meet me and hoped I would come back again.

"If she doesn't come back with me, don't let her in."

Elaine led us to one of the ten tables along the wall, opposite the bar. According to an article I'd read in *Vanity Fair*, these tables were reserved for her favorites. As we sat down, I glanced around. Wherever I looked, I saw faces I had previously seen only on the back of book jackets. I had been married to a man whose face was on book jackets, and now here I was in the company of another man whose face was on the jackets of books. It was like some bizarre dream.

"You don't need menus," Elaine said. "Trust me." She headed for the kitchen to order whatever she'd decided we should have.

"The food's good," he said. "Unless you're a vegan?"

"I eat anything put in front of me. I've eaten buffalo tongue — it's black, and delicious."

"You ate buffalo when you were in Africa?"

"Just the tongue; it was a matter of honor because I was the only woman on an expedition. We were trying to catch poachers who were slaughtering Cape buffalo for their horns. Actually, it's powdered *rhino* horn that's supposed to be an aphrodisiac, but the poachers figured the buyers couldn't tell what kind of horn it was when it was ground into powder." I stopped, embarrassed. "I'm sorry, I'm babbling. Normally, it takes an Act of Congress to get me to tell 'Out of Africa' stories."

"I enjoyed it."

A thought struck me. "How did you know I've been in Africa?"

"Research. I know a lot about you; but don't worry, none of it is bad."

"I wouldn't expect it to be. I mean, other than

mill park terrace

Dobson, Joan D.

Expires: Tue 7/3/12

Love is murder
ITEM: 33133019514538
CALL NO. FICTION Pal

Outreach
On Hold: Mon 6/18/12

the fact that I'm suspected of committing a murder. But then nobody's perfect, right?"

"You looked me up, too. Didn't you?" He smiled in a way that forced me to smile, too.

"Just the basics," I admitted. "You're a criminal psychologist who writes about crime. Your flap copy isn't very informative. It doesn't say whether you prefer dogs or cats. And you're referred to as Kevin Chet Thompson, Ph.D. I don't know what I should call you. Dr. Thompson? Kevin? Kev? Elaine called you 'K.C.' —"

"Definitely not Dr. Thompson. K.C. is okay for pals. Or Kev. I'd like you to call me Chet. My résumé, in brief: no arrests, no convictions, no marriages, no children, no allergies. I like both dogs *and* cats. I'm an Episcopalian, forty years old and I have a younger brother who's a medical doctor in the Navy. Our mother and father are both alive and well and they live in Surprise, Arizona."

"You made up that name."

"No, there really is a Surprise, Arizona, and my parents live there. How are you fixed for folks? I mean, will the man in your life have to deal with crazy in-laws?"

I was saved from answering by the appearance of Sidney Sheldon and his attractive blonde wife, Alexandra. The author was tall, with a full head of silver hair, bright blue eyes and the easy smile of a man who liked to laugh. The couple, who knew my companion, stopped at our table on the way to theirs. Sheldon complimented Chet on his book *Murder in Vermont*.

"Sidney bought a dozen copies to give away to friends," Alexandra Sheldon told us. "And he buys them from different bookstores to stimulate your sales."

Chet thanked him warmly, then he introduced me by saying I was the head writer for *Love of My Life*, and that I was suspected of murdering Damon Radford.

Sheldon's eyebrows went up, his smile widened and there was an unmistakable glint of delight in his eyes. "When I was working in television," he said, "there were one or two network executives I'd like to have killed. Let me know if you need a contribution to your legal defense fund."

I laughed, and at last I began to relax. "That's very kind," I told him.

"Why don't you join us for dinner at our table?" Sheldon asked.

His wife added a gracious, "Please do."

Chet looked at me to see if I was agreeable. I was. We got up and joined the Sheldons, and I had a wonderful time. They were charming company, and Sidney, I discovered, was not only a witty conversationalist but also a good listener. When the check came, Chet wrestled Sheldon for it and won, but it was a struggle. I took a discreet peek as Chet was signing the credit card slip and saw that he had given the waiter a twenty percent tip. Chet Thompson had just passed one of my tests: he wasn't stingy with waiters. *I'm looking for a reason to dislike him. Why?*

We said good night to the Sheldons and got back into the Range Rover.

A few minutes later, when we neared the Dakota, Chet spotted an open parking place across from the entrance. He eased into it and turned off the engine. We sat in the dark for a moment. I felt my right hand begin to twitch from nervousness. To break the silence, I asked, "Are you driving back to Connecticut now?"

He shook his head. "I have a house there, but I'm staying in a sublet down on Waverly Place. I thought about taking you to dinner at my favorite Italian restaurant, Grotto Azura, but I was afraid you might think it was suspiciously close to where I'm staying."

If I was going to become a grown-up again, I would have to stop acting like the only virgin at the Sacrificial Sock Hop and get back into the dating pool. "Would you like to come up for a drink?" I asked. "You'll be reasonably safe."

"Good." He opened his door. "I'd like to talk about the Radford murder."

He got out of the Rover and came around to the passenger side to open the door for me. As we walked through the Dakota's interior court-yard, I opened my handbag and took out a flash-light. "My apartment is on the third floor. I always take the stairs. Do you mind?"

"It's pretty dark," he said. "Are you trying to lure me to my doom?"

"That's not how I do it." I turned on the light as we started up.

We reached the third floor and turned right toward my front door. The hallways in the Dakota are well-lighted, so I switched off the flashlight. "I'm not even breathing hard," he gasped.

"The third floor is only two flights up," I teased him.

I inserted the key in the lock and opened the door. My front door opens into a small foyer that leads into the living room. I had left the lights on, as I always do when I go out at night.

"Nice," he said. He followed me into the living room and glanced around. "I like the fresh flowers."

"I get them every week. When I wasn't working, I'd buy a bunch of daffodils or daisies or whatever was blooming from vendors in the subways. Now I splurge by going to flower shops."

He strolled toward the huge windows that face Central Park and looked out.

"You've got a great view," he said. "What is that light?"

I walked over and tried to follow his gaze into the park. "Which light?"

"That one."

I stared out in the direction he indicated, but I couldn't see whatever it was that had caught his attention. "There," he said. Gently, he put his hands on my shoulders. Still puzzled, I turned to face him. At that moment he leaned down and touched his lips to mine.

It caught me by surprise and I gave an involuntary gasp.

Before my mind could form a thought, his arms were around me. He pulled me against him as his lips closed over mine. Firmly, this time. He kissed me with authority, and his kiss sent unexpected waves of heat all through my body. I lost track of the seconds that passed until he drew his head back slightly. Just enough to look in my eyes. Then he kissed me again. His lips parted, his tongue pushed into my mouth and now I was no longer a woman who was being kissed.

I was a wholehearted participant.

We held on to each other tightly. I could feel my breasts swell against his chest as our mouths locked in mutual exploration. I was thrilled, I was frightened, I was —

BANG!

We sprang apart.

"What was that?" I looked around us and saw a small, round hole in my huge living room window, at a height just slightly higher than my head. *Oh my God.* I was transfixed as the glass began to spider web out from the hole.

"GET DOWN!" Chet yelled and knocked me onto the floor.

As we tumbled to the rug, his foot caught the

base of the small end table that held a crystal vase of flowers. The crystal shattered when it hit the floor, spraying us with water and showering us with broken glass.

# 27

Chet had me pinned beneath him. My face was pressed into the junction of his neck and shoulders, and his arms were wrapped protectively around my head. We lay still — except for my terrified trembling — for the longest minute of my life. This was the *second* time somebody had tried to kill me, and my heart was pounding so hard I was sure Chet could feel it.

"What just happened?" A stupid question, but it proved my voice still worked.

"Somebody shot at us," he whispered. "Are you all right?"

"I think so. Are you?"

"Yes."

Keeping below the level of the shattered window, he raised his torso just enough to support his upper body with his elbows. That took some of his weight off me and I was able to breathe more easily. With his face only a few inches above mine, he looked down at me and joked, "I don't usually do this on the first date."

I managed to smile back at him. "I *never* do this on the first date. That glass is too expensive to replace." Humor is my coping mechanism; I stopped shaking.

"I'm sure whoever did it is gone, but let's not take any chances. Can you inch across the floor with me until we get away from the window?"

"I've crawled for a mile through the African bush after a wounded Cape buffalo; I think I can make it fifteen feet across my living room."

"Tough girl." He gave me a quick peck with his lips on the tip of my nose and then rolled off of me. With Chet in the lead, we started slithering on our bellies toward safety.

"Ouch," he said. "Watch out for the broken glass." A shard from the vase had cut his hand. He was bleeding.

We made it to the archway between the living room and the den and stood up just as the phone rang. It was near where I was standing, on the end of the library table, well away from the windows. I picked it up. "Hello?"

"Mrs. Tyler — it's Frank, down on the desk. Somebody shot at your window."

"I know. I was about to call the police."

"I did already. Are you okay?"

"Yes. Thank you, Frank."

"I was outside on my break, having a smoke. I heard the shot. Jeez. The sniper was across the street, in the park."

*Sniper?* Before I could ask him anything else, we heard the wail of a police siren.

"Here come the cops," Frank said.

"Good. You'll send them up?"

"Right away."

I put the phone back on its stand and turned

to see Chet examining the wall opposite my smashed living room window.

"What are you doing?"

He indicated a place on the wall that was about level with his shoulder. He tapped it lightly with the knuckle of his left index finger. "The bullet lodged here," he said. "The cops will be able to dig it out. If it isn't too damaged, they may be able to make a match."

"I wonder if it'll be from the same weapon as —"

I stopped just in time. I wasn't supposed to say anything about the bullet in Damon's head. So far, the police had managed to keep that piece of information out of the press reports.

"The same as what?"

The ringing of the doorbell saved me. I opened the door and admitted two uniformed officers. "Thank you for coming so quickly," I said. "I'm Morgan Tyler. This is Dr. Thompson."

"I'm Officer Williams. This is Officer Riley."

Officer Williams had very pale skin, blond hair and the bushiest eyebrows I had ever seen. Officer Riley, in spite of his Irish name, was African-American. They were both young and boyishly good-looking. In their immaculate uniforms they looked more like actors we might cast as police officers rather than the real thing.

"Nobody we know has been in this building since John Lennon was killed," said Officer Williams. "I wondered what it looked like inside."

"They say these exterior walls are three feet thick," said Officer Riley.

We led Officers Williams and Riley into the living room. They surveyed the destroyed window. Officer Williams turned to look at the opposite wall and Chet pointed out the spot where the bullet was lodged. Officer Riley asked, "Do you two have any enemies?"

"I don't live here," Chet said.

"What about you, Miss Taylor?"

"It's 'Tyler.' "

"Tyler. You maybe got some 'ex' who's not a good sport about being dumped, Miss Tyler?"

"My life isn't that exciting."

"You mean it didn't used to be," Chet said.

At that moment the familiar figures of Detectives Phoenix and Flynn pushed through the partially open front door. Phoenix quickly looked me over, scanning my face and body for visible signs of damage.

"Are you all right?"

"Just a little shaken up," I said. "What are you doing here?"

Detective Flynn answered. "We're supposed to be notified when something happens to one of the —" Flynn was about to use the word "suspects," but he made a quick course correction and finished with "— uh, when something happens involving the *people* in the Radford case."

Phoenix was staring at Chet. "And you are — ?"

"A friend of Morgan's," he said. "Kevin Chet Thompson." He extended his hand to Phoenix, then realized it was bleeding and pulled it back. "Sorry." He took a white handkerchief from his pocket and wrapped it around his hand.

"I'll clean that cut," I said.

"Hold it," Phoenix said. He turned to the two uniforms. "This room faces the park, so the shot had to come from there. Canvas the neighborhood to see if anybody saw the shooter, and get mounted officers to search inside the park."

Officers Riley and Williams nodded and left. Flynn was detecting in the living room.

"The bullet's in the wall," Chet told him, indicating the location. Flynn went over to examine the entry hole.

"I'd like to take care of Chet's cut," I said.

"I'm okay."

Phoenix was busy judging the angle from where the bullet had entered the room to where it had penetrated the wall. "Where were you standing?" he asked, at last.

"In front of the window, looking out at the park," I said. I felt my face beginning to flush with embarrassment and hoped he didn't notice.

Phoenix turned the chandelier switch to the "Off" position, leaving the room illuminated by a lamp on the end table next to the phone. "Show me *how* you were standing," he said. "Exactly. But don't go near the window."

Chet and I moved to stand within a few

inches of each other, side by side, looking out. My posture was unnaturally stiff.

Phoenix had a skeptical expression on his face. "Is that *exactly* how you two were standing?"

"Not precisely," Chet replied. He moved closer to me, looked down and said softly, "This'll only hurt for a moment." Then he took me in his arms.

Detective Flynn made a sound that was somewhere between a grunt and a chortle. "So you two had a little lip-lock action going," he said.

I could have killed him.

Chet released me. I stepped back a good two feet.

"I don't want to stay anywhere near this window," I said.

"You don't have to. I found out what I wanted to know." With that terse comment, Phoenix-the-tight-jawed went to the window and closed the wooden shutters. I stepped several more feet away from Chet.

Flynn flipped the lights back on and asked, "Do you have any other rooms that face the park?"

"The den and the bedroom."

"Until we find out what's going on," Phoenix said, "keep your shutters closed."

Chet, Phoenix and I stood on our respective spots as though we had taken root. I glanced at Chet and saw that he was trying not to smile at our awkward situation. At least it was awkward for *me*. The only two men I had gone out with in years were, ironically, in the same room, sizing each other up.

And Phoenix was here because someone had just tried to kill me. Again.

The tension was broken by the last person I would have guessed could lighten a mood — Detective Flynn.

"You got any coffee?" he asked.

# 28

My Mr. Coffee machine was brewing freshly ground Kenya beans while Phoenix and Flynn were in the living room, digging the bullet out of the wall. Chet sat at the kitchen table, and I was cleaning, medicating and dressing the cut on his hand.

"You're a good medic," he said.

"I spent a lot of time in places where the nearest doctor was two hundred miles away."

"Your husband was the conservationist photographer, Ian Tyler."

"Yes."

"I recognized some of his work on the walls in your dining room. He was good."

"He was amazing."

"The print you have in the corner — of the young chimp washing his hands — I bought a copy of that at a gallery. It's in my house in Greenwich." He caught the sudden grin of pride on my face. "What is it?" Then he guessed. "Wait a minute! You took that picture, didn't you?"

"It was on the first roll I shot in Africa. We were visiting friends of Ian's in the district of Karen. The chimp was one of their pets. I saw him dipping his little hands into the water bucket and took the picture before I thought about it. Just beginner's luck." I finished bandaging and stepped away from the table. "Try to keep that dry for the next twenty-four hours."

"Yes, ma'am."

I turned and opened an upper cabinet to get some coffee mugs. Chet got up and stood behind me. Too close; he was making me nervous.

"Did you take any other pictures that are hanging in the dining room?"

"No." I moved away to take a package of Oreos out of my big brown cookie jar that was modeled after an ancient, knotty tree stump. I arranged them on a plate. To keep Chet at a safe distance, I handed him the plate of cookies. "Would you put these on the table, please?" I could feel him watching me as I placed half-and-half, sugar, Sweet'N Low, spoons, and napkins on a tray with the coffee mugs.

When I finished, Chet picked up the tray and set it on the kitchen table, too.

In spite of the fact that I had enjoyed his kiss — or maybe because of it — I wanted to tell him we couldn't go out together again. Then I remembered he hadn't *asked* to take me out again.

At that moment, Phoenix and Flynn came into the kitchen. Phoenix carried the bullet in a clear plastic evidence bag. Flynn sniffed the air like a bloodhound, and headed directly to Mr. Coffee. "That smells great," he said.

"Sit down." I gestured to the four chairs

around the kitchen table, and everyone sat. I poured coffee into the mugs and distributed them, then I took the only seat left, between Phoenix and Chet. I looked at Detective Flynn, who was inhaling the Oreos, and asked him what they had learned from the bullet.

Phoenix answered for him. "It's a thirty caliber. Stainless steel jacket."

"A man-stopper," Flynn added, between bites. "Wasn't no kid out there with a BB gun. Our bullet's probably a 30.06 from a five-shot bolt-action Springfield."

Chet asked Flynn, "You're an ex-Marine, aren't you?"

"No, I'm a *retired* Marine."

Phoenix was smiling. "There's no such thing as an 'ex'-Marine."

"You got that right," said Flynn.

"Will you be able to identify the rifle?" I asked.

"The bullet's pretty damaged," Flynn said, "but Forensics will be able to tell us something."

Phoenix turned to Chet and said, rather pointedly, I thought, "We have to talk to Mrs. Tyler. Don't let us keep you from wherever it is you're going."

Chet turned to me and said, "We haven't had a chance to talk yet. Why don't I go wait in another room —"

The front doorbell rang.

"Want me to get that?" Phoenix asked.

"No." I rose and started for the door. Flynn stayed seated and reached for another Oreo, but Chet and Phoenix stood, signaling their good manners. As I left the kitchen, I gave the three men a parting shot, so to speak, "Play nice while I'm gone, boys."

I thought the police officers were back, ringing the bell, but when I opened the door, I saw one of the last people I expected.

"Penny?"

"Hi, Morgan," she said. Even with her face devoid of makeup and tight with worry, she looked much younger than forty-three. "Matt said there'd been a shooting at your apartment." She peered at me closely. "Thank God, you look all right. Were you hurt?"

"No, the bullet missed."

"I hope you don't mind my coming over."

"Of course not. Come on in."

Penny Cavanaugh let me take her jacket and indicated the tote bag she was carrying. "I made sandwiches. Matt and G.G. get hungry when they go out investigating in the middle of the night."

From the stunned expressions on their faces, Phoenix and Flynn were two very surprised detectives when I showed my newest guest into the kitchen.

"Aunt Penny? What are you doing here?"

Chet stood up again. He smiled at Penny. "*Aunt* Penny? You look too young to be a detective's aunt. Hello, I'm Chet Thompson."

219

"Penny Cavanaugh," she said. Penny turned to look at me, her eyes full of questions. I could almost hear her wondering, *Who is this gorgeous man?*

Before I could decide what to say, Flynn spoke up. He indicated Penny's tote bag with a nod of his head, and asked, "Is that roast beef I smell?"

"Yep," she said. "Just the way you like it."

Penny unpacked the sandwiches and I took a platter out of the cupboard. In less time than it takes me to give Mr. Coffee a fresh filter, Penny had arranged the sandwiches on the platter with an artistry that impressed me. When I put cookies on a plate, they look like cookies on a plate. When Penny arranged food, it looked like the cover of *Gourmet* magazine.

Even though Chet had just eaten dinner, all three men attacked the food like NBA players after an overtime game. I had to admit I couldn't blame them. Penny made fabulous sandwiches: perfectly done roast beef piled between thick, soft slices of homemade bread, with spicy mustard, pickles and horseradish on the side. As though her spectacular sandwiches were not enough, she had also made a large bowl of warm German potato salad. The first taste ruined me for commercial potato salad forever.

"You should have your own cooking show," I told her between bites.

Chet looked up from his second meal of the

night, gazed at her soulfully and in a cowboy drawl, said, "Marry me, Penny Cavanaugh."

"I'm already married," she replied. She didn't add that her husband was supposed to be dead but would be coming back.

Flynn, having finished the last of the roast beef sandwiches, burped discreetly and resumed his detecting. "Let's go back in the living room," he said.

Penny gasped when she saw the bullet hole in the window. She glanced around, looking for something. "Where's the yellow crime scene tape?"

"There's only a hole in the window of a private apartment," Phoenix said. He was scowling at everyone in the room, especially Chet. "I want some answers." He started his interrogation with me, "You made it easy for the shooter. Why were you standing in front of the window with the lights on?"

His sharp tone annoyed me. "You make it sound like a crime," I snapped.

"That was my fault," Chet said. "I was looking out at the lights in the park and I asked Morgan to tell me what one of them was."

Flynn snorted and looked at me with pity. "You fell for that? Lady, you don't get around much, do you?"

Phoenix aimed knife-sharp eyes at Chet. "So, getting Morgan to stand in front of the window was your idea."

"No, *kissing* her was my idea. Looking out the window was just my excuse."

Listening to this, Penny's eyes were getting as large and round as silver dollars.

I was angry, but I wasn't sure at *whom*. I started with Phoenix: "Just what are you implying, Detective?"

Chet answered, "He thinks I set you up."

"It crossed my mind," Phoenix said.

"That's ridiculous. I'm on the third floor. Whoever took a shot at us must have been standing inside the park wall, on that hill of rocks. That's a distance of *at least* a hundred and fifty, maybe two hundred yards. Bullets don't keep flying straight-arrow. He'd have to aim slightly upward, calculate the wind, allow for the drop and for the fact that the bullet had to go through glass. He couldn't have been positive which one of us he would hit."

All three men and Penny were staring at me.

Phoenix broke the spell. "You know a lot about guns," he said.

"I know how to shoot."

"I'm impressed," Chet said.

Flynn aimed a suspicious look at Chet and asked, "Just who *are* you? What's your part in this?"

"I write books on crime."

"That's where I've seen you," Penny said. "On *Oprah*."

"I'm doing the story of Damon Radford's murder," Chet told them.

"When did you make up your mind?" I wanted to know.

"While we were lying on the floor together, covered in broken glass."

"Oh," Penny sighed, "how romantic . . ."

Phoenix made a low sound in his throat, something like a growl. We ignored him.

"I'd like you to help me solve this case," Chet told me. Before I had a chance to reply, Phoenix started bellowing.

"That's *crazy!* You want to get yourself *killed?* You write *soap opera* —"

"Daytime *drama*. We don't call it 'soap opera.' "

"I don't care what you call it!" Phoenix snapped. He lashed out at Chet next. "I can't stop you from sticking your nose where it doesn't belong," he said, "but by God, if you get in the way of our investigation, I'll slap you in jail for obstruction." He turned to me again. "I'll arrest you, too."

"Well," I said to Phoenix, "you certainly are persuasive." I gave him my sweetest, most agreeable smile. Then I looked at Chet and asked, "Do you want to go partners on a lawyer when Phoenix ships us off to Rikers Island, the NYPD's version of Devil's Island?"

# 29

Penny asked if she could spend the night, and I was delighted to have the company. It was clear from his expression that Detective Phoenix had mixed emotions about the arrangement. Detective Flynn looked amused; Chet seemed disappointed.

As the two detectives went off to close and secure the shutters on my various windows, I heard Flynn say to Phoenix, "You're getting too involved in this case, Matt. Until you get your poker face back, don't get sucked into a game anytime soon. You'll get wiped out."

"I'd better be going," Chet said. He turned to Penny. "Thanks for the best sandwich and the best potato salad I've ever had."

"You must come to dinner at our house sometime."

"Just let me know when your nephew won't be home," he joked. Then he pressed my hand lightly. "Will you two be okay here?"

"We'll be fine."

"Then I'll see you tomorrow," he said. And he was gone.

Penny sighed. "Oh, I wish he wasn't so good-looking and charming," she said. "Poor Matt.

Well, it's just like in my stories. We'll have to wait to see what happens."

Phoenix and Flynn came into the kitchen and glanced around.

"If you're looking for Chet Thompson, he's gone."

"Watch out for that guy," Flynn said. "Something about him bothers me."

Phoenix grunted in agreement, but didn't elaborate. After instructing us to keep the shutters closed and the doors double locked, he and his partner departed.

Penny and I finished cleaning up the kitchen.

"Elegant china," she said as we dried the plates I'd put out for the sandwiches and potato salad. "I've always thought china patterns are like fingerprints — they're a kind of *identifier*. But you fooled me. This pattern is so formal. I would never have guessed you chose it."

"I didn't. The dishes and silverware and the furniture were all part of the package when I bought the co-op."

"Didn't you get your own china and silver when you were married?"

I shook my head. "Ian and I were always traveling. We never owned anything we couldn't pack up in five minutes and carry ourselves."

"Well, you're settled down now, you have a home. Shouldn't you think about getting some things that reflect who *you* are?"

"I hadn't thought about it," I said. *Who am I?*

"Maybe there are some family heirlooms that will come to you one day?"

"No heirlooms." I couldn't help laughing, but just a short laugh. "No family."

"Oh, I'm so sorry. What happened? I don't mean to pry. I'll change the subject if that's what you want."

"No, it's okay. I was adopted — for a little while. An old couple. They were much too old to adopt through the usual legal channels, so I suspect they got me in some private deal. Anyway, I must have been more trouble than they expected, because they sent me back." Penny looked horrified. I didn't want to make a big drama out of something so long in the past. I smiled to show the memory didn't hurt anymore. "I think of it this way," I said. "It's like the 'no questions asked' return policy the shopping channels have. I guess I didn't fit."

"That's *terrible*."

"Adoption is a really good thing, most of the time. Probably ninety-nine percent of the time."

"If you weren't adopted again, where did you grow up?"

"In a Catholic boarding school. The nuns were very kind to us, and we got a good education. It was so good that I won a scholarship to Columbia."

"But you didn't have a childhood . . ."

"True, but I also don't have the same family problems most people do. Tonight, for instance,

Chet asked if I have any crazy relatives some-body would have to put up with —"

"*Somebody?* I think he was sending you a message," Penny said.

"No, it was just getting-to-know-you, first-date conversation. But the point is I *don't* have crazy relatives. I have no baggage. So, you see, there are compensations." *Like Harrison said about developing a great torso, you win some, you lose some.*

"Well," Penny said, "when my Patrick comes back and we have our own home again, I'll be taking my china and silverware with me. Then Matt's going to have to buy his own. Maybe you'll help him pick them out."

"Maybe you'll help *me*," I said. "I mean, when I'm ready to get things of my own."

"Count on it, Morgan."

I gave Penny the bed, and handed her a new pair of red silk pajamas that were a birthday present from Nancy, but that I hadn't worn yet. I put on my Bruce Lee T-shirt and the satin pa-jama bottoms I like to sleep in, then I pulled something out of the closet that resembled a backpack. Penny looked at it with curiosity.

"What's that?"

"An extra bed. One of my late-night TV pur-chases," I said. "It's an inflatable mattress. Watch." I fiddled with a lever and — whoosh — just like in the commercials, it filled with air and expanded into a full-size mattress in seconds. As

I dressed it with sheets and a comforter, I told Penny, "The bed linens and towels didn't come with the apartment. I picked those out."

"They're pretty," she said. "I knew you had good taste."

Penny turned out the bedside lamp. After a few minutes I heard her deep, even breathing and knew that she was asleep.

I was still awake an hour later, my mind full of questions.

*Who fired a bullet through my living room window?*

The person must have been trying to kill me, because this is my home. How could anyone have known Chet would be here tonight, when I didn't even know myself that I was going to invite him in? Is it possible, as Phoenix suggested, that Chet set me up by drawing me to the window, where I would be a perfect target?

*Ridiculous.*

But did I believe in Chet's innocence strongly enough to bet my life on it?

I honestly didn't know. All I knew for certain was that I would have to step up my efforts to find out who killed Damon. Because the police didn't seem to be having much success, and their list of suspects still included me at the top. The problem was I didn't have a lot of time to play sleuth. I had professional obligations to fulfill. In the eyes of television network brass, the fact that I was suspected of committing a murder (and that someone was trying to kill me) would *not* be an acceptable reason for falling behind our taping schedule.

So I began making a mental list of problems I had to solve for the show.

Sean O'Neil's character "Nicky" needed an exciting new story line. Although not the right love interest for Kira, his portrayer had an army of devoted fans. How to turn him into an asset . . . *Who is Nicky?* A young man from a wealthy family yet to find a focus for his energy. *What is he going to do?* Something to make him interact with most of the other characters. *What are his talents?* Not established. Into what metaphorical pool of sharks can I toss him?

I had a sudden inspiration.

Nicky, who has family money but no profession, was going to buy a failing nightclub in Greendale. Against the advice of everyone (except Kira, who believes in him even as she realizes she doesn't love him), Nicky will renovate the place, rename it and turn it into the town's hot spot. Nicky's struggle to make his club a success would give Sean something meaty to act: challenges to face, obstacles to overcome. Some of them could be physically menacing. I would have organized crime try to get a foothold in Greendale, USA. Nicky's nightclub would greatly expand the show's storytelling possibilities, and with a nightclub set, we could give the show an injection of live music, something the younger fans loved.

There was another thing this new plot was going to do.

It would give me the opportunity to begin my own covert investigation of Damon's murder — and I'd start by making a visit to Kitty Leigh.

I didn't want to disturb Penny's sleep, so I got up, took one of my white legal pads and a pen from the night table and went quietly from the bedroom to the den. I settled into a corner of my big, comfortable sofa and propped the white legal pad against my knees. On the first page of the pad I wrote the title of this particular project. I called it "Who Killed D.R.?"

This was going to be *my* list of suspects.

I paused for a moment, one of my favorite blue ink Pilot Rolling Ball pens poised over the legal pad. There were eight people I believed wanted Damon gone from the earth, but three of them could not have done the deed.

The first of these three was Helen Marshall. Everyone who saw her at the funeral commented on her heavier than usual drinking since she lost her job on *Trauma Center*. Her friends (the few, the thick-skinned) were so worried about her, I'd heard they'd banded together and tried an intervention, with no luck. While she might have been able to shoot Damon, I don't know how Helen, small as she is, could have gotten his body over the balcony railing — not without help. Even if she had performed that miracle, it was highly unlikely that a sloppy drunk could have gotten out of his apartment without leaving evidence.

Damon's killer had to have both physical strength and a clear head.

The next name that thankfully couldn't go on my suspect list was Harrison Landers. His hatred of Damon had not diminished since his stroke, but Harrison was confined to a wheelchair. It was impossible for him to have killed Damon and tossed him over the balcony.

The third name I could not include was that of Rick Spencer, the executive most likely to inherit Damon's job. Because of his ambition, Rick *would* have been my favorite candidate, *except* for the fact that he had an absolutely unbreakable alibi. He was at a dinner party for twelve, at the palatial home of the chairman of the board of the Global Broadcasting Network. I had no trouble believing that Mr. Yarborough, or Mrs. Yarborough, would lie to protect Rick, or to protect GBN's image and its stock price. But it was inconceivable to me that the other guests that night — wealthy and prominent people all — would risk arrest for Rick Spencer, or for GBN. And each of those other guests was adamant that no one left the Yarboroughs' house before 1 A.M.

That left the five people I was going to investigate.

Five people who had no solid alibis and powerful motives to murder.

In alphabetical order, my five suspects were:

Johnny Isaac
Kitty Leigh
Serena McCall
Teresa Radford
Tommy Zenos

Any of those five people could be the "who."
My job was to find out which one of them had
the most compelling "why."

# 30

Next morning, I had already showered and was mostly dressed for the day in an oversized periwinkle blue cashmere sweater and black jeans. As I was pulling on my favorite pair of black suede ankle boots, Penny called out from the bathroom, "Do you have an extra toothbrush somewhere?"

"Guest brushes to the left of the sink, in the bottom drawer," I said.

Penny appeared in the doorway holding a large handful of new toothbrushes, tied together with a red ribbon. "Which one should I use?"

"Take any one. They were a present from my friend Nancy, when I moved in. She said she wanted me to be prepared with 'guest amenities' for when I was 'ready to date.' Those were her euphemisms."

"How many toothbrushes did she give you?"

"A dozen."

Penny counted them quickly. "They're all still in their wrappings."

"I haven't been ready."

While Penny was brushing, I called a neighborhood glazier and arranged to have my living room window replaced. A few minutes later I was in the kitchen making coffee. When the doorbell rang, I assumed it was Matt Phoenix coming to make sure I hadn't let anything terrible happen to Penny. When I opened the door I saw that — as G.G. Flynn might have put it — I was "wrong-o."

Chet Thompson was on the other side of the threshold.

Hefting a grocery bag, from which came the unmistakable aroma of fresh-made bagels, he said, "Breakfast. Fresh orange juice, bagels and cream cheese. I didn't know if you preferred smoked salmon or sturgeon, so I brought both."

"Come on in," I said, starting to salivate. "I like it all."

I stepped aside, just as I heard the distinctive *ping* of the main elevator. I saw the ornate door slide open, and had mixed emotions about what I saw next.

"I hope you brought enough bagels for five," I said to Chet.

Chet turned around to follow my gaze. Detectives Phoenix and Flynn were approaching my front door. Flynn pulled out a folded paper from his inside jacket pocket. I noticed it was the same jacket he was wearing the night I met him at the hospital, but the missing button had been replaced and his tie was knotted correctly. Mrs. Detective Flynn, the lady Penny had described as "terrific," must have inspected him before he left home this morning.

Phoenix said, "Good morning, Morgan. And

Thompson." When he said Chet's last name, his tone was icy enough to chill the orange juice.

"Good morning to you, Detectives," I said. To Phoenix, I added, "Penny's getting dressed."

I stepped back so that everyone could enter.

As soon as I closed my door, Flynn said, "We got a warrant." He indicated the folded piece of paper.

"Shall I get you a lawyer?" Chet asked me.

"She's not under arrest," said Phoenix.

"Please don't refer to me in the third person," I told Phoenix. Then I turned to Chet. "I have a lawyer," I said. "The gorgeous blonde super-model you noticed at the funeral, remember?"

"Your lawyer's a supermodel?" Flynn asked. "She ever been in one of the swimsuit issues?"

I ignored that as, from the corner of my eye, I saw Penny coming down the hall toward us.

"What's the warrant *for?*" I asked Phoenix.

"You've got a nine-millimeter Glock," he said. "We want to see it."

"What model?" Chet asked.

"Nineteen."

"Good piece," he said, impressed. "The safe-action trigger system's got the fastest accurate first shot on the market."

"That's the shot that counts," I said.

As Chet and I discussed the virtues of the Glock, Flynn was swinging his eyes back and forth between us like a fan at a tennis match.

Penny's eyes were wide with surprise. "You have a *gun?*" she asked me.

"A pistol, yes, and I have a valid permit to have it here for protection."

"We're not questioning your permit," Phoenix said. "Maybe your sanity," he added in a low mutter.

"Why do you want to see my pistol?" I asked.

"The bullet that was in Radford's head," Phoenix said, "came from a nine millimeter."

Penny gaped. "You mean that man who was pushed over the balcony — he was shot, too?"

Chet was also surprised to hear about the bullet. "This case gets more and more interesting," he said.

"The Glock is in my bedroom," I said. "Follow me."

Phoenix and Flynn refused to let Chet accompany us, so he went to the kitchen with Penny as I led the way. When I opened my bedroom door, I saw that Penny had made the bed. Judging from the fresh pillowcases, she had also changed the linens. Moreover, she had managed to collapse the inflatable mattress and put it back into its carrying case. Glancing into the bathroom through the open door, I noticed she had replaced my almost-empty roll of toilet tissue with a fresh roll, and had folded the first square into a perfect triangle.

I was in awe of Penny Cavanaugh.

"Where do you keep it?" Flynn asked.

"Here," I said. I opened the top drawer in the night table and took out my semiautomatic pistol. The Glock's overall length of seven and a quarter inches (four and a half of those inches were the barrel) was the right size to be comfortable in my hand. It's a light weapon, about a pound and a half with a full magazine. The stock grip is made of a single piece of injection-molded plastic.

I handed the pistol to Phoenix, who sniffed the barrel.

"It hasn't been fired in at least a year," I said.

"You should keep it locked up," Phoenix said. "A child might find it."

"I don't even *know* any children."

Phoenix removed the magazine, saw that it was full. "Where did you get this?" he asked as he passed the pistol to Flynn for his examination.

"My husband gave it to me. In Africa. We were in dangerous places sometimes."

"This baby couldn't stop an elephant," Flynn said. He tested the grip in his large hand.

"I didn't need protection from elephants."

"How did you get it into the country?" Phoenix asked.

"In my carry-on. I was very upset when I came back to New York; I didn't remember that I'd packed it. Security must have been careless because it wasn't spotted. Anyway, it's registered now," I told them. "And it's completely legal."

"That's how we found out you had it," Flynn said. "You didn't tell us you had a piece."

"You didn't ask me."

Phoenix wanted to know where I had fired the Glock last.

"About a year ago I went up to practice at the shooting range. Targets, it's in Spring Valley."

"I know where it is," Phoenix said. "How good are you?"

"I'm okay," I said. *Actually, I'm a lot better than okay.* "I used to go up there once a month to shoot with my old boss, Harrison Landers. Before his stroke. I don't much enjoy going alone."

I instantly felt uncomfortable. I had just told them Harrison had a pistol, too. As though he read my mind, Phoenix said, "We know about Landers's nine-millimeter Beretta. He had a residence permit. According to our records, he reported it stolen two years ago."

I was relieved. "Two years ago . . . someone must have taken it while he was in the hospital," I said. Detective Flynn had been scribbling something on a piece of paper. Now he handed it to me. "This is a receipt for the Glock," he said.

"You're taking it with you?"

"You'll get it back when the lab finishes with it," Phoenix told me.

"*If* you get it back," Detective Flynn added.

He put my pistol in a clear plastic evidence bag, signed his name on the label and shoved the bag into an outside pocket of his jacket. Then, his nose quivering, Flynn followed me to the kitchen from whence wafted the enticing aroma of fresh-brewed coffee and toasting bagels. Detective Phoenix brought up the rear. The expression on his face could have been used to define "grim."

Our party of three entered the kitchen to find Penny arranging the items Chet had brought for breakfast. Chet was standing next to the sink, slicing tomatoes and sweet onions.

"Thank you, Penny, but you shouldn't have changed the linens," I told her. "You're supposed to be the guest."

She was smiling as she took the slices of onions and tomatoes from Chet and added them — artfully — to the platter of smoked salmon and sturgeon on the center of the kitchen table. "It wasn't any trouble," she said. "Matthew says I'm a compulsive nester."

The Windsor chair with the tapestry cushion from the dining room had been added to the four plain oak chairs around my kitchen table. I was sure it was Chet who had done the lifting. Penny Cavanaugh was not the kind of woman men allowed to carry things. I made a mental note to find out how she did that.

As I watched Chet pouring orange juice into glasses, it occurred to me that he was being very helpful to Penny. She was only a few years older than he was, and lovely, like those Italian actresses of a certain age who always end up with the leading men in foreign films. It wasn't inconceivable Chet might be attracted to her. *Was I glad Penny was convinced she was still a married woman?*

"Let's have breakfast," Penny said.

She indicated where each of us should sit. She assigned the elegant dining room chair to Chet. "I thought it would be fun, and a little different, to have a candlelight breakfast," she said, "but I couldn't find your candles, Morgan."

"I don't have any candles," I admitted.

"That's all right," she assured me. "You're very busy creating."

I made a mental note to buy some candles.

Everybody consumed the smoked salmon, cream cheese, sturgeon, bagels, sliced tomatoes, orange juice and coffee. Only Detective Flynn ate the onions. Everything was cordial, until Chet and Phoenix got into an argument over who was going to drive Penny to work. I thought they might come to blows, but was spared from having Penny teach me how to clean blood off floor tiles when Phoenix's pager buzzed. The two detectives were called to a crime scene. Chet got to drive Penny to Natasha's.

Since the glazier was coming, I worked in my apartment. I used the dining room table as a desk while I edited two scripts and roughed out three new Cody and Kira scenes to be inserted into existing scripts. When I finished, it was eleven-thirty, time to leave for GBN, and the glazier hadn't arrived yet. Typical.

I asked Luke, the chief of maintenance, to let the glazier in. I slipped Luke a twenty to stay with the glazier while he was in my apartment. I realized I wasn't as trusting as I used to be. Getting shot at will do that to you. The window could be replaced; it wasn't as easy to restore my sense of safety in my own home.

I resented whoever shot at me for blasting that away.

# 31

When Kitty opened the door to her dressing room at noon that day, I was sitting on one of her chintz-covered chairs, waiting for her. She taped her daily hour-long talk show in Studio 26, two floors below where we taped *Love of My Life*. Nathan Hughes's secretary had given me her arrival, rehearsal and taping schedule when I told her I wanted to invite Kitty to appear on *Love*.

The moment she saw me, her face went pale with dread. Her huge green eyes — those eyes that, when she was a child movie star, were so beguiling in close-up — filled with tears. Concerned, I got up from the chair. "Kitty, are you all right?" I started toward her, but she shrank back against the door, as far away from me as she could get.

"What do *you* want from me?" She emphasized "you."

"I don't want anything from you," I said. "I'm here because —"

"Then you're not by?"

"By? By what?"

Kitty stared at me until she realized I truly had no idea what she was talking about. Then she started to laugh. It was a weak laugh, about two breaths short of hysteria. "Bi-*sexual*," she said. "I thought you were here because . . . you know."

*What?* Every time I think I can't be shocked anymore, something happens to shock me. This was a biggie. "Why in the world would you think *that?*"

"You were there that night, you saw what happened, too." Her voice had become like a child's.

"At Damon's?" I was beginning to understand. "Has somebody who was there that night . . . threatened you?"

She didn't answer in words. Tears began running down her cheeks, cutting little trails through the thick TV makeup. I flashed back four months to Damon's apartment.

I had gone to his party only because Tommy had pleaded with me, saying Damon would take my no-show out on *him* if I didn't. I offered him a deal. "I'll go, but only if you'll be my escort." Tommy agreed. We arrived together, and were paired at the sit-down dinner for twelve, but then Tommy disappeared immediately after coffee was served, leaving me to handle whatever might happen next.

What happened next was nothing I could have predicted, or even imagined.

There were four guests remaining: Kitty, Rick Spencer, Joe Niles — whose scowling wife had stalked out earlier — and me. The staff had been dismissed, and we were in the living room. I was talking to Joe about the technical difficulties of an upcoming episode when I realized Joe wasn't listening. Instead he was looking past me. I turned, following his gaze, and saw Damon sitting in one of the large club chairs that flanked the fireplace. His legs were stretched out in front of him, and they were slightly apart. With one hand gripping Kitty's hair and the other pulling her by the arm, Damon was forcing Kitty to kneel down in front of him.

Kitty was crying, "No, Damon. No, please, not here."

"Yes, right here. I want our friends to see what your greatest talent really is."

Damon forced Kitty's head down to his open fly — and I got out of there so fast I forgot to take my evening bag. I was the only one who left.

Rick Spencer and Joe Niles stayed for the show.

I walked home as fast as it was possible to walk in evening shoes. My keys were in the bag I had left behind, so when I reached the Dakota, Frank, the night security man, let me into my apartment. The first thing I did was telephone an all-night locksmith and have the locks on my apartment and my office doors changed. What I could not change was the image of Kitty Leigh's forced public humiliation.

"Kitty," I said, "I came to see you because I'm

writing a new story line for *Love of My Life*. I'd like you to be in it. Do you watch the show?"

Surprised and relieved, Kitty wiped her eyes. A little color began to seep back into her face under the smeared makeup. Catching a glimpse of herself in the mirror, she sat down and picked up a small triangular sponge. "I tape it and watch it every night when I go home," she said. She deftly began repairing her face. "Your show, and *All My Children*, although I'm not too crazy about what's happening on *All My Children* right now." She glanced up at me before reapplying her mascara. "What did you have in mind?"

"Since you watch the show, you've seen Nicky —"

"He's a cutie," she said. "A sweet puppy dog. I could go for him, but honestly, I don't know what Kira sees in him."

*You and most of our audience.* "I'm fixing that," I said. "Don't miss any shows this week and next. Now, here's my plan: I'm going to have Nicky buy a nightclub and turn it into the town's hottest hot spot. I'd like you to come to the club and sing — you can appear as yourself, or I'll write a character for you to play. Your choice. And we'll make sure the tape schedule doesn't interfere with your talk show. What do you think?"

"I like it," she said.

She seemed genuinely pleased, but she was cautious.

"I don't want to be me. Create a character — after all, I'm an *actor*." She paused for a moment, put down the mascara wand and looked up at me. "One thing." There was a flash of fire in her eyes. "I don't care what you pay me — scale, whatever . . . if the part catches on with the audience, you can talk to my agent. And I won't need a private dressing room or any special treatment when I'm upstairs with you guys — *unless* the part catches on, of course. Then we might make some *adjustments*. But there's one thing that I *do* want right now. It's the deal-breaker for me."

"What is it?" I asked.

"How many of your shows does Joe Niles direct?"

"One out of every four. Sometimes one out of three if he has an overhang episode."

"He cannot — can *not* — direct me. Ever. Will you promise me that?"

"Tommy Zenos is the executive producer," I said, "but having you on the show will be such a coup, I know he'll honor your request."

She nodded, turned away from me and went back to fixing her makeup. I sensed she wanted to say something else, so I waited quietly until she was ready. "That son-of-a-bitch stayed and watched," she said into the mirror. "You left. That's why I'm talking to you."

She gave me the opening I needed. "Kitty, when you came in, why did you think . . . what you thought?" I asked.

Her eyes met mine in the mirror. "Niles and the other little shit, Rick Spencer, have been blackmailing me. They won't spread the story, they say, if I . . . *favor* them. When I found you in my dressing room, I thought . . ."

"Those creeps. Kitty, I'm disgusted at both of them. At all of them."

"Since I was eight years old," she said softly. She had finished her makeup and now sat staring at the mirror, gazing into the dark infinity of her own eyes as though mesmerized. "You never get over it," she whispered, "being treated like that."

I didn't know if she was talking to me or to herself. I remembered thinking, as I was walking home the night of Damon's grotesque party, that if Kitty decided to kill Damon, I would volunteer to give her a phony alibi. "She was right here with me at the time of his death," I would swear. Now someone *had* killed Damon, and watching the emotionally fragile woman staring at herself in the mirror, I was sure it had *not* been Kitty. She looked as though she was one stiff breeze away from a nervous breakdown, and I sensed that she knew it, too.

Mentally, I struck Kitty Leigh off my list of suspects.

*And then there were four.*


I left Kitty's dressing room and headed for the fire stairs to walk up the two flights to the *Love* studios. Cybelle was scheduled to tape some inserts, and I wanted to see how she was feeling. Also, I wanted to talk to Tommy Zenos about the new Nicky story line, and about my idea for Kitty Leigh's involvement.

All the bright lights were on in Kitty's talk show studio, which was right next to the door to the interior stairs. As I passed through the studio, I saw Kitty's new audience (all of whom had written to the network for tickets) being led to their seats by interns. The TV lights were so blinding that when I pulled open the heavy emergency door and stepped onto the landing, it wasn't until the door clanged shut behind me that I realized the fire stairs were in total darkness. I pushed down onto the horizontal steel bar that opened the fireproof door to return to the corridor.

That's when I discovered the door locked automatically when it swung closed.

*Uh-oh.* Now that I was locked in the fire stairs, I remembered — obviously too late — a memo that had gone out. It had explained that due to security concerns, the fire stairs were henceforth going to lock from the inside, and that they were to be used only for purposes of evacuation. Because I worked at my office in the Dakota and seldom went to the Mother Ship, I'd barely scanned the memo before tossing it into the trash with the other memos that came from the network. Since I was stuck anyway, and would have to pound on a door until someone heard me and let me out, I decided I might as well make my way up the two flights to where our show was taped. If I am going to be embarrassed, I prefer to be embarrassed among friends.

Much as I dislike clichés, it truly was so dark on those stairs that I couldn't see my own hand in front of my face. I gripped the railing along the wall and started up the concrete stairs, careful not to slip on the protective waterproof sealant that made the surface of the concrete slick to the touch. Ian used to say admiringly that I had the steady nerves of a burglar, but it's a lot easier to be brave when you can see where you're going. Caught in the darkness, I was feeling more than a little uneasy. My heart was beating faster than normal, and it wasn't from exertion. When I reached the landing on the floor above Kitty's studio, I let go of the railing and stretched my hands out in front of me, moving them around, using them like the whiskers on a cat. I was trying not to bump into the wall as I fumbled to reach the next flight of stairs.

Suddenly my right foot bumped against a large, soft object.

Disoriented in the darkness, I stumbled and fell forward across what felt like a duffel bag. Reflexively, my hands shot out in an attempt to break my fall. They smacked hard against the floor, but instead of keeping my torso upright, the palms of my hands were sliding. Without traction, my hands could not brace me and my full weight collapsed on top of the soft object. I realized with a powerful jolt of horror that I was sprawled across the back of a *human body.* The slippery substance that covered my hands and wrists was faintly warm. To my exploring fingers, it had the texture of blood.

I screamed.

As I scrambled to my feet in the darkness, my hand brushed against a hard object. Reflexively I picked it up. Whatever it was weighed several pounds and was inside a fabric that stretched. Like a sock. Something heavy inside a sock . . .

*Oh my God. What if this is the weapon?*

Immediately, I dropped it.

It fell with a metallic *clunk* onto the sealed concrete floor and I managed to stumble a few steps away from the body before I bumped up against the emergency door. I pounded on the door with my fists. I grabbed the steel bar and rattled it. I yanked at the bar as I threw myself against it — and nearly fell out into the corridor as the heavy fire door flew open. Because my head was down, a small, creased cardboard rectangle at my feet caught my eye. It was the front flap of a green matchbook cover, folded lengthwise.

It lay on the floor near the doorway.

Had it been wedged into the door by someone who wanted to keep it from locking automatically?

I looked up, trying to adjust my eyes to the sudden assault of bright lights, and realized I was just outside Studio 31, one of the two large facilities where *Trauma Center* was taped Monday through Friday. The powerful lights from the floor flooded the landing behind me. I turned to look, and saw that the body I had fallen over was a woman's. She was lying face-down. Blood had pooled around her head, blood that had been smeared by the palms of my hands when I stumbled over her. It wasn't necessary for me to see the woman's face because I recognized her as soon as I saw her platinum hair.

The unmistakable platinum hair of a former daytime diva.

The woman lying dead, whose blood covered my hands and stained my clothes, was Serena McCall.

# 32

A woman with glasses on top of her head and carrying an armload of scripts was the first living person I saw in the corridor. She took one look at me, her eyes bugged out in horror and she started shrieking. I couldn't blame her. My hands were covered with blood, there was blood on my clothes, and there was a body lying behind me.

Drawn by her screams, people were coming at us from all directions. It was chaos. I noticed an actor I had a passing acquaintance with — Jack something. He was standing in the gathering crowd, staring at the body on the floor as though in a trance, holding a coffee mug, unaware that he had tilted it and coffee was spilling onto the floor. "Jack." I spoke to him sharply to break through his dream state. "Call nine-one-one. NOW, JACK! *Call nine-one-one!*"

The commanding tone of my voice woke him up.

Accustomed to following directions, he sprinted for a phone.

Then I caught sight of Anthony Howell, one of *Trauma Center*'s directors. He had directed some of our episodes when we were caught short; he was a good man in a crisis. "Tony, have some of your crew block the doors," I said. "Nobody's to leave here until the police say so." Tony sprang into action and began herding people away from the door to the fire stairs and used the walkie-talkie clipped to his belt to summon his technical team.

I took two steps back to the landing and scanned the floor until I spotted what I had touched (besides Serena) when I was trying to stand up in the dark. It was indeed a thick athletic sock, bulging with something rounded like a cylinder. It might have been a short length of pipe, or . . . rolls of quarters? I bent down close, but didn't touch it again. I kept myself from looking at Serena.

*And then there were three.*

First on the scene were uniformed officers. They relieved Tony Howell's crew, secured the floor and calmed the *Trauma Center* people down.

A few minutes behind the blue wave, Detectives Phoenix and Flynn arrived on the scene, accompanied by other plainclothes detectives from the Twentieth Squad. With all that had happened in the past few weeks, I was beginning to think of the Twentieth as *my* precinct. It's one of two police precincts known collectively as Midtown North, and its territory encompasses the three most important addresses in my life: the Global Broadcasting building, the Dakota

253

and the building where Nancy lives and Damon Radford died.

Soon, members of the Crime Scene Unit arrived. They were all over the fire stairs, doing their meticulous photographing and spraying and hunting for fibers. I watched one of them bag Serena's hands in plastic, to preserve any possible evidence of her attacker. Two other detectives from the Twentieth were "doing the canvas" — as they called it — to find out exactly *who* had been *where* at the relevant time. According to the medical examiner, Serena had been dead only a short time when I found her.

Detective Flynn called me to join him and Phoenix in *Trauma Center*'s makeup room. As the lead detectives on the case, they had commandeered it for their on-site interrogations. I had the honor of being the first interrogat*ee*.

"What were you doing on that landing?" Phoenix had not been thrilled to learn I had discovered Serena's body.

"You messed with the crime scene," added Detective Flynn.

"Not intentionally," I said. "I've already explained what happened."

"You talked to the uniforms," Flynn said, "not to us."

"We'd like to hear your story firsthand," said Phoenix.

My *story?*

Briefly, I told them about going to see Kitty

Leigh, how I wanted to go up to our floor to talk to Tommy Zenos about Kitty's role, and to check on how Cybelle was doing. "This is her first day back in the studio," I said.

"So what were you doing on the fire stairs?" Phoenix asked.

"I always take stairs. Unless where I'm going is higher than the sixth floor."

Flynn grunted with distaste. "You got some kind of phobia?"

"No," I said. "Taking stairs, and walking as much as possible — that's my exercise. The more I walk, the less I have to worry about what I eat. Unfortunately, I forgot that the fire stairs lock automatically from the inside."

"Except down on the ground floor," said Phoenix. "That door is kept unlocked."

"Obviously," I said. "The stairs are for emergency exit."

"So," Flynn said, "a person can go *up* the fire stairs from the ground floor, or down those stairs and out of the building, but they can't get onto any of the floors unless somebody opens the door from the other side."

"Yes," I said. "But — did you see the folded matchbook cover on the floor? I think it was used to keep the door from locking."

Flynn narrowed his eyes to slits as he looked at me. "Sounds like you got a theory of the case."

"The beginning of a theory," I said. "I think Serena went into the fire stairs to meet someone

— and used the matchbook cover to keep from getting locked in. And that someone killed her, maybe with that sock that looks like it's full of quarters. He — or she — couldn't have left through the door that Serena had kept from locking, or the matchbook cover would have fallen out and I wouldn't have been able to open the door." I paused, to see if they were still following me. They were. "Now, the killer *might* have wedged open the door to another floor in the building, but I think that would have been too big a risk. They didn't want to be seen, right? So my guess is that he or she walked down to the ground floor and slipped out through the heavy foot traffic in the lobby."

"Where'd you get the quarters?" Flynn snarled.

"What?" I asked.

"The three rolls of quarters taped together in the sock. Did you roll them yourself, or did you get the rolls from a bank?"

"I didn't put quarters in that sock."

"Then how'd you know what was in it?" Flynn demanded

"It felt round, like rolls of quarters, and it was heavy."

Phoenix was galvanized by my admission. "You *picked it up?* When?"

"In the dark. Accidentally. Come on, guys, you can't think that I —"

"We're going to have to take your clothes," Phoenix said.

I responded with a lifted eyebrow. I thought he was joking.

His tougher-than-thou façade cracked and he blushed. "Fiber evidence," he said, a little louder than necessary.

"I *told you* I fell over Serena! Of *course* you're going to find her fibers on me. And mine on her. So what do you need fibers for?"

"G.G.," Phoenix ignored me, "find a female officer to take her clothes and check her body for scratches or any other marks that might indicate a struggle."

My mouth dropped open.

Flynn grunted and left.

Phoenix quickly closed the door and turned to me. His voice was low and urgent. "Get yourself a lawyer, quick," he said. "We found the vehicle that almost ran you down; we were able to trace it through the paint it left when it side-swiped the parked car. It was stolen — no surprise — but I had the lab boys go over it for anything they could find. Just before the call came to come here, we got the report. There was only one print on the inside of that car that shouldn't have been there. It belonged to Serena McCall."

I felt my eyes go round as an owl's.

"She's the one who tried to kill you, Morgan," Phoenix said.

As though that was not a big enough shock, he threw another one at me. "After the police-woman checks you over and takes your clothes,"

257

he said, "we need you to come to the Twentieth to give us a formal statement."

"And you want me to do this . . . naked?"

He almost laughed, but he managed to stop himself. "I saw a room here that's as big as an apartment and it's full of clothes."

"It's *Trauma Center*'s wardrobe department."

He smiled as he said, "I bet you'd look cute in a nurse's outfit."

I didn't return his grin.

# 33

One of the wardrobe women put together an outfit in my size: a sweater, slacks, a jacket and a pair of shoes. I asked for a looser sweater, and she made the exchange. Then she gave the clothes to a nice young policewoman whose name tag identified her as Officer Martinez. Officer Martinez accompanied me to an empty dressing room and watched me strip down to bra and panties.

No suspicious marks.

Having passed inspection, she handed me the change of clothes. As she was folding my blood-stained clothing into a plastic bag, I used my cell phone to call Nancy at her office. Nancy's assistant, Miriam, told me Nancy was in conference, but when I said a police officer had just taken away my clothes, Miriam got Nancy on the line.

"Are you all right?" Nancy asked as soon as we were connected.

Bless her heart, she didn't ask what I had done; she was too loyal for that. Her immediate assumption was that something had been done to me. Briefly, I told her about finding Serena McCall's body, and about accidentally handling what might be the murder weapon. I finished up with, "So I'm on my way to the Twentieth Precinct, to give a formal statement."

"Don't tell them anything," Nancy commanded. "We'll meet you there."

"Who's 'we'?" I asked. But Nancy had already hung up.

The Twentieth Precinct is a squat building at One Hundred and Twenty West Eighty-Second, a tree-lined street between Columbus and Amsterdam Avenues. The two pale gray stone upper decks sit on a base of charcoal gray bricks. Once they might have been a lighter color, say back around the time George Washington still had his own teeth. Whether for purposes of information, or intimidation, it identified itself in big metal letters affixed to the front of the building — **20TH PRECINCT**. No one walked through those doors by accident.

The detectives' squad room was on the second floor, up a flight of wooden stairs that creaked with history. The large, open area where they worked looked pretty much the way I expected the place to look, having seen many reruns of *Law & Order* and *NYPD Blue*. There were a lot of desks, a lot of telephones and nothing that could be confused with decorative charm. Separated from the detectives' bullpen, at the far end of the room, was a glass-enclosed office. I saw slatted blinds on the inside and guessed that they could be closed for privacy.

I entered the squad room with Officer Olivia Martinez still by my side, still carrying the large plastic bag that contained the clothes and shoes I had worn at the Global Broadcasting building. Nancy had already arrived. As usual, gorgeous Nancy was the focus of all eyes in the room, including those of Detectives Phoenix and Flynn. She was wearing a dressed-to-intimidate steel gray Versace suit with a neckline that hinted at more than it revealed, and her favorite strand of seven-millimeter natural pearls.

Dazzling as she was, I was used to my pal, so my eyes went directly to the man standing next to her. He was a good three inches shorter, in his late thirties, with a boyish face, a high forehead and dark hair that was beginning to thin. Black-rimmed glasses accented intelligent brown eyes. His black Armani suit and his gray silk tie were so elegant they could have been featured on the cover of *GQ* magazine. He carried a handsome black calf-skin briefcase.

Nancy saw me come in and hurried over. The two detectives and the man in Armani were right behind her. "Are you sure you're all right?" she asked.

"I'm fine," I said. "Thanks for coming."

"Where else would I be?" She looked truly worried.

I gestured to Phoenix and Flynn and asked Nancy, "Have you met the two lead detectives in my life, Matt Phoenix and G.G. Flynn?"

"Yes," she said, the chilly tone of her voice implying the experience had not been a thrill. Then her tone warmed dramatically as she said, "Morgan Tyler, I'd like you to meet the head of our Criminal Defense Division, Arnold Rose." Her eyes sparkled as she pronounced his name. "I told you about him," she said softly.

*But not nearly enough.* I extended my hand, Arnold Rose took it, and we acknowledged the introductions. He had a nice firm handshake.

"So you lawyered up," Flynn said, scowling at me. Phoenix said nothing, but I saw the same worried expression in his eyes that I saw in Nancy's.

Arnold Rose, Esquire, ignored Flynn and addressed Phoenix. "Is there someplace where I can speak to my client in private?" he asked.

"Interview One is empty," Phoenix said.

Officer Martinez, who had been standing next to me, indicated the plastic bag she carried and asked Detective Flynn, "What'll I do with this?"

"It's my clothes," I told Nancy, indicating the bag with a nod of my head.

Arnold Rose went into action. "I would appreciate it, Detectives," he said, "if you would wait a few minutes and then inventory those items in my presence."

"No problem," Phoenix said. He took the bag from Officer Martinez and put it on top of what I guessed was his desk. He nodded at Flynn. "I'll show them to One."

He led us down a hallway to an unmarked wooden door, opened it and then left without a word.

Interview Room One was a cheerless rectangle painted pea soup green, about eight feet by twelve feet, with a scarred wooden table in the center. Three mismatched wooden chairs had been placed around the table, with a fourth chair next to the door. A steel ring attached to a dangling handcuff was bolted to one end of the table. I pictured my wrist locked in that cuff and I shuddered. Nancy saw me looking at it, guessed what I was thinking — *fearing* — and reached out to give my hand a comforting squeeze.

The first thing Arnold Rose did when we entered the room, even before we sat down, was stare at the six-foot-by-four-foot mirror that was set into the wall next to the door. Arnold Rose went over to the mirror and rapped with his knuckles. He addressed unseen ears in a raised voice, "There had better not be anybody out there listening to us. If there is, turn off any microphones and or cameras, or risk the legal consequences of violating attorney-client privilege."

He waited a few seconds, assumed that he was being obeyed and then turned his attention back to Nancy and me. He indicated that Nancy was to sit on one long side of the table and I was to sit opposite her. He pulled the chairs out for both of us, then he took the seat he had chosen for himself. It was next to Nancy and across from me. When he placed his briefcase on the table, I noticed it had a five-number combination lock.

Needing something to lighten the mood, I decided to test a bit that I was about to use on the show, in my Jillian and Garrett story. "May I see your briefcase?" I asked.

The request surprised Rose, but he pushed his briefcase across the table toward me. I stroked the soft leather admiringly. I studied the combination lock for two seconds, then I twirled five numbers: six-two-five-seven-three. I pressed the release button . . . and the lid of the case snapped open. Two startled gasps erupted from the other side of the table. Immediately, without looking at the contents, I closed and locked the case again. I twirled the numbers to other digits, and pushed the case back.

The two attorneys stared at me, astonished.

Then Arnold's ears began to grow red with embarrassment.

"How did you do that?" Nancy asked. Arnold was silent; he knew how.

"Lucky guess," I said. Then I smiled at Nancy. The numbers I had used to open the lock stood for June twenty-fifth, nineteen seventy-three. The month, the day and the year of Nancy's birth. I wondered if Nancy knew her birthday was the combination; since she was looking puzzled, I guessed she did not. So Arnold Rose was as crazy about her as she was about him. It had to be true; after all, I had just caught him doing the upper-income equivalent of carving initials on a tree.

Arnold must have been flustered, but he was a good poker player. He arranged his face in a criminal-defense-attorney expression and got us back to business. "Tell me everything you did, Morgan, from the moment you arrived at the Global building today."

I obliged. Mostly. I told him about my visit to Kitty to talk about her appearing on *Love,* our discussing whether it would be as herself, or as a character I would create for her. What I did not tell Arnold and Nancy was about Rick Spencer and Joe Niles blackmailing Kitty. Nor would I tell them, or anyone, about Damon humiliating her. When I left Kitty's dressing room, I remembered a line that I heard or read. It went something like, *What is necessary for evil to triumph is for good men to do nothing.* I had done nothing for four months too long.

"Morgan? Morgan, where are you?"

The voice of Arnold Rose snapped me back to the present.

"I'm sorry," I said. "My mind wandered for a moment."

"Would you like some coffee?" Nancy asked. "Or something cold?"

"No, thanks. I'm with you again. Where was I . . . ?"

"Kitty Leigh agreed to be on your show," Arnold said.

"And she wants to play a character," Nancy added. She turned her head to watch Arnold question me. When she looked at him, she positively glowed.

"Right," I said. "I left Kitty's dressing room, and was going upstairs to the *Love of My Life* studios to talk to our executive producer, Tommy Zenos. We're only two floors above Kitty's studio, so I did what I usually do — instead of using the elevator, I took the stairs."

"That's true, Arnold," Nancy said. "Everybody who knows Morgan knows she uses stairs whenever it's possible."

Arnold Rose nodded. "Confirmation, that's good."

I explained I didn't remember that the fire doors now locked from the inside until I was stuck. "Do they know why there weren't any lights in the stairwell?" I asked.

"Someone unscrewed the bulbs on the landing where you found the body, and on several floors above and below," Arnold said.

"The police told you that?" I asked.

"Not officially." He smiled with satisfaction. "I have a source here."

"So do I," I said. "And *un*officially, I was told Serena was the person who tried to run me down a while back."

Nancy was shocked. "What do you mean — tried to run you down? *When?*"

"A while ago," I said. "I didn't say anything because I didn't want to worry you. There's something else I didn't tell you, Nance, for the same reason. Last night someone fired a bullet through my living room window — apparently at me."

"Morgan!" Nancy was beyond shock now; she was terrified. "You're coming to live with me, that's it, no argument."

"Yes, argument," I said. "I appreciate your offer, but I won't hide, and I won't let what's going on destroy the life I've built."

"We can get you bodyguards," Arnold Rose said. He was still maintaining his professional calm, but I saw worry in his eyes, too.

"No bodyguards. I can take care of myself." I smiled at them and joked, "I'm still alive, so I must be doing a good job."

"I don't want to lose my best friend," Nancy said.

"You're not going to."

"Tell me *exactly* what happened last night." Arnold said.

I told them about going to dinner at Elaine's with Kevin Chet Thompson, and then inviting him upstairs after dinner, to talk about Damon's murder. I told them about looking out into the park, and about the bullet through the window. That it was a 30.06, but that the detectives weren't confident they'd be able to match it to a particular rifle.

"You're leaving something out," Nancy said.

She was as smart as she was good-looking, and she knew me too well.

"Well . . . Chet was kissing me when it happened," I admitted.

"Hallelujah," Nancy said, softly.

"I hardly think that's the proper response to my being shot at." I tried to sound aggrieved, but Nancy gave me one of her "you-know-what-I-mean" looks.

Arnold Rose was a man who refused to be thrown off the track. "Two attempts on your life. Did you report them to the police?"

"The shooting," I said. "Police officers came to the apartment, and then Detectives Phoenix and Flynn arrived. They classified it as vandalism since there was no proof the gunshot was a murder attempt."

Nancy made a sound of disgust, but let Arnold ask the questions.

"And when you were nearly run down . . . ?"

"Penny Cavanaugh told Detective Phoenix about it. She's his aunt, and I had just had dinner with her when that happened."

I told them that Serena's fingerprint was in the stolen car. I also told them that Phoenix and Flynn had come to my apartment this morning with a warrant to examine my nine-millimeter Glock, and that they took it with them. Arnold Rose revealed that his mystery source had already informed him of how Damon Radford really died.

"It's a mess," Nancy said.

Arnold Rose aimed comforting smiles at us both. "I've found that in confusion and chaos there is opportunity," he said. "The DA won't risk charging you, Morgan, until they have a theory about these crimes. They won't dare claim that the two murders aren't connected, because it's a virtual certainty they are. They'll look ridiculous if they say anything else. Now, what they *can* say is that your motive for killing Radford was to inherit several million dollars."

"Which Morgan didn't know anything about," Nancy said.

"She can't *prove* she didn't know," Arnold told her.

He turned back to me. "Next, they can say you killed Serena McCall because she tried to kill you."

"I didn't know it was Serena at the wheel until after she was dead!"

"But you can't *prove* that," he said.

"Even if I did know that Serena was driving, I'd have to be crazy to kill her in our building," I said. "I'd have had to lure her into the stairwell, probably by phone. Even if I asked her not to tell anyone she was meeting me, how could I be *sure* she wouldn't tell someone? She'd already tried to kill me, so why wouldn't she be suspicious of my invitation to meet her inside an emergency exit?"

"That's right," Nancy said.

Arnold agreed; the scenario that had me killing Serena didn't make sense. "It would be an easy case to defend," he said. "But I want your troubles to stop here. We have to turn their spotlight in another direction."

"Last night I made a list of suspects," I told them. "Those people who don't have alibis that I think might have murdered Damon. Serena was on it, but with her dead, that reduced my list to three names."

"Who?" Arnold asked.

"Johnny Isaac, Teresa Radford and, as much as I hate to consider it because I like him — Tommy Zenos. And whoever killed Damon probably killed Serena, too."

Arnold nodded. "I agree, that is likely," he said.

"I don't know where Teresa was today, but Johnny Isaac and Tommy were probably in the building . . ." I said.

"From what I've learned," Arnold said, "Serena McCall was dead for a few minutes, at *most*, before you found her."

A horrible thought turned my spinal column to ice. My stomach muscles clenched in fear. "If that's true — about the time of her death — then the murderer must have been in the stairwell at the same time I was," I said. "Maybe going down when I was going up . . ."

"Oh, God," Nancy whispered. She reached across the table and gripped my hand.

"It's okay — nothing happened to me." I said that to reassure both of us. "My luck is still holding."

Neither Nancy nor Arnold replied to that.

We all knew that luck had a way of running out.

# 34

After our private conference in Interview Room One, Nancy, Arnold Rose and I watched Detective Phoenix make a list of the clothes I was wearing when I found Serena's body: black slacks, ivory silk shirt, green suede blazer and black leather ankle boots. All were stained with blood.

"How long are you going to keep these things?" Arnold asked.

"I don't want any of them," I said before Phoenix could reply. "Keep them as long as you want, then give them away, or burn them." The thought of wearing something that had been soaked with Serena's blood revolted me.

"Okay," Phoenix said. "They stay bagged and tagged in the evidence room until the case is over. Then we'll have them cleaned and give them to the church around the corner."

I nodded agreement.

Finally, with Arnold Rose sitting next to me, I gave my statement. Arnold insisted that Phoenix telephone Kitty Leigh immediately, to ask if I had been with her, and how long we had spent together. He did. Kitty told him the same thing that I had, and put her floor manager on the phone to back her up. After the calls, Phoenix and Flynn told me I could go home.

Matt Phoenix escorted us to the head of the stairs. As Arnold and Nancy started down, Phoenix touched me lightly on the arm. "Two murders — this isn't some daytime plot you can control," he said softly. "Watch your back."

I was about to reply with a joke, but I looked at his eyes and saw they were dark with genuine concern. The quip died on my lips. I told him I'd be careful, then I hurried down the stairs to catch up with Nancy and Arnold. Out on West Eighty-Second Street, while Arnold was hailing a cab, I still felt the touch of Matt's hand on my arm.

Arnold and Nancy dropped me at the corner of Seventy-Second and Central Park West and continued on to their office in midtown. I was within two feet of the Dakota when a large, blond uniformed chauffeur who looked like a "Come to Bavaria" poster suddenly blocked my path. "Mr. Yarborough would like to see you," Mr. Bavaria said. "Will you come with me, please?"

*The Chairman of the Board of Global Broadcasting wants to see me?*

The chauffeur opened the door of a new silver Lincoln Town Car. When I climbed inside, I sank back against black leather upholstery as soft as a baby's skin. I thought I was going for a short ride down Central Park West, but when

273

we turned left at Sixty-Sixth Street to go through the park, I realized I wasn't going to the Global Broadcasting building.

I leaned forward, "Where are we going?"

"To see Mr. Yarborough."

*Duh.*

Robo-Driver was not inclined to tell me anything else, so I relaxed and idly stroked the soft black leather. I hoped we weren't going all the way up to Greenwich, Connecticut, because I needed a major injection of coffee, and soon. Also, I was getting hungry. Thanks to Chet I had had breakfast, but now it was late in the afternoon. On a day during which I had fallen over a dead body, lost two suspects on my short list, been summoned to give a command performance at the Twentieth Precinct and acquired a criminal lawyer — well, all of that had burned up the breakfast calories long ago.

Our destination turned out to be Seventy-Sixth Street and Madison Avenue, The Hotel Carlyle. In addition to his home in Greenwich, Winston Yarborough also keeps a permanent suite at this elegant Manhattan landmark.

The Carlyle has a distinctive white wood canopied entry, trimmed in gold, with a straight white canvas drape on each side that falls almost to the sidewalk. The drapes serve to frame the black and gold façade of the entrance. For anyone who doesn't recognize it on sight, "The Carlyle" is spelled out in gold script on each side of the canopy and above the revolving door.

I had never been upstairs to one of the high-priced rooms, or to one of the suites which were priced in the stratosphere, but I had been to the Café Carlyle several times with Nancy and one of her pre–Arnold Rose insignificant others. And once, during one of Tommy Zenos's short-lived engagements, I had met him and his fiancée-of-the moment at The Carlyle's Bemelmans Bar for a drink to celebrate another rise in our ratings. Tommy told me Bemelmans was his favorite hangout because he loved the whimsical murals of author and artist Ludwig Bemelmans, who had also created Madeline, the precocious children's book character. On that night Tommy had had a little too much to drink and confided to his fiancée and me that, as an only child, he liked to pretend that Madeline was his sister, and that he talked to her in the middle of the night. His admission was touching, but then he made the mistake of adding that he still did this. I could hear the sound of another of Tommy's engagements breaking even as he spoke.

Mr. Bavaria was not content to deliver me to the entrance. He whisked me through the revolving door and across The Carlyle's opulent lobby. With a key he took out of his pocket, he opened the door to a private elevator and pushed the button for the twenty-second floor. He stepped back out into the lobby just as the elevator door closed. For twenty-two floors I was a bird all alone in this gilded cage.

When the elevator stopped, the door slid open

with barely a whisper of sound. I stepped directly into the foyer of one of The Carlyle's luxurious Tower Suites, and found myself facing Winston Yarborough. He was dressed like a London banker on a casual Friday, in superbly cut pale gray wool slacks, a white shirt with French cuffs, a textured silver tie and a black cashmere cardigan. The cuffs were secured by his signature platinum links, embossed with the Global Broadcasting logo.

"Thank you for coming, my dear," he said. He stepped forward and wrapped his arms around me in an avuncular embrace. I was so startled I went stiff in his arms. He must have sensed my discomfort because he quickly took his arms away. "Forgive me, if that was inappropriate. It's just that I think of you almost as a daughter, Morgan."

*A daughter?* "That's very flattering, Mr. Yarborough." *This is the first conversation we've ever had!* "But I'm afraid I don't understand." *Am I in The Hotel Carlyle or the Twilight Zone?*

He put his hand on my arm and gently guided me into the raised living room. It had cathedral ceilings, and a magnificent picture window view over Central Park. The room was furnished with museum-quality English antiques that I guessed belonged to Winston Yarborough personally. Nor were the paintings that hung on the walls likely to be hotel-supplied; I recognized two large and glorious scenes by Turner. With a sweep of one manicured hand, the chairman of the board — *Bwana Macubwa* I'd have called him in Swahili — indicated he wanted me to sit down on the silk upholstered sofa to the left of the concert grand piano.

I sat.

A picture-perfect English high tea had been laid out on the low antique table in front of the sofa.

Yarborough took a seat next to me, indicated the tea service with a small nod of his head and clasped his hands on his knees. "I sent my butler out on an errand so that we could be alone," he said. "Do you mind pouring for us?"

"No, not at all," I said. I picked up the fine china teapot and put the antique silver tea strainer that was next to it over his cup. As I poured the steaming tea, I recognized the scent. "Darjeeling," I said. "From Ashby's, in London?"

"Yes, Ashby's." His smile told me he was pleased I was aware of Ashby's. "Do you know London well?" he asked.

"No, I'm sorry to say. I've only been once, and not for nearly long enough." I handed him the filled cup.

"Perhaps we can do something about that. Send you on business, perhaps to assess daytime television in Britain. We could arrange theater tickets for you while you're there. You'd stay at the Connaught, of course," he said, mentioning an exquisite hotel in Mayfair — more like a club — where staff members outnumber the guests.

This meeting was getting more and more bizarre. He was offering me a fabulous trip, but in exchange for *what?*

Glancing sideways at him, I put the silver strainer over my own cup and proceeded to pour. "I don't think you invited me here to discuss the wonders of London," I said delicately. "Is there something I can do for you?"

"Yes, there is. But first I must apologize to you, Morgan." There was pain in his voice. "If I had known you and Damon were to be married, I would have taken you up to Greenwich immediately, to stay with us for as long as you needed."

That statement almost made me spill my tea. I decided to listen instead.

"I was so deep in my own grief," he said, "I didn't think about anyone else. Except Jeremy, of course, but Jeremy still has his mother. You have no one."

I decided my best course would be ambiguity — at least until I learned what was on his mind. He was silent, so I arranged my mouth into what I hoped looked like a brave smile and I prodded a little. "Feeling about Damon as you did, this must be terrible for you, as well," I said sympathetically.

He nodded, but did not reply immediately. I was even more certain now that I was not here simply because he wanted to comfort me, the unofficial widow. "You said there was something I can do to help, Mr. Yarborough . . . ?"

"Please, call me Win." He took a sip of tea and then set the cup down.

*Here it comes.*

He took the teacup out of my hand, set it down on the tray and took both of my hands in his. His eyes stared into mine. "Damon was like a son to me," he said. "The closest I ever came to having a son. I loved him as though I were his father."

I kept quiet, listening for the reason this wealthy and powerful man had asked me to call him "Win."

"My wife and I had a daughter . . . but we lost our little girl to a drug overdose. That was more than twenty years ago. It happened only a few weeks before Damon wrote his audacious letter to me, analyzing the flaws in my network's programming . . . But you know the story. To come directly to the point, my dear Morgan, I want to say that I know Damon was not perfect. He had his . . . well, I called them his little weaknesses. Now that he is gone, I want to protect the splendid image the public had of him."

He was looking closely at me, gauging my reaction, perhaps even trying to determine how much I really knew about Damon's "little weaknesses." I kept a sympathetic expression on my face. "I understand," I said.

"No, you don't. Not yet. When the person who killed Damon is found, I intend to make a bargain with — with this person. I will pay all expenses for the finest legal talent in the country — secretly, of course — in exchange for one thing. That person must swear to give one particular explanation to the authorities."

"What explanation?" I asked.

"That's the story *you* will write, my dear."

My eyes widened with surprise. "The story? I'm sorry . . . ?"

"I need you to create a motive for the crime." As he spoke, he was patient, intense, focused. "A reason that reflects well on Damon. This will be the most important tale you have ever created, Morgan." A dark, furious light burned deep in his eyes; his grip on my hands tightened. "In exchange, I'll give you anything you want," he said. "A longer and more generous contract? To become a producer? Would you like to create your own daytime drama? You would have my written commitment to put it on the air and to keep it there for at least five years, regardless of ratings. Whatever you want. Name it."

I needed to be sure I understood what he was asking of me, so I repeated it back to him, carefully. "You want me to devise a motive for Damon's murder that will reflect well on Damon. You don't want the killer to put up a defense that smears him."

"That's it precisely," he said. "I knew we could do business. You are discreet."

There must have been question marks in my eyes.

"Yes, I investigated you, Morgan." He said it as casually as someone else might have told me what time it was. "I know I can trust you," he added. Deep in his carefully nonthreatening tone was the clear implication that if I betrayed his trust, he could, and would, crush me. For all of his courtly manners, Winston Yarborough had not become chairman of the board of a major media conglomerate by being Mr. Nice Guy.

"It's probable the person who killed Damon also killed Serena McCall," I said.

"I don't care." He let go of my hands. "Whatever will be said will be said about the unfortunate Ms. McCall."

"Do you have any idea who killed Damon?" I asked.

"My private investigators have reached no conclusions. My personal theory? I believe Damon was murdered by his former wife. She's a most unhappy woman, and, I believe, emotionally unstable. If I'm correct, it should be fairly easy to devise a convincing insanity defense for her. Let her get some treatment, then go free."

I raised my brows, and he continued, "Punishment won't bring Damon back. What I want is damage control. You will create a scenario to accomplish that objective." He leaned forward, "Now, what can I give you in return for protecting the reputation of the man we both loved and lost?"

*Whew.* Winston Yarborough was offering me himself as a wish-granting genie in a bottle. He

281

may have been a titan among the media gods, but he wasn't God, so the one thing I wanted most was something he was powerless to give me.

But my *second* choice was an easy one.

"Win," I said, tasting his name on my tongue. "I appreciate your generosity. And there is something I want, but it doesn't involve money or a new title, or my own show. There are two men in your organization who could seriously damage Global's reputation if the tabloids found out about what they're doing." I was looking into his eyes and saw the silent alarm bells go off in his head.

"Rick Spencer and Joe Niles — Niles is a director on *Love* — are blackmailing one of the stars on your network to keep quiet about . . . something they saw," I said. "Your star didn't steal or hurt anyone, this was something personal and embarrassing. It's something *you and I* wouldn't want made public either."

I was Salome, he was King Herod, and I was asking for the heads of Rick Spencer and Joe Niles. Yarborough assessed my words carefully, parsing them for every bit of meaning. I was sure he got the hint that this "something" might not reflect well on Damon. He set his teacup down with a gesture of finality.

"I'll handle the matter. Discreetly."

"Thank you," I said. I put my cup down too, prepared to leave.

"You don't want anything for yourself?" he

asked. He took my hands again and looked into my eyes. "Nothing?"

"With Damon gone . . ." I lowered my eyes and shook my head with what I hoped he would interpret as sadness. There *was* one more thing I wanted from my new friend Win; I smiled up at him. "After the hit-and-run, when he was in the hospital, Damon told me" — I was taking a big leap — "that he owed his financial security to *you*. He was about to explain, but then we were interrupted." I shrugged, and gazed at Yarborough for a moment. "It was so important to Damon, what you did for him, but now I'll never know what it was." I was doing my best to look winsome. Some older men melt like butter on a grill for winsome.

Pride swept across Yarborough's face. He gave my hands a conspiratorial squeeze. Even though we were alone, he lowered his voice. "Damon was a tremendously astute programmer," he said. "From the time he left UCLA and started working at our affiliate station in Los Angeles, I let him view the prime-time pilots and read scripts for proposed series. Of course, my programming people knew nothing about it. The shows Damon championed, I told my head of programming I wanted to try on the air. I only gave that order *if* the show's creator was agreeable to giving up a small cut of his personal fee. To Damon, of course. If the show was a hit and stayed on the air long enough to begin eternal life in syndication, then Damon's remuneration in time would amount to millions. The series creators realized having the largest share of something was preferable to having one hundred percent of nothing. I think it was rather clever of us — finding a way to reward Damon for his prescience without attracting the attention of the FCC. Or the stockholders who monitored salaries."

*Kickbacks.* That was the source of Damon's "royalties." And the founder and chairman of Global Broadcasting was describing what amounted to extortion as just a creative form of executive compensation! "That's so . . . imaginative," I said.

"It was a much better arrangement than giving him the title of head of programming, where the media would watch him and snipe. As Vice President in Charge of Daytime, he was able to stay somewhat below the radar, continuing to be groomed by me until the day when I retire and . . ." His animation died out and his voice trailed off.

I gave Winston Yarborough my best big-eyed imitation of a Stepford Fiancée, thanked him for our talk, and said good-bye.

"My door is always open to you, Morgan," he said. A hint of tears glittered in his eyes. "I'll be in touch."

# 35

I left the Carlyle through the revolving door and there was Mr. Bavaria, waiting in front of the silver Lincoln Town Car. He was on his cell phone. When he saw me, he nodded and said, "She's here now, sir . . . Yes, sir." He clicked off and approached me. "Mr. Yarborough instructed me to take you wherever you'd like," he said.

I thought about it for a moment.

"Take me to the nearest big video store," I said, "and then back to the Dakota."

Thirty minutes later, carrying a bag full of DVDs, I unlocked the door to my apartment. It was pleasantly warm. The glazier had not yet replaced the living room window, but he had patched the hole to keep out the late October chill, and he had left a scrawled note saying he would put in the new glass tomorrow afternoon. I took off my shoes and picked up the phone to punch in a familiar number. When Nancy came on the line, I thanked her again for meeting me at the police station, and for bringing Arnold Rose.

She lowered her voice to a whisper. "Isn't he wonderful?"

Reflexively, I began to whisper, too. "Yes, he is," I said. "I was very impressed — but why am I whispering?" I shook my head at the absurdity of it, resumed my normal tone of voice and asked, "Are you two seeing each other tonight?"

"No, he's preparing for a major trial."

"Then come over here. I picked up a stack of Teresa Gleason's old movies."

"Teresa Gleason from your short list of suspects? What will we be looking for?" she asked, her voice back at its normal level.

"Like pornography, we'll know it when we see it."

"Oh!" Nancy said. She began whispering again. "Arnold found out from his source that somebody telephoned Serena in her office about half an hour before she was killed. Serena's secretary told officers that the call sounded personal. When Serena left the office, the secretary thought she was going to the bathroom because she didn't take her purse, *just a book of matches.*"

"Good work, Nancy Drew. Thank your Ned Nickerson for me."

On the other end of the line, I heard Nancy laugh. "Ned Nickerson was never my type," she said. "I prefer brains to brawn. I'll be there at seven."

"I'll order Chinese."

"No MSG."

"Cross my heart," I promised. "I think I'll invite Penny Cavanaugh, too."

"Good idea," she said. "I'm curious to meet Detective Neanderthal's aunt."

"Do you really dislike Matt Phoenix as much as you seemed to this afternoon?"

"Of course not. I was just being imperious on your behalf — letting 'da fuzz' know you have friends who will not stand for you being abused. Actually, I think your detective is very sexy," she said. "He's a little on the grim side, but you can fix that."

She hung up before I could respond. I called Penny and told her my plan.

"I'll be there," she said. "Can I bring anything?"

"Absolutely not. Do you like Chinese food?"

"Adore it."

"Seven o'clock, then," I said.

The phone rang as soon as I put it down. I picked it up and heard Harrison's voice asking, "Doll. Are you all right?" before I could even say "hello." "I'm fine," I said, flooding with warmth at his concern. "So you've heard about Serena?"

"The show's producer called," he said. "The prick wanted to be sure I'd have the scripts in on time." He let out a disgusted snort. There was sadness in his voice as he added, "I wonder if anybody in that place even cares about her."

"I think she was killed by the same person who killed Damon."

"I don't. Serena was a troubled lady — into some risky stuff. Told me she was doing the bar scene to meet new guys. I warned her . . ." He expelled a sigh full of frustration, then took a calming breath. "They told me you found her, and that the cops questioned you."

"They thought they caught the killer — me — but Kitty Leigh confirmed the two of us were together in her dressing room at the time Serena was killed, so they let me go home."

"You've had a rough day, sweet face. Want to have dinner? Agata loves an excuse to cook a civilized meal of more than one course."

"No, thanks. Nancy's coming over here, and a new friend — Penny Cavanaugh — is joining us. We're having Chinese takeout and a film festival."

There was something else I wanted to say, but I hesitated. It seemed a little crass under the circumstances, but I decided I had to ask. "Will you take over *Trauma Center* officially now?"

"I suppose so."

"If it doesn't work out, you can always come back to *Love*."

"Let's see what shakes out. I'll talk to you soon. Have fun tonight. What are you girls doing, giving yourselves a Mel Gibson orgy?"

"Don't I wish," I laughed. "No, we're watching old Teresa Gleason movies."

He was silent for a beat. "If I remember, she was a better actress than the lousy pictures she was in."

By the time I took a shower, changed and set up three portable snack tables in front of the

288

big-screen TV in the den, it was nearly seven o'clock. Nancy, who was never late, arrived first, carrying a bottle of wine. She had changed into designer sweats, but was still wearing the strand of pearls. Penny arrived two minutes later, simultaneously with the delivery man from the Chinese restaurant. She was carrying a thin package, wrapped in crisp white tissue paper.

I introduced Nancy to Penny and then paid the delivery man.

Penny and I took the food into the den and Nancy went to the pantry for glasses. Nancy rejoined us in the den just as Penny handed me the small package. "I have no shame," I said, ripping off the tissue paper. "I love presents."

"It's a copy of that old Judith Viorst poetry book I told you about."

I looked at the title, and showed the cover to Nancy. "*How Did I Get to Be 40 and Other Atrocities.*"

Penny said, "I know you two aren't anywhere near forty yet, but I was only twenty-five when I read it for the first time and loved it. Just read the top of page forty-one, you'll see her sense of humor."

I flipped through the little book and found the page. It was a piece called "The Sensuous Woman." I read the first few lines aloud:

I'm giving up nice and becoming a sensuous
   woman.

The kind of woman who wouldn't wear bed-
    socks to bed.
I'm giving up going to places like Saks and
    the cleaners
And going wherever my appetites lead me in-
    stead.


"Words to live by," said Nancy as she eased
the cork out of the bottle of wine. She lifted one
eyebrow at me and said with significance,
"Memorize that piece, Morgan. It's time to
forget the lightbulbs and buy candles again."

"Ignore her," I said. "She's in love so she
wants everybody else to be, too."

"There's nothing better than loving someone," Penny said softly.

I agreed, but it wasn't something I wanted to
talk about. "Thank you for the book, Penny. I
know I'm going to enjoy it." I began to open
the array of dishes I'd ordered for dinner.
Nancy spotted the stack of Teresa Gleason
movies. "Let's see . . . What'll we watch first?
We've got *Pirate Queen*, *Pirate Island*, *Bonnie
Annie* —"

"That one's about the real female pirate,
Anne Bonney," I said.

Nancy went on, "*Lady Godiva's Daughter*, *The
Red Head from Montana*, *Fool's Gold*, *Belle of the
Comstock Lode*, and *Hot Ice*."

"I particularly want to see her action scenes,"
I said. "She was supposed to have done a lot of
her own stunts."

I pulled the double-wide ottoman in front of the sofa from its usual place beneath the window — the now-shuttered window. Penny scooped portions of cashew chicken, beef with oyster sauce, steamed giant shrimp with fresh garlic, chow mein, and fried rice onto plates and added an egg roll apiece. Nancy poured the wine and passed out chopsticks. I put in the first DVD.

Like teenage girls, we plopped down against the cushions, put our feet up on the ottoman, and ate while we watched the opening scenes of *Pirate Queen.*

Young, flame-haired Teresa Gleason was take-your-breath-away gorgeous in Technicolor. She burst into her first scene swinging on a rope from the mast of her pirate ship down onto the deck of the helpless vessel the pirates had captured. As soon as her feet touched the deck, she was slashing her way through a violent sword fight. It was one long shot from the top of the mast to the middle of the fight, with no cuts, no cutaways. No possible stunt double; that was all Teresa.

"Yeow," Nancy said, swallowing a mouthful of chow mein, "I don't think I'd want her mad at me."

"She still fences," Penny added. "A couple of weeks ago I recognized her coming out of the fitness academy across the street from Natasha's, carrying foils and a mask. She's in great shape."

"If Damon had been run through with a rapier, mystery solved," I said.

When the fighting scenes stopped, the dialogue was so bad I hit "Fast Forward" until the next battle scene. More swinging and slashing, and a spectacular dive over the side of the pirate ship. I was sure that the diver was a double, but it was clearly Teresa herself doing all the underwater swimming.

We'd had enough of *Pirate Queen*.

We watched selected parts of three more bad costume pictures. In the DVD narration that accompanied *Belle of the Comstock Lode* we learned that to prepare for the movie, Teresa had become an expert pistol and rifle marksman.

"It sounds like she became the man women used to want to marry," Nancy joked. "So why did she end up twenty years later looking whipped?"

"Damon slapped some of his women around," I said, "but I never heard that he hit Teresa. The story is she was a huge asset to him when he was starting out. She elevated Damon socially, got him invited to lots of A-list gatherings where he made industry connections he couldn't have gotten near without her popularity and social contacts."

"Men have all sorts of ways to hurt the women they're supposed to love," Penny said quietly. "I see a lot of well-known socialites who've been devastated psychologically by their husband's cheating on them, belittling them. Sometimes I spend a facial hour not just restoring skin tone, but trying to persuade a client that she's a person of value."

"I can't understand why a woman would stay in a marriage like that," I said.

"From what I see, most of them stay for the money and the social position," Nancy commented. "But in my opinion, women who sell themselves like that deserve what they get. I'm not sympathetic to weaklings."

It was nine-fifteen and we had just finished the last of the egg rolls when I slipped *Hot Ice* into the machine. Unlike most of Teresa's movies, which were set either on the high seas or in the Old West but shot on studio back lots, this picture was a contemporary caper, and had been filmed mostly on the streets of Los Angeles. It was obvious from the opening scenes — which were shown without the intrusion of credits — that the filmmakers were attempting to make a movie that was a lot better than its low budget would suggest.

In it, Teresa plays a desperate young woman who thinks she is stealing diamonds from the man who destroyed her father's business and crushed his spirit, but the gems actually belong to a professional killer. Fleeing from the killer, Teresa loses valuable escape time when she rescues a six-year-old boy who is being badly abused by his stepfather. At nail-biting risk to her own life, Teresa decides to reunite the little boy — whose name is Jeremy! — with the biological father who has been searching for him ever since the boy's trashy mother and vicious stepfather stole him away.

"It's a pretty corny story but I like it," Nancy said. She passed some Kleenex to Penny and to me. We were both teary-eyed as we watched the scene where Teresa discovers terrible bruises all over the child's body.

"The dialogue is very good," I said, sniffling. "She named her own son Jeremy — I wonder if she named him after the character in this movie?"

We watched *Hot Ice* all the way through, without making fun of it. At the climax, when Teresa saves little Jeremy, but is shot by the killer, the three of us cried out in dismay. "Oh, no," Penny moaned. "She doesn't deserve to die!" Shock was followed by sighs of relief as we learned Teresa would survive the wound — and would probably end up happy with little Jeremy and his real father.

"That's what a movie's supposed to do," Nancy said as the final scene faded out. "Give us characters to like and worry about."

I looked at my watch. "And let us spend most of eighty-five minutes not thinking about what's going on in our own lives."

"Amen to that," Penny said.

The credits began to roll. I wanted to see who wrote *Hot Ice*. When I saw the credit flash on the screen, I sat up so fast I almost spilled half a glass of wine.

"What's the matter?" Nancy asked, taking the

wineglass out of my hand. Penny stopped cleaning up our dinner debris.

"Look at this," I said. I pushed "Rewind," searched backward to the writer credit and pushed "Pause." The three of us stared at the words that were frozen on the screen:

"Written by Harrison Landers."

# 36

"Harrison Landers?" Nancy said, looking at the name frozen on the screen. "Isn't he your old boss?"

"I didn't know he'd been a screenwriter in Hollywood," I said. "I knew he used to write for *Another World* . . ."

"I loved *Another World*! Especially Linda Dano," Penny said. "I watched almost every episode from the time I was in junior high."

I acknowledged Penny with a nod and told her, "I buy Linda Dano's tote bags from QVC." But I wanted to stay focused on what we'd just learned. "If Harrison wrote *Hot Ice*, then he probably knew Teresa from way back when." I said.

"What are you thinking?" Nancy asked.

"There are so many little pieces to this puzzle, and there's no picture on the box to give us a hint about what piece to put where," I said. But as I spoke those words, a part of the picture was actually beginning to take shape in my mind.

I turned to Penny. "Will you play a role for me?"

She gasped in horror. "On *Love of My Life*? Oh, I couldn't —"

"No, I mean here in the den, on the phone? Would you call someone for me and pretend?"

Penny sighed with relief. "Oh, sure. What do you want me to do?"

I took my personal phone book from the small desk in the corner of the room and flipped pages until I found the number I wanted. "I'm going to dial Teresa Radford on my cell. Then you'll get on the phone and ask to speak to her. Say that you're calling to confirm her appointment for a facial. If she's home and gets on the line, pretend you've made a mistake, apologize for bothering her and get off the line. I just want to know if she's at home."

Penny nodded, Nancy looked puzzled and I began to punch in the number.

"I don't get it," Nancy said.

I shushed her because the phone was ringing on the other end. I handed the cell phone to Penny just as someone at Teresa's picked up.

Penny startled us by playing her part with a German accent. She introduced herself as "Elke" and asked to speak to Mrs. "Rotford" about her *"Schoenheitspflege."*

Her *what?*

We moved in closer, Nancy on one side of Penny and me on the other. We held our collective breath as "Elke" listened to the other end of the line. "Ach!" Penny said into the phone. "Mus' be mistake . . . *Danke . . . Guten Abend."* She quickly disconnected the line and replaced the receiver.

"The boy answered," she told us in her normal voice. "He said his mother isn't home, and asked me to call back tomorrow." Penny smiled impishly. "He didn't want to take a message — he probably couldn't spell *'Schoenheitspflege.'*" She saw our quizzical looks and said, "It means 'beauty treatment' in German."

"You speak German?" Nancy asked.

"Just a few words; we have a German masseuse at Natasha's. What do we do now?" Penny asked. The excitement in her voice indicated she was eager for another assignment.

"Nothing tonight," I said. But I was lying. I looked at my watch and saw it was ten minutes to eleven. I needed to get rid of them as quickly as possible. "You two go home," I said. "I'll think about the next step and we'll talk tomorrow."

Penny and Nancy decided to share a cab. I called downstairs to Frank at the desk and asked him to please get one for them. As soon as they left, I threw a black suede blazer on over my sweater and jeans, grabbed my keys and the little emergency money change purse that snapped around my wrist and slipped out of the apartment. I stayed in the shadows of the courtyard until I saw Nancy and Penny get into a cab. As soon as it was out of sight, I hurried out and had Frank flag down one for me. A yellow cab screeched to a stop in front of Frank, and I climbed into the back.

"Central Park West and Sixty-Fifth Street," I told the driver.

He grunted disapproval at the short ride and subsequent small fare, but slammed the vehicle into gear, punishing the metal for his bad luck in getting stuck with me. I was going to see Harrison. Since he was habitually a night owl who never went to bed before 2 A.M., it wasn't likely I would disturb his sleep. I was beginning to think Winston Yarborough might be right, Teresa *had* killed Damon. Physically, she would have been able to do it. And she knew the layout of the building because she had lived there. I wanted to know what Harrison thought. I needed to see his face when I asked the question. If he had known Teresa years ago in Hollywood (which he never mentioned in the years we worked together), he might have some reason to feel protective of her. He was a man who, if he had lived in the days of King Arthur, would have had a seat at the Round Table. If there was a woman in need and a dragon to be slain, Harrison was — or at least he had been — the man for the job.

The cab screeched to a stop at Central Park West and Sixty-Fifth. As I leaned over the front seat to pay the driver, I caught a glimpse of someone coming out of Harrison's building. A woman. The moment I saw her, I ducked back into the shadow of the cab's rear seat, but I may not have been quick enough. There was at least a fifty percent chance that the woman — *Teresa Radford!* — had seen me. She stepped backward into a pool of darkness near the building's entrance.

And waited.

In a whisper, I told the driver to take me back to the Dakota.

Grumbling, he started the motor again and made an illegal U-turn. In a cloud of exhaust fumes, we were on our way back up Central Park West. I leaned against the well-worn and heavily patched imitation leather of the back seat, listing in my mind the questions that had to be answered before I would be able to see the whole picture. Was Teresa Radford "the lady" Agata mentioned, whose visits made Harrison feel better? And, if so, would she have told Harrison she had killed Damon? *If* she had? If she was guilty, it would be the answer to Winston Yarborough's prayers. And, had Teresa lured Serena into the stairwell and killed her with a sock full of quarters?

Here was where I hit the wall. *Why* would Teresa have killed Serena?

Maybe Harrison was right, Serena's death wasn't connected to Damon's. Maybe she really was killed by a psycho she met in a bar?

There was one more question, and it hit me with the force of a blow: *If* Teresa was the murderer but *didn't* tell Harrison; *if* Harrison figured it out, would she kill him, too?

I had the driver stop at the nearest payphone, got out and told him to wait for me. As fast as my fingers would work, I deposited coins into the slot and dialed.

"Hello?" It was Harrison's voice. Holding my hand tight over the mouthpiece, I sighed in relief.

"Hello?" he said again, annoyance in his voice. I disconnected the line. Because I'd called from a public phone, Harrison would have no way of knowing who had just rung his number.

I didn't sleep very well that night.

At seven o'clock the next morning I called Chet Thompson's number at his Waverly Place sublet. When he answered, he sounded fully awake. "I was just thinking about you," he said.

I let that pass without comment and got right to the point. "There's something I want to talk to you about, but not on the phone. Can we get together this morning? Just for a few minutes."

"I've got a meeting with my publisher on the East Side," he said. He thought for a moment. "How about the Central Park Carousel at noon."

"The *carousel?*"

His voice was warm as he said, "I'll treat you to a ride on the horse of your choice, then I'll buy you a hot dog with everything."

"An irresistible offer."

"One of many I hope to make you," he said. His voice was soft; it made me remember his kiss, and my pulse accelerated. This was verbal foreplay, and another time I might have enjoyed it. There wasn't time right now.

"Noon at the carousel," I said, keeping my voice light.

We hung up and I started to work. There was one script I had to write, another that needed to be edited, plus I had more advance story to rough out. It was going to be a busy day, and I wouldn't be able to work this evening, because whether or not Chet agreed to help me, I was going to be out stalking a murder suspect.

I lost track of the time creating a romantic courtship scene for Kira and Cody. It was ten minutes after noon when I arrived at Sixty-Fourth and Fifth Avenue, the entrance to the Central Park Carousel. I spotted Chet right away. He was pacing — it was more like marching — up and down just inside the park, frowning and speaking into his cell phone.

His obvious impatience annoyed the hell out of me.

I was only a few minutes late!

I was not going to allow some man I barely knew to become possessive. When he looked up, our eyes connected, and a powerful wave of *relief* spread across his features. It was then that I realized it wasn't impatience I had seen; Chet had been *worried*.

"No — it's okay, she's here," he said into the phone. "Thanks." He disconnected and hurried toward me. "Are you okay?"

"Were you talking to someone about me?" I asked.

"Penny — I called her at Natasha's to see if you were there. I was going to call your friend

Nancy next, and if you weren't there, I'd have called that Phoenix guy."

That made me mad. "Are you *crazy?* I'm only ten minutes late!"

He waved his cell phone at me. "You have all my numbers, you should have called! Two people have been murdered . . ." He didn't add "and you could be next," but I saw it in his eyes. My anger evaporated.

"I was working and I lost track of the time," I apologized. "Next time I'll call."

He took me by the arm, gently. "Maybe I overreacted."

The Central Park Carousel is housed inside a squat, round building. I had passed it many times, but this was the first time I had ever gone inside. There were dozens of large horses and two elaborate chariots, so beautifully carved and painted they took my breath away.

Chet paid our admissions. "What's your pleasure?" he asked.

"Those two," I said, pointing to a pair of caramel-colored horses with their heads thrown back. We mounted them and grasped the poles. The carousel started to revolve, and an organ began playing "And the Band Played On." The horses and chariots circled a large central drum, which was adorned with beautiful, intricately carved figures. My favorite was a big, black circus seal with a shining coat, balancing a bright, red ball on the tip of his nose.

*And the band played on . . .*

When we were having hot dogs and soft drinks on a quiet bench outside the carousel building, I got right to the reason I'd called. "You told me you know Teresa Radford. How well do you know her?"

The hot dog stopped an inch from Chet's mouth. "What exactly are you asking?"

"Not . . . something deeply personal —"

"The answer to 'did I ever sleep with Teresa' is *no*," he said. I was glad to hear it, but I shrugged to convey the pretense it didn't matter.

"Do you know her well enough to call and invite her out to dinner tonight?"

"Yes," he said. "No guarantee she'd accept. What's this about?"

So far, I hadn't seen anything in his eyes that made me think he would protect Teresa. "I'd like you to call and ask her to dinner tonight. If she says yes, then I want you to call twenty minutes before you're supposed to meet and cancel the date. Tell her you have some emergency. But if she turns you down because she already has plans, that's good."

"You've lost me," he said.

"I want us to stake out Teresa's building and follow her when she goes out."

"What makes you think she'll go out if I break our date?"

"She'll be all ready. My guess is she won't want to waste the preparations."

He was staring at me, comprehension in his

eyes. "You think Teresa murdered Radford, don't you?"

"I think it's possible," I said. I used my fingers to tick off several reasons. "She hated Damon. I just found out she's an expert with a rifle and pistol. She knows Damon's building. She's in terrific physical shape, so twenty flights of stairs aren't beyond her capabilities. Last, if I die within six months, her son inherits Damon's entire estate."

He was looking at me as though he didn't know whether to laugh or be impressed. "You've got reasons," he said. "If not very good ones."

I dismissed his skepticism with a wave of my hand. "If Teresa is the killer, I'm afraid she might go after someone else."

"This plan of yours has holes in it you could fly an airbus through, but count me in. At least I'll get to spend time alone in my car with you."

"In the *front* seat," I said, "with our eyes on her building and your hands on the steering wheel."

I'd finished my hot dog and was wiping mustard off my fingers with a napkin. Chet had eaten only half of his, but he folded the uneaten half into a napkin, balled it up and then tossed both our napkins and empty soda cups into the nearest trash can.

"I'll keep my hands on the steering wheel *tonight*," he promised, "but I can't guarantee how I'll behave in the future."

# 37

Chet telephoned at 7 P.M. and told me he was parked across the street from the front entrance of Teresa's apartment building.

"How did you get such a perfect spot?" I asked.

"I bought it," Chet said. "For fifty bucks the guy who had just pulled into the space was willing to vacate. When will you be here?"

"Fifteen minutes." I gave him my cell phone number. "Call me if Teresa goes out before I get there. You follow her, let me know where you are, and I'll catch up."

"Aye aye, Captain," he said.

A cab let me out at the corner of Seventy-Seventh and Lexington, and I walked the rest of the way to Chet's Range Rover. Holding two thermos bottles of hot coffee against my chest, with my free hand I rapped my knuckles against the front passenger's window. When Chet, who had been keeping his eyes on Teresa's building, saw me, he reached across the seat and opened the passenger door. I climbed in and handed him a thermos.

"What's this?"

"Hot coffee," I said. "Essential for stakeouts, according to my favorite cop shows."

"You're the perfect partner. Thanks." As he unscrewed the top of the thermos, he indicated Teresa's building with a nod of his head. "I know she's still in there because there's no back entrance. Deliveries go in through the walk-in door to the garage, and that's over there, at the far corner of the building, in the front. Whichever exit she uses, we'll see her." He took a sip of coffee and smiled his approval. "Gourmet coffee on a stakeout." Then he screwed the cap back on and set it down between us.

"Could she have gone out earlier?" I asked.

He shook his head; negative. "I phoned her when I got here, to apologize again for breaking our date. I said I wanted to make another one, but she said she was going out of town soon and would let me know when she got back."

We had been watching Teresa's building for more than an hour when Chet began squirming in his seat, as though he was trying to find a comfortable position. I wondered if he needed a bathroom break. Since no one in daytime drama ever has to relieve themselves, this wasn't something I had planned for. I was about to ask him if he wanted to find a restroom, when I noticed his forehead was beaded with perspiration.

"Are you all right?" I asked.

"I'm fine," he said. But his voice was tight with pain, belying his words.

Automatically — I think this must be encoded

in female DNA — I reached out and put the palm of my hand against his glistening forehead.

"My God, you're burning up!"

"My . . . stomach . . ." He was panting now, his breath horribly labored. He gagged mightily, threw open his driver's side door, leaned way over into the street and vomited. As soon as he tried to straighten up, I grabbed his shoulders and guided him back inside.

"I'm sorry . . ."

"Don't be silly," I said. I found the little package of tissues I carry in my handbag, pulled out a handful and gave them to him. He groaned in pain as he wiped his mouth. It was obvious something was very wrong. I opened the door on my side. "Scoot over into this seat," I told him. "I'm taking you to the hospital."

He started to protest, but I was already out of the Rover and heading around to his side. Careful not to step where he had just emptied his stomach, I climbed into the driver's seat as he maneuvered his body into the shotgun position. "Lenox Hill is on this street," I told him, naming one of the best hospitals in the country, a teaching facility affiliated with NYU Medical Center. It was on Seventy-Seventh, only three blocks west. I was very familiar with it; I'd had my wrist surgeries there.

Hoping to attract a police escort, I made an illegal U-turn and sped as fast as traffic allowed toward Lenox Hill Hospital, but no patrol car spotted me. It was true; there never seemed to be a cop around when you wanted one. I screeched to a stop at the Emergency entrance, leaped out and pushed through the door.

"Help! Please! I have an emergency outside!"

A doctor and two orderlies rolling a gurney swept past me. I ran behind, pointing to the Rover. In a matter of seconds, they had Chet on the gurney and were speeding him into the E.R. The doctor shouted that I had to get my vehicle out of the Emergency lane. I didn't want to leave Chet, but I rushed outside to move it.

I was back in three minutes and grabbed the first nurse I saw.

I asked where Chet was and she directed me to where they had taken him.

He was in terrible pain, but was managing to gasp out answers to the doctor's questions. He even summoned a grimace when he saw me.

"What's the matter with him?" I asked the doctor.

Chet answered, "Ap . . . appen . . . dicitis."

"We're taking him in to surgery," the doctor told me.

Chet groped in his jacket, pulled out his wallet and handed it to me. "Take this . . ."

Then he passed out.

"Oh my God."

"He's going up to the O.R.," the doctor told me as a nurse drew the curtain separating us. "You'll need to fill out some paperwork — ask at the desk."

★ ★ ★

Chet had been in an operating room for two hours.

I couldn't find out anything about his condition.

I sat, then I paced, then I sat again, all the while holding tight to his wallet and his watch. When the cell phone in my jacket pocket rang, I jumped. I fished it out and answered it to hear Tommy Zenos's voice. He was rushing his words together in an unintelligible jumble.

"Morgandoyouknowwhat'shappened?"

"I'm in the hospital with a friend —"

He raced on, "RickSpencerquitandJoeNiles'sbeenarrestedwithanunderagehooker!"

"What? Tommy, calm down. I can't understand what you're saying."

I heard Tommy expel breath in four quick bursts. He sounded like a Lamaze coach. He cleared his throat loudly in my ear. I was about to protest when he said clearly, "Rick Spencer quit, and Joe Niles got arrested with an underage hooker."

My heart began to thud in my chest. "Tell me everything you know," I said.

He did, and I didn't believe a single word of it. In a press release that came as a shock to the industry, Rick said he had decided to leave television and follow his dream of going back to school to become an architect.

"An *architect?*"

"That's what he said," Tommy affirmed. I

could tell by the tone of his voice Tommy didn't buy it.

"Tell me about Joe."

"This is really juicy," Tommy said. "It was on the news! Cops busted Joe in a hot-bed hotel with a *thirteen-year-old* hooker. He claims he was drugged in a bar and has no idea how he got to the hotel, or who the girl is, but the girl tells a different story."

*I'll bet she does.* I asked Tommy, "Did she swear Joe sought her out, and told her he wanted her because she was so young?"

"Something like that," Tommy agreed.

"I bet somebody's going to find child porn in his apartment or on his computer."

"Really?"

Winston Yarborough hadn't wasted any time. With resources at your command, justice was swift. At that moment I saw Chet's surgeon, still in scrubs, coming down the hall toward me.

"Tommy, I can't talk anymore." I said a quick good-bye and hurried to meet the surgeon. His photo badge identified him as Doctor Karl Wenders.

"How is he?" I asked.

"Mr. Thompson is out of surgery, in the recovery room. You're the woman who brought him in?"

"Yes."

"You got him here just in time — that appendix was about to burst."

"But he's going to be all right?"

"We'll want to monitor him closely for two or three days, but I expect he'll be good as new. Or better; he won't have to worry about his appendix."

The doctor explained Chet's appendix was removed by a surgical procedure called arthroscopy. "While we were inside, we looked around. No blockages, no problems. He's in great shape."

I thanked the doctor and asked when I could see Chet.

"In about an hour, but just for a few minutes."

It was nearly 1 A.M. when I was finally allowed into the ICU.

Chet was groggy, and it was hard for him to talk, but he smiled when he saw me. He grabbed my hand and held it. "Do you think we'll ever have a normal, dull evening together?" he whispered.

"Don't talk," I said.

"Thanks . . . for . . ." He was fighting to stay awake, but sleep was what he needed most.

"I was looking for an excuse to drive the Rover," I joked. "Go to sleep. I'll see you in the morning."

"Do you . . . have your appendix?"

"Lost it when I was eleven."

"You show me your scar . . . an' I'll show you mine . . ."

"No deal. You won't have a scar, Chet — you

had arthroscopy. And the doctor says you're in great condition."

"I could've tol' em that . . ." He yawned, and closed his eyes.

I stayed with him for a few minutes longer, until his breathing was deep and steady and I was sure that he was asleep.

*What a night.*

I drove the Rover back to the Dakota and found a parking space half a block from the entrance. Seventy-Second Street between Central Park West and Columbus was empty of people. The only footsteps I heard on the pavement were my own. I greeted Frank at the desk, then hurried through the courtyard, taking the flashlight out of my handbag as I approached the stairs. I was so tired I was operating on adrenaline.

Three flights and I was inside, home, safe.

The living room lights were on, as I'd left them, and I could see that the glazier had replaced the glass in the window. But he'd left the shutters open, so I closed them. I felt lonely. I wished Nancy was here tonight, or Penny. Or Chet.

Or Matt . . . I still hadn't figured out what his grandfather invented . . .

The phone rang, shattering the silence. It seemed as loud as a shrieking fire alarm in the empty apartment. I snatched up the receiver even before I took time to wonder who would be calling me at this hour. "Doll?" It was Harrison. "I hope I didn't wake you."

"No, I just got in," I said.

"You been out club-hopping?"

"A friend's in the hospital," I said.

I heard the concern in his voice. "Serious?"

"It's going to be all right, but it's been a long night."

"Doll, I hate to bother you, but there's something I was hoping you could do for me. I wouldn't ask, except I really need it."

"Sure, what is it?"

"Remember back four years ago, we were thinking about doing a story line on MS? You used to keep everything up in your office — I called you the filing fairy. Hope you haven't changed."

"No, I still have all that. It's in my 'What Were We Thinking?' file."

"Can you let me have it? I figured out how to make the story work."

"I'll bring it over first thing in the morning, before I go back to the hospital."

"Well . . . that's a problem, Doll. I need it right now. I've got a messenger standing by to pick it up from your reception desk."

I let out a deep, exhausted sigh, but I held my hand over the receiver so Harrison wouldn't hear it. "I'll go upstairs and get it now," I said.

"I wouldn't ask if this wasn't really important. Thanks, Sweet Face."

"Tell your messenger it'll be in an envelope downstairs in twenty minutes."

We said good night. I took the keys and a

flashlight, locked the apartment door behind me and started up the stairs. When I reached the fifth floor, I saw that the light had burned out. That's why God made flashlights, I said to myself as I flicked it on and continued up to the sixth floor.

The light was burned out up there, too.

Both lights . . .

I was only a few feet from the door to my office when a figure sprang out of the darkness and grabbed me from behind. Before I could scream, a ferociously strong man clapped a hand over my mouth and the cold steel barrel of a pistol was pressed hard against my cheek.

"I'm going to take my hand away from your mouth," the man whispered, "but if you try to scream, I'll kill you before you can utter a sound. Understand?"

I nodded my head; yes, I understood. And understanding broke my heart, because I recognized the voice hissing at me in the darkness.

"Unlock the door to the office," Harrison Landers said.

# 38

Fumbling, I managed to insert my key and open the door. Harrison shoved me inside, kicked the door shut and flipped on the lights.

"How — ?" That one word came out of my mouth as a faint croak.

"I called you from my cell phone." He patted the pocket of his navy blue windbreaker with his free hand. The other hand held a nine-millimeter Beretta; he was pointing it right at my heart.

I gaped at him, dumbfounded.

"Much as I dislike stating the obvious," he said, "you're surprised to see me walking."

Still not trusting my voice, I nodded. I was even more surprised to see the madness in his eyes.

"I've been able to walk for almost two years," he said. "That's how long I was planning to kill Damon. That's why I reported this pistol as stolen, when it just went into hiding."

Propelled by the Beretta, I backed up into the room until the corner of the desk jabbed me in the derriere. It hurt, and that made me realize my brain cells were reassembling themselves; I was beginning to form coherent thoughts. *Keep him talking until I can think of something to do.* I tried my voice again. "Why . . . are you here?" It wasn't steady, but my vocal cords were working.

"There's something you're going to do for me," he said. "Sit down and turn on the computer."

I moved behind the desk and lowered myself carefully into the chair, and did as instructed. As I waited for it to boot up, I said, "I'll do whatever you want — you don't have to threaten me."

"Ah, Doll, I wish that were true."

"I hated Damon as much as you did —"

"Nobody hated Damon as much as I did," he snapped. "He turned me into a vegetable."

The computer was whirring; in a few moments it would be ready to use.

"What did he do — to bring on your stroke?" I asked.

Harrison pushed a pile of scripts out of the way and perched on the corner of my desk, where he could see the monitor and keep the gun on me at the same time. "Teresa and I fell in love on a movie set. She'd been married to Damon for a year, but she already wanted a divorce. He refused — said he needed the image of being married to her. He threatened her so badly she was terrified to leave him."

The desktop image appeared on the screen.

"Go to your Letters file," he said.

I did as directed. "He found out about you

and Teresa the day you had the big fight?" I asked.

"He'd known for years, since he caught me visiting Terry in the hospital when she had Jeremy."

There was something in Harrison's voice — an unexpected softness. "You're Jeremy's real father, aren't you?" I guessed. "I used to wonder how such a terrific boy could be . . ." For a moment I forgot a gun was pointed at me. "Oh God — did Damon know that?"

Harrison nodded. "That's how he kept her so frightened. He threatened to take Jeremy away. I would have died before I let that happen. I was about to strangle Damon but I collapsed with a stroke instead . . ." He paused, his face twisted into a grimace of remembered fury. "*That's* when Damon finally let Terry have the divorce, when he thought I was as good as dead."

Harrison gestured toward the monitor with the Beretta. His voice was lighter, almost teasing, as he said, "Take a letter, Ms. Tyler."

My fingers hovered over the keyboard, ready to type, but covertly I was looking for anything on my desk I could use as a weapon. The only loose object within grabbing distance was a ballpoint pen that lay between the mouse pad and the keyboard.

He started dictating, "Type the date. Then 'Dear Jeremy.' "

Midway through the word "October," I stopped.

"Harrison — I love you like a father. I'll keep your secret."

There was a flicker of sorrow in his eyes. "I can't afford to bet my life on that." Then they hardened as he said, "You saw Terry outside my house, but you didn't ask me about it. Then you and that writer she knows were parked across the street from her house. We saw you. You're a danger to everything I've worked for."

He paused for a moment, remembering something that amused him. A hint of a smile played at the corners of his mouth. "Serena was the one who hit Damon with the car. A jealous fit. If she'd been a better driver, I wouldn't have had to shoot him." His smile disappeared. "I'm sorry you were the one who found her. I heard you fall and scream; I was still in the stairwell."

"But why —"

"Serena came over unexpectedly and saw me walking. I had to kill her; I waited two years, I couldn't let her spoil my plans. I'm genuinely sorry for it. I made it quick, She didn't suffer."

With my left hand hovering over the keyboard, the thumb and little finger of my right hand gripped the pen as I concealed it beneath the palm of my hand and my wrist. "How did you kill Damon without anyone seeing you go in or come out of his building?" I asked, playing for time. *Praying* for time. And inspiration.

Amused again, he said, "Terry called and *purred* about the days they were happy together. She hinted she wanted to come back to him. It was a great performance, and the egotistical idiot believed her." He made a sound of disgust before continuing. "Damon sent everyone away so they could be alone. Then she and I slipped in through the delivery entrance and went up in the service elevator. Terry let herself in with a key she'd kept, and left the door unlocked for me. We both left the same way. No one saw us."

"Jeremy told the police they were together that night," I said.

Harrison smiled with pride, and for a moment I glimpsed again the Harrison I knew. "He's a good boy. Terry told him she'd gone out to a movie by herself and was afraid the police would suspect her. Jeremy protected her. That's what a man should do." He had begun to relax into a conversational posture but caught himself and straightened up. "Story time over," he said. "Let's write that letter to Jeremy."

"What kind of a letter is this going to be?"

He looked at me with regret. "Your suicide note."

Sweat born of fear was beginning to make my hair damp. I felt it beading on my forehead and brushed a few drops away with my left hand. My right hand was next to the keyboard, gripping the pen as my insides roiled with nausea. His tone was reasonable, conversational. Professorial. Once again he was instructing me, but this time it wasn't in the craft of daytime drama.

"In this letter to Jeremy," he said, "you're going to confess to killing Damon and Serena.

You're going to apologize for the pain you've caused him. And then I'm going to shoot you so that it looks like you took your own life — with my Beretta. You'll say in the note that you stole it from me while I was hospitalized."

"Harrison." I forced myself to swallow the bile that had risen in my throat. With determination, I managed to keep my voice steady, and my tone as conversational as his. "So many murders go unsolved. No one suspects you. You could keep up your pretense of being paralyzed and let this case get cold. Colder."

I made myself smile at him, hoping he'd think of me as a co-conspirator. "Any moment a celebrity — much more interesting than a daytime TV executive — will do something stupid, get in big trouble, and the media will be all over it. Damon will be forgotten. He's almost forgotten now."

"No," he said.

His voice was cold. His "no" was my death sentence. He truly was insane.

"Terry and I want to take Jeremy and leave New York. We're going to make a new life, together. In order to do that, this case has to be solved. No loose ends. I'd trust you with my money, Doll, but not with my life. Or Terry's." There was sadness in his eyes, but I saw something else, too. I saw resolve. "I'm sorry," he said.

That was it. He wasn't going to let me go, so I had nothing to lose.

"I'm not going to write this note. You're going to kill me anyway."

I was surprised to hear the cool, firm tone of my voice. Sheer bravado.

"If you don't write it, I'll kill you anyway, but there'll be a double funeral. I know your friend Nancy. I can get to her, and I will, unless you start writing."

His voice was hard as stone. There was not even a trace of pity in his eyes. I knew in the pit of my stomach that he meant every deadly word. I lifted my shoulders slightly and rotated my neck as though trying to relieve stiffness between my shoulder blades. What I was really doing was using the motion to glance around the office for anything I could use as a weapon. I saw one object that might be able to save me. It was sitting on the shelf to my right, just inches beyond the desk. All I needed was to get to it . . . I had to keep Harrison talking.

"You win," I said. I laid the pen down at the edge of the keyboard, my hands hiding it from his line of sight. I typed the note, reading it aloud to him as I composed. I was trying to make it as convincing as possible. He liked what he heard.

"You always did write well under pressure," he said.

When I finished, I put a piece of my personal stationery in the printer and clicked "Print." I palmed the pen as the two of us watched the printer. *Is this how I will spend the last few mo-*

322

*ments of my life, staring at a printer?* "Who fired at me from the park?" I asked. "Teresa?"

"No," he said. "She's not a good enough shot — she might have killed you. I was a sniper in the Corps — I could part your hair with a round from eight hundred yards and not draw blood. We didn't want to hurt you, just scare you away from poking into Damon's death."

The letter slowly emerged from the printer.

"Pass it over," he said. With my left hand, I removed the page from the tray. I started to hand him the letter, then raised my curled right hand and hurled the pen at him. At most, I'd hoped to distract him for a moment, but it was an extraordinarily lucky throw. The pen hit high on his cheek, dangerously close to his eye. Instinctively, he touched his face. That instant gave me the precious second I needed to reach the shelf next to my desk and grab the gleaming brass Emmy that sat there. Harrison emitted a primitive roar, dropped his gun and lunged at me, ready to kill me with his bare hands. I swung the heavy brass award with all of my strength and smashed him on the side of the head with it. He groaned, staggered backward and then fell.

There was a loud crack as the base of his skull hit the window ledge.

I stood over him, stunned at what I had done.

Time was suspended as I clutched the Emmy. Harrison lay unconscious. Once I'd said the golden statue should have his name on it. Now it had his blood on it. Loud sounds in the hallway pulled me out of my trance. I heard feet pounding, people running. A man's voice shouted, "Morgan!"

The door burst open. Matt Phoenix and G.G. Flynn were there, guns drawn.

I looked at them. Fighting back tears, I tried to make a joke. "It's me again," I said. "With another body. But this time I really did do it."

# 39

Harrison was alive, for which I thanked God.

He'd been taken to the trauma center at Bellevue.

The sun was just beginning to rise in the east, beyond the tranquil beauty of Central Park. One by one, electric lights were going off as nature's light took their place. I was watching this phenomenon with Matt. We were strolling through this oasis in Manhattan to clear our heads, since the park is at its most enchanting at dawn, when the leaves and the grass all look fresh and clean, when there are no other human beings around.

I had given my statement, telling *most* of the story, but leaving out two details.

I didn't tell Matt that Teresa was there with Harrison when he killed Damon. I didn't want Jeremy to be left without a mother. A perfect person would have turned Teresa in, too, but I'm not a perfect person. In effect, I allowed her to get away with murder. Let God punish her for what she did, I thought. Maybe God will punish me, too, but Jeremy deserves a chance to be better than his parents. I had to give him that chance.

The other detail I left out was that Jeremy was really Harrison's son. That was Teresa's secret to keep or tell; it was not mine.

It was early enough so we could hear birds chirping as they began the activities of their day. We spotted a pair of gray and white mockingbirds on the branch of a tree, having a loud dispute. We stopped to watch them.

"Two guys arguing over a female," Matt said.

"Male *and* female," I countered, with my own theory of the scene on the branch. "A couple in love, having their first fight."

He smiled at me. "You're an incurable romantic."

"Is that a compliment or an accusation?"

"I like it on you," he said. "It's clean and nice. I don't see a lot of that."

We were strolling again. My head was clear, and my emotions were mostly under control. I asked Matt how it happened that he and G.G. came to my office.

"Penny," he told me. "I got home about one in the morning, and she hadn't been able to sleep, so we met in the kitchen. I was fixing us a pair of my special grilled cheese and tomato sandwiches — I'll make one for you sometime. Anyway, while I was smearing butter on the grill, she was telling me about the movies you saw, and how Harrison Landers had written one of them. Then she said something about *Another World* — she wondered if Landers was the writer who came up with one of her favorite old stories, about a man who only pretended to be paralyzed. It was as if a firecracker exploded in my head. I called G.G. and told him we had to go see Landers immediately. We found he wasn't home, but his wheelchair was. I called you, but you didn't answer. Frank, at reception, let us into your apartment and you weren't there. He told us you had a little office on the sixth floor. I didn't know that — I thought you wrote in your apartment. Anyway, that's how we found you."

"Just in time," I said.

"You did fine all by yourself."

I was barely listening, because a fragment of memory was nagging at me. I forced my mind to replay the confrontation with Harrison, and the fragment expanded into a picture. With my free hand I reached into the pocket of my jacket and my fingers closed around the little ballpoint pen I'd thrown. I couldn't remember when I'd picked it up, or why, but now I took it out and stared at it.

"Bic," I said. "That's it."

Matt stopped walking. He looked at me quizzically, but there was a glitter in his eyes. "That's *what?*" he asked.

"Your grandfather," I said. "Was his invention the ballpoint pen? Was he Mr. Bic?"

Matt stared at me with respect. "Granddad *perfected* the ballpoint pen. It was invented so Air Force pilots could write at high altitudes. Later, the Bic Company bought out the various patents."

"I win," I said.

"I'm impressed. Nobody ever guessed right before."

"Just how many women have tried?" There was an edge in my voice.

Matt took my arms and eased me around to face him. He looked down at me, and suddenly I found it hard to breathe. He pulled me into his arms and kissed me. A deep kiss, a kiss that felt as though hot liquid was shooting all through my body.

It was a kiss that seemed to last forever, and not long enough.

When we gently disengaged, Oliver Twist's famous line sprang into my head, "Please, sir, I want some more."

I felt it, but I didn't say it.

"I'd like to keep kissing you," Matt said, "but we can't do this." He dropped his hands and stepped back a few inches. "A couple of hours ago you were almost killed. You've had a traumatic shock and you're vulnerable. I can't take advantage of that."

I opened my mouth to protest, but heard Matt's voice again. "Think about it — when one of your characters goes through something big, you don't let her behave as though nothing's happened."

Matt Phoenix had just confessed to a secret vice. I gave him a "gotcha" smile. "You watch *Love of My Life!*"

"Penny tapes it every day, and leaves it in the

machine." He was trying to sound casual. "*Sometimes* I turn it on accidentally."

"You're busted!" I said. "The big, strong homicide detective is embarrassed to admit to watching my —"

"Someday," he said, ignoring my sarcasm, "when I kiss you again —"

"If I *let* you kiss me again!" I felt prickly and suddenly confrontational.

"*When* I kiss you again," he said softly, "I want to know that it's *me* you need, and not just *someone* to comfort you." He squared his shoulders, all business once more. "I've got to get back to the squad. Do you feel like coming with me to sign your statement?"

"I'll be there later, after you've gone home. Leave the statement with anybody."

"You're not mad at me, you're really mad at Landers, but you can't vent to him, so you're striking out at the nearest target. It's okay — I understand. I'll call you in a week or two," he said.

"I won't be home."

"I'm a detective, I'll find you," he said as he turned and strode back toward the place where he had parked his car.

# 40

When I got back to my apartment, I called Bellevue to find out about Harrison's condition. The operator connected me to the floor that held incarcerated patients.

The nurse who answered told me that a police detective named Flynn was there, getting the latest medical report. She couldn't answer my question, but perhaps he could. She put G.G. Flynn on the line.

"Landers is in a coma," he said. "Things don't look too good."

I felt sick to my stomach. "Then I've killed him."

"No, not you," he said. There was a gentleness in his voice I'd never heard before. "The doctor said it's because of his previous stroke and coma. That's why they think he probably won't come out of this one."

"Thank you, Detective."

"Call me G.G.," he said, which made me think Penny was right. G.G. Flynn *was* nicer than he seemed the first dozen times you met him.

"I'll come to your precinct house later, to sign my statement," I told him, and we said good-bye. I had two more calls to make.

First, Teresa Radford. She picked up immediately.

"It's Morgan," I said. "I'm afraid I have some bad news."

There was a pause, and I could hear her breathing. Then, "What's happened?" Her voice was barely a whisper.

"Harrison's been hurt. He tried to kill me and I defended myself. The police have taken him to Bellevue."

She gasped, then dropped the phone. I heard the clatter as it crashed against some hard surface, and then desolate sobs. She, or someone with her, replaced the receiver without another word. I had no doubt Teresa loved Harrison as much as he loved her. I wished I could have written a happy ending to their story.

My next call was to Winston Yarborough at The Carlyle. As soon as I gave my name, the hotel operator put me through to his apartment. No questions. No, "I'll check to see if he's available." Like Teresa, Yarborough answered on the first ring.

"I need to see you," I said.

"How soon can you be here?"

"I'll leave my apartment in half an hour."

"My car will be downstairs waiting for you."

That was exactly what I needed at the moment: a no-frills conversation.

I heaped coffee into Mr. C's filter-lined basket, and flipped the switch to On. I would need drinkable jet fuel to get myself through the next few hours. While the coffee was brewing, I brushed my teeth, showered, and grabbed the first outfit in my closet, a chestnut brown suede blazer with matching suede pants. I opened my drawer and pulled out an apple red cashmere sweater. Although I might still be shaking a little inside, the sweater would signal, "This woman is in control."

I thought about that as I headed back down the hallway, inhaling the revitalizing scent of Southern Pecan roast as I went. When I got to the kitchen, and was about to pour the coffee, I put down my supersize *Love of My Life* mug and did something I had not done in the five years since I returned from Africa.

I tucked my too-big sweater into my pants.

I am a size thirty-six C, with a small waist; it was time to stop wearing tops meant for someone who's a size sixteen.

When I came through the courtyard of the Dakota, I saw Winston Yarborough's chauffeur waiting for me at the entrance. I could have walked across Central Park faster than the Town Car made it through morning traffic, but I used the time to plan what I was going to say when I saw Global's founder and chairman.

Yarborough was waiting for me when I stepped out of the elevator.

Through one of his many contacts, he already knew that Harrison had been arrested for the murders of Damon and Serena, and for attempting to kill me. And that Harrison had been taken to Bellevue. It saved me a lot of talking.

He led me into the living room, where we sat next to each other on the most comfortable sofa. Refusing his offer of breakfast, I got right to the point. "Harrison's in a coma, and he's not expected to recover. He won't be able to contradict the story I have in mind to tell, nor will he be able to say anything negative about Damon."

Yarborough leaned forward. "What story?"

"Harrison Landers killed Damon and Serena because of a mental disorder resulting from his previous stroke. It's simple, and as far as the media's concerned, it's not sexy. This makes it nothing more than a one-day story. It will help if you can find a respected neurologist to state that's what happened."

"I'll get two," he said. "Thank you, Morgan. Now, tell me what I can do for you."

"Pay Harrison's medical bills. Please don't let him be sent to some institutional warehouse. It doesn't look as though he's going to wake up, but will you make sure that for however long he's alive, he has the best possible care?"

He nodded. "You may count on it," he said.

Robo-Driver was so well-trained in keeping his face impassive he showed no reaction when I told him, "Bellevue. Four Sixty-Two First Avenue."

Agata, Harrison's longtime housekeeper, was in the waiting room, clutching two women's coats against her chest. One was an elegant number with a golden sable collar. Her eyes were red and swollen from crying. She tried to smile when she saw me, and I devoutly hoped she didn't know I was the one who put Harrison back in a coma. Or why I did it.

"Have you been able to see him?" I asked.

"No. The lady is with him now."

*The lady.* "Do you mean Teresa?" I asked.

Agata nodded. She began to cry again.

"Is there anything I can do for you, Agata? Do you need a job?"

"No, I am going to be with Mrs. Teresa now."

"Good." I patted her shoulder, relieved she would be taken care of. "You'll love her son, Jeremy." I reached into my bag for my card. Slipping it into her hand, I told her to call me if she ever needed anything.

I had come to the hospital because I wanted to see Harrison. On the slim chance that he could hear me, I had hoped for the chance to say a soft good-bye to the man who had been my friend and mentor. The Harrison in my office was *another* man, one I would try to forget. But Teresa was at his beside. I had no doubt that she really loved him, so I wouldn't intrude. With one last smile at Agata, I left quietly.

It was a little before 10 A.M. when the Town Car dropped me off at Lenox Hill Hospital. At the reception desk, I learned Chet had been

334

moved to a private room on the fourth floor an hour earlier.

He was lying in bed with his eyes closed, apparently sleeping. I was standing in the doorway, and he must have sensed my presence; he opened his eyes and said, "Hi, Beautiful. Did you bring the gang to spring me from this hellhole?"

"Lenox is the best hospital in Manhattan." I moved to the side of his bed. "How do you feel?"

His smile turned into a grimace as he clenched his teeth against a sudden jab of pain. "I'm okay," he said.

"That's a huge exaggeration."

"No, really, I'm fine — thanks to you. The surgeon was in here a little while ago . . . told me what a close call I had." He moved with effort into a more comfortable position. "What did I miss after my lights went out?"

"The big finish," I said.

He put on an exaggerated expression. "Who done it?" he asked. "Were you right about Teresa?"

I said, "Harrison Landers killed Damon, and Serena McCall."

"How?"

"He was only pretending to be paralyzed."

Chet's eyebrows shot up in surprise. Cocking his head, he studied my face. "What's the rest of the story? Why? Why would he kill them?"

"He despised Damon," I said. "Serena, because she discovered he was faking his paralysis."

Chet stared at me with the skepticism of a skilled psychologist who knows when a patient is sanitizing a story. I tried to divert him with another piece of information. "It was Harrison who shot at us. He wasn't trying to hurt me — hurt either of us — he wanted to scare me so I'd stop asking questions."

"So we staked out the wrong suspect."

"Guess I'm not as good a detective as I thought I was."

"There's a lot more to this story," Chet said, staring at me. His voice was strong; his writer's curiosity was tougher than his post-appendectomy discomfort. "What are you saving it for?"

I hesitated for a moment, then I let out a sigh that seemed to come up all the way from the soles of my feet. I sat down hard on the chair next to his bedside "I haven't been to bed since the day before yesterday, and a few hours ago somebody I trusted tried to kill me. So bear with me. I'm a little cranky."

"Were you in love with Landers?" His voice was tender.

"Not *in* love with him, no, but I did love him for his kindness to me. I had no idea what I was going to do with my life after Ian died. Harrison trained me in his world, and then he shared it with me."

He lay silent for a while, staring at the wall in

front of him. Sitting there in the silence, in the warm hospital room, my eyes began to close. In spite of all the strong coffee I'd consumed, I was almost asleep.

"I'm not going to write the Radford book," he said.

My eyes popped open. "What made you decide that?"

"When I tackle a story, I go for the full picture, wherever the investigation takes me. In order to make sense of the murders, I'd have to uncover whatever secrets Landers had. I won't do that to you."

I felt tears of relief well up and fought them back. Before I could reply, Chet reached for my hand, turned it over palm up, drew it to his mouth and kissed it. He released me, saying, "They're throwing me out of here tomorrow. I'll need to spend a few days up in Greenwich, then I'll come back down. Are you free for dinner Sunday night?"

Robo-Driver was standing beside the Lincoln, outside Lenox Hill Hospital.

"I'm going to the Dakota," I told him, "but there's one more stop I want to make first." He nodded and opened the back door of the car for me.

I directed Mr. Bavaria to a boutique on Madison Avenue. While he waited, I bought two sweaters and a silk blouse in my correct size.

Then I went home and slept for twelve hours.

# Epilogue

Three nights later, Nancy, Penny and I were sitting with our shoes off and our feet up on my big ottoman, having Japanese takeout in my den.

Nancy maneuvered several grains of white rice onto her chopsticks. "I made an appointment for you to see my financial guy at two o'clock Monday afternoon," she told me. "You'll be getting eight million dollars in a few months, so we have to figure out how to keep as much as possible away from the tax monster."

"I haven't decided whether or not to take the money," I said.

Penny looked up from her salmon teriyaki, horrified. "You've got to take it," she insisted. "Even if you don't want it for yourself, you could use it to help people."

With so much happening, I hadn't really considered this, but Penny's idea appealed to me. *Maybe I should take the money.*

Nancy speared a piece of shrimp tempura. "Two o'clock Monday at my office. Had to rearrange my whole schedule to be there."

"All right," I said. Then, partly to get Nancy

off the subject of the money, I added, "I'm having dinner with Chet this Sunday night."

Penny frowned, and put down her chopsticks. "Matt better get off his duff."

"It's just a casual dinner," I told them. "I'm not going to do anything rash."

"Please *don't*," Penny said, "because Matt really likes you."

Nancy flashed her "I win" smile at me. "I'm proud of you, Morgan — you've got two hunky guys to juggle, *and* you're finally wearing clothes that fit."

Aiming my chopsticks at one of the last three shrimp on the tempura platter, I tried to make my tone sound casual. "At the age of thirty," I said, "I'm finally beginning to date."

I was more excited at the prospect than I was willing to admit.

# About the Author

**LINDA PALMER** was a wildlife photographer in Africa before she turned to writing. She teaches screenwriting classes at UCLA Extension, and lives with several pets in Studio City, California.